AGNES

Visit us at www.boldstrokesbooks.com

AGNES

by
Jaime Maddox

2014

AGNES

ISBN 13: 978-1-62639-032-4

This Trade Paperback Original Is Published By
Bold Strokes Books, Inc.
P.O. Box 249
Valley Falls, NY 12185

First Edition: January 2014

CREDITS
EDITOR: SHELLEY THRASHER
PRODUCTION DESIGN: STACIA SEAMAN
COVER DESIGN BY SHERI (GRAPHICARTIST2020@HOTMAIL.COM)

Acknowledgments

It is easy to type words on a keyboard and then tuck them away in a computer file, away from the scrutiny of others. Far harder a task is finding the courage to allow another to read your words and infer your thoughts and feelings. I was hiding there in my comfort zone, happy to write stories for my eyes only, until my partner forced me out of the literary closet. If not for her, *Agnes* would still be a very large document on my Zip drive instead of a published novel. Thanks, Carolyn, for your always-gentle encouragement.

While this book was written mostly between the hours of ten p.m. and midnight, it was edited at all hours of the day and night, and I am very grateful to Carolyn, Jamison, and Max for sharing me with *Agnes* during that process, and for only whining a little.

Agnes is a work of fiction based on an event that really happened. I've heard the stories my entire life, and while the tale of Sandy and Jeannie is a creation of my mind, I have no doubt it could have really happened. Thanks to all of my family and friends who shared their memories of the flood and the little town of West Nanticoke; it is all of those stories that are the foundation of this novel.

I have relied on people's memories, now fading after forty years, as well as multiple sources to create the story and verify details. Everything from the newspaper to videos on YouTube was used to help me put the pieces of that time back into place. I'm sure there are errors; they are unintentional and not meant to be offensive.

After that little push from Carolyn, my manuscript still needed a home. Thanks to Len Barot for reading it and offering me the opportunity to turn it into a book, and to my editor, Shelley Thrasher, for showing me how. Thanks, too, to everyone at Bold Strokes Books who helped in this production.

To Carol, Linda & Karen—
my fabulous, much older sisters
for guiding me through all of life's disasters

CHAPTER ONE
THE OBITUARY, MAY 23, 2011

Northeastern Pennsylvania

Nellie Davis Parker

Nellie Davis Parker of Mount Pocono passed away peacefully yesterday at Pocono Medical Center. At 98 years of age, she lived a long and full life. Although she spent her early and last years in the Poconos, Nellie lived for 40 years in West Nanticoke, leaving only after Hurricane Agnes destroyed her home.

Mrs. Parker was the daughter of the late William and Matilda Barnes Davis, of Mount Pocono. Her father was the holder of many engineering patents, and she inherited his thirst for knowledge and learning. She was valedictorian of Mount Pocono High School, class of 1931, and a graduate of the Fitzgerald Mercy School of Nursing. She married her childhood sweetheart, Dr. David Parker, and until his death, she worked beside him caring for their patients.

A former president of the Anthracite Golf Association, Mrs. Parker continued golfing into her eighth decade. She was the first female board member of the Nanticoke State Hospital and later also served on the board of directors at Pocono Medical Center. While she was president of the Tilbury Volunteer Fire Company in West Nanticoke, she spearheaded the effort to secure the funding for the town's first ambulance. She supported many charities and was active in her community both in West Nanticoke and in Mount Pocono.

She was preceded in death by her husband, Dr. David Parker, and her son, David Parker Jr., as well as her brothers William, Joseph and Arthur. She is survived by her granddaughter, Sandy Parker; her great-granddaughter, Angela Key and her great-great-grandson, Leo Key.

There will be no calling hours. Memorial contributions may be made to the charity of your choice. Interment will be beside her husband and son at Riverview Cemetery, West Nanticoke.

The sun had barely begun its ascent over Harvey's Lake when Dan Parker sat down to breakfast. An architectural masterpiece, his house was designed to capture both the morning and evening sun through the glass walls that formed the front and both sides of the house. A fastidious man, he placed the crisply pressed linen napkin in his lap, carefully protecting his silk suit. His breakfast menu—two eggs over medium with fried potatoes and four slices of bacon—hadn't changed in over fifty years. Each of the chairs at the shiny table was pushed neatly into place, and the vase of fresh flowers at its center sat upon a plate to prevent staining the wood. It was all very orderly, just as he preferred.

He was used to having things his way. Groomed from boyhood to run the Parker Companies, he had begun issuing orders to his parents' household staff when he was barely old enough to ride a bike. He was just a teenager when he followed his father and grandfather into the family business, learning the ropes from them as he worked after school and on weekends. He stayed home and earned his business degree from King's College in just three years, and began working beside them as soon as he did. Upon his father's untimely death, it was a natural transition for him to run the multitude of companies his family controlled.

He took a sip of his black coffee and opened the newspaper. The financial news was no different than what he'd seen on the television the evening before. He skipped that section completely and, instead, studied the headlines, determining if there was anything worth reading. Next, he pored over the national and local news before turning to the obituary section. When he saw Nellie Parker's name, he closed his eyes and sighed. When he opened them again, he didn't change his facial expression to match the elation he felt inside.

Dan leaned back into his chair as a tremendous weight fell from his shoulders. For forty years he had held his breath, awaiting Nellie Parker's discovery of the secret that only he knew. He had wondered what she would do to his little empire if she ever learned the truth. Quite simply, the old lady could have destroyed him. She could have brought down his entire branch of the family tree. At last he could let out that long-held breath in a sigh of relief.

He rose, placing his folded napkin beside his empty plate. He would begin his workday as he always did, by visiting his family companies. With a bounce his sixty-year-old legs hadn't shown in quite a while, he picked up his briefcase and did something else he'd been doing for fifty years—he went to work.

❖

The gravedigger didn't enjoy cooking, and unlike Dan Parker he didn't employ a housekeeper with kitchen skills. Hell, he didn't even have someone to help clean up after him, not that he'd have wanted someone poking around in his private things. The primitive kitchenette in his cabin high up on the edge of the mountain wasn't designed for much more than boiling water for instant coffee. Consequently, he took most of his meals out of house.

After showering and dressing in his typical work uniform—overalls and work boots—he climbed into this oversize pickup truck and headed to the Flamingo Diner. By reading the free newspaper at the diner the gravedigger calculated that he saved about five hundred dollars a year. His father had grown up in poverty, and his own early life had been the same. Even though he now had more money than he could ever spend, his frugal ways were engrained and habitual. The understanding that he was saving money made his breakfast of pancakes with artificial maple syrup all the sweeter.

Always a shy man, the gravedigger said few words to the other diner patrons. Keeping his nose hidden in the newspaper assured that no one spoke to him. In truth, most of the locals kept a polite distance and wouldn't have said more to him than a friendly "hello" even if he gave them the opportunity. He had lived in West Nanticoke his entire life and everyone in the town knew him, but no one in town really knew him at all.

The gravedigger was never sure whether he chose his job at the Riverview Cemetery, or the job chose him. He only knew that it was perfect for him, appealing to his need for solitude and quiet. He only wished he could see more of the bodies. As he grew older, with more arthritis and less flexibility, digging up graves and opening caskets had become more difficult for him. Consequently, he had to cut back on his nocturnal activities at the graveyard, and he missed it terribly.

As much as death fascinated him, he was naturally inclined to jump to the obituary section of the newspaper, bypassing world news and sports headlines. He controlled this urge, however, allowing the excitement to build as he leafed through the pages, each turn bringing him closer to the news he craved to know. Who had died? Whose grave would he have the pleasure of digging? Whose casket would he cover with soft brown earth? Who could he then pull back out of that same earth to help satisfy his peculiar cravings?

The Nellie Parker obituary jumped right at him, as if her name were printed in color on the otherwise black-and-white page. He didn't recognize the face staring at him, but the name sure was familiar. He read through to the bottom, to be sure this was the right Nellie Parker, and when he finished reading, he leaned back into the cracked vinyl of the booth and let a small smile form at the corners of his mouth. It was indeed the right woman. And she was coming to Riverview!

At last! Oh, how long he had awaited word of her death! How many hours had he spent worrying, wondering what he would do if Mrs. Parker had shown up at his door and confronted him with the truth. Strangulation? A bullet? He could have easily murdered her and then buried her among the dead at the cemetery, where no one would ever find her. He had done it before.

The questions no longer mattered. At long last he could rest, knowing that Nellie Parker would take his secret with her to the grave. He signaled the waitress for a second cup of coffee—refills were free—and he was whistling as he walked back to his truck. He was going to dig Nellie Parker's grave.

❖

Jane Bennett stirred her second Bloody Mary of the day with a thick stalk of celery. Standing in the kitchen of her home in Mountaintop, Pennsylvania, she stared unseeing through the large window across from her. Conscious of the time, and knowing she was breaking a promise to herself, she swallowed a mouthful of the spicy mix. Fuck her promise to cut back on her alcohol consumption! She needed this drink, and probably another afterward.

Nellie Parker was dead. The woman had lived for a fucking century, and of course she had to die now, when Jane couldn't afford to have any trouble. And the trouble Nellie's death could cause her was potentially catastrophic. In just another few weeks, Jane would have her life back on track. She just needed a few more fucking weeks to get everything in order. Was that too much to ask? But then again, why would the gods change course and start treating her kindly now?

Nellie's granddaughter Sandy had left Pennsylvania years ago and had never looked back. Thank God for Jane and her family for Sandy's absence. Her grandmother's burial at Riverview Cemetery would very likely be the reason to end her exile. This had been worrying Jane for years because inevitably the woman was going to die. Now that the moment of truth was here, though, Jane wasn't prepared. Since reading the news, she'd been suffering palpitations of the heart and felt like she might pass out.

The spicy cocktail did nothing to calm her frazzled nerves. She retrieved a Xanax from the bottle she kept handy in her purse and swallowed it. She couldn't face this trouble now. She just didn't have the strength to deal with it before noon. Slugging the last of her drink, she decided to go back to bed. Unless she was prepared to take very desperate measures, Jane was powerless to control the events about to unfold. The sight of the medicine bottle sitting beside her cocktail reminded her that things in her life had indeed gotten pretty desperate.

CHAPTER TWO
WEDDING DAY, JUNE 17, 1972

West Nanticoke, Pennsylvania

It was going to be a beautiful day. It was going to be a beautiful summer. It was going to be a beautiful year. It was going to be a beautiful life.

Although not devoid of tragedy, Sandy Parker's life had been one of comfortable privilege that had helped forge the optimistic perspective with which she viewed the world. Her family had been in the anthracite business, and the fortune the first American Parkers had amassed had been carefully invested and would sustain their descendents for generations to come. She had never wanted for anything, and her needs were really quite few.

Sandy had been awake for nearly an hour on this spring morning, considering with youthful anticipation all the wonders life held in store for her. Even as her mind had been so active, her body had been still so as not to disturb the girl who lay sleeping beside her. Now she felt movement and turned to look at her lover.

Sun rays peeked through the narrow space between the window's frame and the shade, pulled all the way down in an effort to impede their entrance. Minute particles of dust danced through the morning light, carried along on invisible waves. Shadows were cast, and as the sun followed its course through the morning sky, they dissolved and re-formed before her eyes. Birds chatted outside the window, ignorant of the sleeping humans.

It was going to be an especially beautiful day for a wedding. Sandy felt so happy to have been invited to one. She was happy because of the girl beside her. She was happy to have been given so many blessings. She was just plain happy.

Jeannie still slept, but Sandy moved close to her, snuggling against her back, their heads sharing a pillow. She studied the room that had been hers since she came to live in this house at the age of three. On the precipice of her life, Sandy had recently found her thoughts more reflective and sometimes somber, in spite of the joy she felt for the good things in her life and the good things she was certain lay ahead.

Deep down she felt a fear of change, of letting go of all that was so good for the potential of gaining something better. But that is how it must be, she thought, and how it always must have been—young kids like her, venturing off to college, leaving behind safety and comfort for things unknown. For her, though, the stakes were probably not as high as for most. Those other kids probably enjoyed the freedom to love who they pleased, but Sandy would never enjoy that privilege if she stayed in West Nanticoke. Even though the prospect frightened her, leaving home was the only path that could lead her to the life she craved.

Would she miss this place? Truly the only home she'd ever known, its walls and floors were the canvas of her life, and over the years she had been quite an artist. Working beside her grandfather and the laborers he hired for home repair, Sandy had learned how to paint and run electrical wiring, unclog a drain, care for the garden, hammer and screw and sand and spackle. The house now had her fingerprints everywhere, from the roof to the cellar, and she loved it even more because she knew it so intimately and her own hands had performed the labor of love to care for it. If her college studies in finance didn't go well, she could make a living as a contractor building homes.

She studied the room that had changed so little in fourteen years. The big four-post bed was crafted from cherry and sat so high off the floor, she'd required a booster just to climb in when she first claimed this room as her own. The bed had been her great-grandmother's and was given to her grandmother when she set up her house here along the canal. There were two matching nightstands in a dark stain, a dresser, a chest, and a vanity. Even with all that furniture, the massive room still appeared uncluttered. The wallpaper was the same faded floral print, and although she detested the pattern, by the time she found the courage to tell her grandmother it should be changed, she'd grown accustomed to it.

The ten-foot-high ceilings were framed with crown molding darkly stained to match the hardwood floor. A similar molding bordered the room at the doorways and at the floor. Pocket doors opened to an adjacent sitting room, which she had recently converted into a closet. The craftsmanship of the room, and of the house, was incomparable.

Her grandfathers had built it over a hundred years earlier, in a time when money was being hauled out of the coal mines by the ton, and had spared no expense. The wood and glass used throughout were carved and cut and stained, marble surrounded all three fireplaces, and all of the twelve rooms were expansive.

Warned by some that a house built so close to the river was sure to flood, her grandfather's grandfather had consulted a team of engineers about the construction of his home. They had recommended a thick foundation of stone built so high that the first floor of the house actually sat nearly a story above ground. Periodic spaces in the stone, which appeared at a distance to be windows, were actually left open to allow the Susquehanna to flow through and relieve some pressure on the structure. Though enclosed, this cellar was left empty. It had often taken in water when the river came up, but the Parkers had rarely suffered anything more than an inconvenience due to flooding.

With a Greek Revival element at its heart, the great front porch with columns supporting the roof afforded a magnificent view of the river rolling just a hundred yards away. A magnificent front staircase of stone stretched across the entire porch, and whether it was intended or not, it served as the perfect seating for guests at the many Parker spring and summer social events. The boxy design sported a long central hallway with a grand staircase of wood to the right, and the seven rooms on the lower level all opened off this corridor. Of the five grand bedrooms on the second floor, Sandy's room in the rear of the house opened to a corner balcony facing woods and river, and her grandparents' suite at the front opened over the porch onto their own private balcony. The unique style was functional and beautiful, perfect for this setting beside the Susquehanna.

Yes, she'd miss this house. It would always be her home. She couldn't imagine calling another room her own, or having a Christmas without the tree in the center of the window in the parlor where her grandmother played carols on the piano. She had never eaten a Thanksgiving turkey that wasn't served on her grandmother's "good" china from the dining-room table that overlooked the river, where an original Norman Rockwell painting hung on the wall.

She looked back at the beautiful girl beginning to stir beside her on the bed. It was the desire to share her bed and her life with this girl that would force them both to flee this town and all that was so comfortable and familiar.

Jeannie's curvaceous body was naked, and as she rolled away Sandy admired the shapely calves, the round bottom, and the long back draped with chestnut hair that fell in curls across the pillow. She couldn't see the large breasts with the nipples that sprang up under her tongue, breasts that fit perfectly in her hands and her mouth. She couldn't see the speckled green eyes with the long dark lashes, the cute nose, the full lips, or the round face of the girl she loved, but she had spent so much time of late studying them that she could probably have sketched them from memory.

Although only two inches taller than Jeannie, Sandy was all angles and hard muscle, the product of the sports she played and the work she chose to do, whereas Jeannie was soft, every inch of her feminine. Sandy was blond and fair, with blue eyes the color of the depth of the ocean. Jeannie was dark, both skin and hair, and occasionally her temper, too.

The two of them had just celebrated their seventeenth birthdays. Sandy and Jeannie Bennett were destined to be together, she mused, since they had first met in the nursery at the Nanticoke State Hospital on the day they both came kicking and screaming into this world. Sandy didn't know if she fell in love with Jeanie that day, but she certainly did three years later when she saw her again, playing in her mother's flower garden and wearing her Easter dress. Sandy promptly joined her there, and they successfully rid the garden of most of its tulips before they were discovered and dragged away in opposite directions, both of them screaming. In her mind's eye she could still see Jeannie in that muddy pink dress. Sandy could still see the tears that she understood were not cried over the trouble she was in but over the separation from her new friend.

That was Sandy's first memory. Of course she had no memory of the father who died in a car accident before she was born. Nor were there any of the mother who buckled under the weight of raising a little girl alone and unceremoniously dropped her off with her late husband's parents one Easter Sunday and left, never to be seen again. She had a million happy memories after that first one, for she had lived a blessed life with her grandparents, growing up in the hamlet of West Nanticoke, along the west bank of the Susquehanna River, in the house next door to Jeannie Bennett.

Sandy treasured these mornings when Jeannie was with her,

knowing how precious they were. They'd been best friends since the age of three, lovers for two years now. Though their personalities were opposite—Jeannie outgoing and adventurous, Sandy reserved and cautious—they liked all the same things. They possessed that rare chemistry that allowed them to understand each other's unspoken feelings and finish each other's sentences. They could do anything together, but could do nothing just as well. They could talk or enjoy the quiet where not a word was spoken and the only sounds were the turning of pages or the whistling of the wind.

Since that first play date in the flowerbed, they spent every moment they could together, only ever wanting to be with each other, never questioning the forces that pulled them together. Riding bikes, swinging on swings, fishing, hiking, playing, working, studying, exploring the amazing little world they shared, they were always together.

The norm was nightly sleepovers during the warm summer months, almost exclusively at the Parkers'. Once school started in September, though, their nights together were limited to weekends and holidays. Precise planning and cunning were required from September to May, when they had to squeeze in alone time according to opportunity. They welcomed June like rain after a drought! June, with the warm weather that allowed them to hike in the mountains and make love beside streams. June, with the long days that allowed them more time together to play tennis or basketball at the park. June, with the relaxation of the rules that allowed Jeannie to spend every night in Sandy's bed.

As their final year of high school approached, Sandy's growing sense of excitement was ever harder to contain. So soon, it would all be in motion, like a Radio Flyer speeding down the mountain path at top speed, gliding atop the snow. Right now she was climbing the mountain, with Jeannie beside her, pulling the sled behind them, but they were fast approaching the summit and the ride of their life.

Enjoying June, and July, and August—that was Sandy's goal for the summer. She wanted to savor each moment, taste each morsel of time, allowing them to spread across her tongue like a bite of chocolate. After she left for college in a year, Sandy would never be able to call this place home again. This house she loved and the friends she'd known all her life would no longer be her sustenance, only a sweet dessert enjoyed on rare occasions. She wanted to make memories of her home and friends, and especially her grandmother, enough to last her a lifetime.

She and Jeannie were both applying to colleges, and while the

Bennetts planned for their daughter to enroll at College Misericordia in nearby Dallas, she and Jeannie had secretly written to colleges in New York City so they could study there. There had to be other girls like them, other lesbians, but she and Jeannie weren't likely to find them in their small town. If they went to college in the big city, they hoped they could find them and a place where they would fit in.

Jeannie wanted to study medicine and Sandy wanted to study money. That Sandy's grandfather had been a physician and Jeannie's dad was an accountant only reinforced for both of them the belief that they were destined to spend their lives together. Having grown up in a family doctor's house, with the office occupying two rooms on the first floor, Sandy understood medicine. Jeannie understood finances. They were a perfect match.

Since both of them were at the top of their class, and Sandy was the best basketball player in school history, they were hoping for scholarships to pay the way through college. Both families could afford the tuition, but neither girl anticipated a favorable reaction when they announced their decision to head to New York. They might be on their own. However, as long as they were together, they would never be alone, or lonely. They would make it.

The sun continued its advance across the room and finally reached the pillow where Jeannie rested her head. When it reached her left eye, she rolled out of its path toward Sandy. Smiling, Sandy opened her arms and pulled Jeannie closer. It was still hard for her to believe that Jeannie loved her and that they could find so much pleasure in each other's bodies and such joy in the love they shared.

Sandy had waited long enough for Jeannie to awake. Gently, she kissed each of Jeannie's closed eyelids. "Open," she said to each of them in turn.

Like their owner—spirited, independent, defiant—they refused. "It's too early," Jeannie complained.

"It is early," Sandy whispered as she kissed Jeannie's temple and then her ear, slowly winding her way to that very sensitive place just behind it. In response, Jeannie moaned softly, tilting her head back, and Sandy took advantage by kissing the newly exposed flesh.

"Awakening before the rest of the world does give one certain benefits," Sandy suggested.

"Such as?" Jeannie liked to tease Sandy. In spite of her earlier protest, Jeannie was now fully awake and anxiously anticipating the benefits Sandy had mentioned.

"It would be best if I demonstrate." Gently, Sandy pushed her onto her back and continued to place soft kisses around her ear, venturing over to her lips for a moment before jumping back to Jeannie's neck. Just this teasing had Jeannie so excited she had to fight to keep still, but she tried, wanting to prolong the pleasure and savor the wonderful sensations Sandy's mouth was bringing her.

The intensity of their passion was still as strong as it had been on their first night together. Jeannie hadn't grown tired, or bored, and still wanted Sandy so badly she could hardly concentrate on such matters as algebra and history or washing dishes and waxing furniture.

By the irregular pattern of Sandy's breathing, Jeannie knew Sandy was equally excited, yet she maintained her slow and deliberate pace. She eagerly welcomed Sandy's tongue in her mouth, and she delighted in the soft caress of her breasts. Sandy's knowing fingers expertly tweaked Jeannie's perky nipples, stimulating the hardened tissue to grow even more erect. Jeannie moaned in response and opened her eyes as Sandy's mouth left hers and found her breasts. She watched through eyelids heavy with desire as Sandy licked them, teasing with her tongue before trying to take one entire voluminous breast into her mouth. Sandy alternated from one breast to the other as Jeannie held her head, caressing it at times and at others holding it fast where she wished it to stay.

With her head held firmly against Jeannie's breasts, Sandy's hand began its own venture—along her ribs, the side of her breast, across her stomach, and to the mound of curls at the bottom of her abdomen. As this movement continued, Jeannie could no longer keep still. She released Sandy's head and she lifted her hips in welcoming anticipation of Sandy's hand.

A knowledgeable finger parted the hair and found its way to the outer folds of Jeannie's sex, where it softly circled the perimeter, edging ever closer to her core with each revolution. By the time Sandy plunged that finger inside, Jeannie's hips were dancing to the rhythm of her rapid breathing and pounding pulse. Moaning, thrusting, she wrapped both arms around her lover, attempting to draw in the entire hand that was giving her such pleasure.

Sandy lifted her head to look at Jeannie and was, as always, overcome with emotion. Jeannie was absolutely gorgeous, but never more so than when they were making love. Her head thrown back, her hair in disarray, and the burning desire in her eyes all filled Sandy with love and longing beyond words. The ache between her own legs was growing with each movement of their bodies, and Sandy ground her hips against Jeannie's, relishing the pleasure that contact gave her, driving her more wild, giving her more determination to bring them both to the place they needed to go.

Thrusting her finger in and out, Sandy matched the rhythm of Jeannie's hips and they moved together, taking Jeannie higher and higher and Sandy right along with her. Sandy turned slightly, moving just enough to find Jeannie's mouth with her own, and their tongues clashed. Jeannie's arms wrapped even tighter around her, pulling her closer, closer as she thrust against Sandy and moaned. The pressure in Sandy's clit was exquisite, her wetness creating a puddle on Jeannie's leg. Jeannie pulled her face back to look at Sandy. Sandy thought for the millionth time how beautiful Jeannie Bennett was, how lucky she was to be her lover.

Jeannie's eyes were only half-open and unfocused and her mouth was half-open as well, and Sandy could feel heavy breaths against her face. Hazy eyes met Sandy's. "I need your mouth on me." It was both request and a demand, whispered with so ragged a breath that had Sandy not known her partner so well she might not have understood her.

Pushing up with only one arm she was between Jeannie's legs in the span of a heartbeat and plunged into her wetness. She thrust her finger wildly, adding another as she sucked Jeannie's swollen, throbbing clit into her mouth and licked it with her lips and her tongue. Burying her fingers in Sandy's hair, Jeannie pulled her closer, tighter. Instantly Jeannie began to moan, and then she groaned loudly. Sandy continued the movements of her tongue and her fingers, pushing Jeannie further until Jeannie's spasms began to subside. Still Jeannie gripped Sandy's head, not releasing her hold until the final shudder ceased. A moment later Sandy felt her lover collapse onto the pillow, her body still except for the heaving chest expanding and falling with each quick breath.

Sandy didn't move from the place between Jeannie's legs, but she stilled her hand and tongue. She simply rested her head upon Jeannie's thigh, inches from her swollen, dripping labia, drinking in her intoxicating smell as she tried to regain control of her own breath.

"Holy shit," Jeannie murmured. "That. Was. Amazing."

"Yes, it was." She didn't enjoy anything as much as giving Jeannie such pleasure. And even though she hadn't climaxed yet, Sandy was calm, enjoying this incredible connection they shared, knowing her time would come, and when it did, it would be well worth the wait.

They were quiet and still for a minute. Then, just as Sandy

anticipated, she felt the gentle squeezing against her fingers as Jeannie began to tighten around her, still not quite satisfied. The rocking of Jeannie's hips soon followed as she again initiated the motions that would help her find the release she craved. Sandy shifted just slightly and kissed Jeannie's inner thigh, at the spot just where it joined her groin. Shifting further, Sandy kissed all of Jeannie's sex, her clit and labia, sucking and licking, and as she did, Jeannie nearly broke her fingers with the strength of the contractions in her vagina as she orgasmed for the second time, laughing softly after the groaning.

This time, Sandy didn't hold her position and rest. Understanding that Jeannie could continue to orgasm indefinitely if Sandy encouraged her with further attention, she pulled back, anxious now for her own pleasure. At that moment, after bringing Jeannie to two orgasms, the throbbing between her own legs was becoming unbearable and she needed some attention herself. Rising, she kneeled and positioned herself above Jeannie's mouth, and holding the headboard for balance she began a gentle rocking of her hips against her lover. Jeannie wrapped her arms around Sandy's thighs, pulling her closer, and allowed the hot, wet tip of her tongue to meet Sandy's clit. As she felt the heat Sandy began to shudder, coming almost instantly, and her legs collapsed so that only her arms clinging to the heavy cherry headboard supported her.

Collapsing back into Jeannie's arms, Sandy shared teasing laughter with Jeannie. "You're so easy," Jeannie complained. "I don't get to have any fun!"

"No fun?" Sandy tickled her.

"Well, maybe a little," Jeannie conceded, and her response resulted in an even more vigorous assault.

Afterward, they lay side by side, studying each other. "I love you," Sandy said, brushing a lock of the unruly hair that had fallen across Jeannie's forehead and covered a sparkling green eye. She pulled her closer and kissed Jeannie's forehead, a gentle kiss that spoke of all the love she felt for her.

Jeannie smiled, and a sigh of contentment escaped her lips. "I love you, too."

Loving Sandy from their first moments together in the garden all those years ago, Jeannie could have lived happily without another friend or playmate for all of her life. Her needs were few, her tastes simple. She had been fortunate in her life and had never been hungry or had to do without. The only thing she'd ever really craved was Sandy

Parker. For most of her life she didn't question it. As a child she didn't understand there was something unusual about her feelings for Sandy. She only knew that her moments with Sandy were her happiest and that she spent her moments without Sandy thinking about nothing but Sandy.

At the advent of adolescence, as the other girls she knew began the tireless pursuit of the opposite sex, Jeannie first understood there was something different about her. While her friends spoke endlessly about the wonders of boys and their desires to kiss said boys, the only one Jeannie had any desire to kiss was Sandy. Intuitively she understood that this information was something to hold private, that she could share it with no one, even Sandy. She didn't believe Sandy would share those feelings. She kept them to herself, certain that no one would understand her attraction to her best friend.

Uncertainty caused her to pull away from Sandy. Or, at least, to try to pull away. She really couldn't stay away from Sandy for more than a little while. Sandy was the one Jeannie wanted to talk to, to laugh with, to look at, to be with.

By occupying her mind with school and sports, helping her dad prepare taxes in his office, and running the student council, Jeannie was able to keep these feelings in check, only having to worry about them when her mind was still, like when she tried to sleep at night. Or on those magnificent occasions she was alone with Sandy and would have liked more than anything to kiss her.

For two years Jeannie went on this way, suffering silently, closely observing the other girls in their mating dances, pretending she shared their fantasies about football players and wrestlers. Jeannie was mostly quiet and others thought her suddenly shy, and she was sometimes teased, but no one suspected the truth she kept so carefully hidden within her heart.

She was terribly sad, and only being with Sandy helped. Enveloped in a blinding fog, wandering without direction or hope, Jeannie was lost, unsure how to control feelings she knew were wrong. She knew she needed to avoid Sandy and that she didn't have the will to do it. She would have died without her.

Then in an instant, the fog was blown away by a gust of wind, opening the portal to the sun, and all was suddenly clear.

It was the summer of 1969 and evening in the Bennett household, on one of those occasions when her parents had decreed the need for family time. Jeannie loved her parents dearly, but she wasn't particularly close to her overbearing mother. She much preferred to spend time with her more intellectual and laid-back father. And as far as her sister went, Jeannie was sure Jane must have been adopted, because they had absolutely nothing in common. They were civil to each other, and like most siblings, they were united in the war against their parents, but they didn't hold common interests or views. Jane was currently in lust with at least a dozen boys, and while Jeannie was forced to tolerate that nonsense from her friends, she had no such obligation with her older sister. When Jane and her mother started talking, Jeannie ran in the other direction.

The Bennetts were gathered in their den. The television was turned on, but no one was paying it any attention. The reporter talking was more background noise to her parents' conversation than family entertainment. Jeannie and her sister Jane, home after her first year of college, had quickly exhausted their supply of conversational topics. Jane sat reading while Jeannie wrote in her diary. Suddenly, as if shot like a clown out of a cannon at the circus, Helen Bennett jumped from her chair and rushed to the television. In the instant between Jeannie noticing her mother's brisk and unusual movements and the disruption of power to the television set when her mother unplugged it from the wall outlet, Jeannie heard a few fragments of a newscast that would change her life.

"Police." "Riots." "Homosexuals." "Greenwich Village."

All three Bennetts in the room were stunned by Helen's actions as they observed her storming from the room mumbling about "unnatural sinners" and "the decline of society" and "the nerve of the television to broadcast such filth."

Jeannie looked at her older sibling and without words asked for an explanation of what had just happened. Her sister silently responded that she'd fill her in later.

As soon as they were alone, Jeannie begged Jane for details. Her reserved mother's behavior had been markedly out of character, and Jeannie knew that whatever had been discussed on that television program had been monumental. Jane's synopsis, though brief, gave Jeannie the missing piece of the puzzle that allowed her to finally see herself clearly.

"The police in New York beat up some queers, and now they're rioting in the streets."

Jeannie studied Jane's face, trying to discern the meaning of this without asking. She couldn't. "What are queers?"

Jane shrugged and sighed as if asking how she could be cursed with such a pathetic sibling. "Homosexuals!"

Jeannie, having lived a somewhat sheltered life, and only having lived it for a short fourteen years, hadn't yet learned the meaning of this word, either. "What's homosexuals?"

Jane just shook her head in seeming disappointment. "Homos. Queers." She lowered her voice and looked over her shoulder at her mother, who obviously wasn't listening. "Men who have sex with men. Women who have sex with women."

Jeannie's astonishment had to be mirrored in her face, and misinterpreting her response, Jane shook her head in agreement with Jeannie. "I know, I know. It's the most vulgar and disgusting thing I've ever heard of, but believe me—there are sick people in this world. I hope the police shoot every last one of them!"

The look of shock on Jeannie's face seemed to amuse Jane, who was sometimes caught up in a sibling rivalry that Jeannie refused to sustain. Jane's knowledge about the Stonewall Riots seemed to make her feel powerful, though, and with her gloating she didn't see the truth—that this knowledge didn't appall Jeannie. It intrigued her. Her feelings for Sandy were suddenly validated by the simple act of naming them and the knowledge that others like her existed. Jeannie's head was spinning and her heart was pounding, and she didn't know what to do next, but she was sure of one thing—her feelings were something she could never share with her sister. To her great relief, Jeannie was quite sure Jane was clueless.

Upon Jane's retreat to her room, as was her custom on summer evenings, Jeannie escaped to Sandy's house. Unable to suppress her excitement, she couldn't wait to talk to Sandy. There was a name for what she was! She wasn't the only one in the world like this. She was a homosexual, and there were other people like her, far away in New York City. Suddenly, Jeannie had a great hope—that if there were other homosexuals in New York City, there might be one living right next door. She loved Sandy, of that fact she had no question, and she felt like Sandy loved her. Sandy had never given Jeannie any indication that her feelings ran any deeper than best-friend kind of feelings. But maybe, just maybe, they felt the same way.

"Did you hear about the homosexuals in New York City?" Jeannie asked when she burst breathless into Sandy's room. In her excitement, she had sprinted all the way from her house, through Sandy's, and up the flight of stairs to reach her. Sandy was lying on her bed reading while the Beatles sang in the background.

"What?" Sandy asked.

"The homosexuals!" Jeannie exclaimed.

"Jeannie, what are you talking about?" Sandy sat up and was staring at her. It was summer and Sandy wore only a skimpy halter and short shorts, so Jeanne concentrated on looking into Sandy's eyes and not at her hard, lean, sexy body.

Jeannie studied her face, and her own fell with disappointment. It was clear Sandy had no idea what she was talking about. Jeannie had been wrong. Sandy wasn't like her. *They might have millions of homosexuals in New York City*, she thought, *but I'm the only one in West Nanticoke.*

Over the course of the coming months, Jeannie found it increasingly more difficult to deal with her new identity. Her feelings for Sandy were real and seemed to grow stronger, despite her attempts to control them. Failing to rein in her hormones, Jeannie finally decided she either had to do something about this or go mad. She opted to confront Sandy and learn if she reciprocated the desire that had been tormenting her for three years.

As was their ritual, Sandy and Jeannie spent a Saturday evening playing bridge with her grandmother and a neighbor. They had been welcomed into the game when Sandy's grandfather passed away a year earlier and the other member of the foursome suffered a stroke. Of course, they played for money. Sandy and Jeannie were connecting that night and, with delight, Jeannie hauled in her share after a winning hand. "I need to start saving my money," she announced. "I'm going to the prom."

Sandy's eyes flew open in wonder and then—or did Jeannie imagine this?—they clouded over. She wasn't sure Sandy heard another word she said after that, and she certainly lost the ability to concentrate on her cards. Soon after, they retired to Sandy's room, having surrendered nearly all of their earlier winnings. Jeannie felt a chasm between them that she'd never known in their dozen years of friendship.

"Is something wrong?" she asked Sandy after she exited the bathroom, turned off the light, and quietly crawled into bed beside her. She didn't reach for Jeannie, as she normally would. She didn't try to touch her. She just seemed to sink into the mattress and disappear.

After a moment's silence, Sandy responded in a whisper. "No."

Jeannie knew Sandy well enough to know she was lying. It killed her to think she'd brought such despair to the girl she loved. Suddenly, her plan didn't seem so smart. Yet she didn't have a way out except by moving forward. "I have a problem," Jeannie confessed, inching next to Sandy in the dark.

"What's that?" Sandy was polite but didn't sound very interested in Jeannie's response. Sandy seemed somewhere far away, lost in her own thoughts.

"What if he tries to kiss me?" Jeannie asked.

"That's disgusting!"

Sandy's reply was so abrupt that it took Jeannie by surprise and she tried to laugh at the harsh response, but she was too nervous. Why did this have to be so difficult? "I've never kissed a boy before," she confessed.

Sandy was silent.

"I was wondering if we could practice?" Jeannie whispered, afraid to speak the words out loud.

"Practice?" Sandy asked, sounding confused.

Jeannie hardly knew what she was saying, so she wasn't surprised that Sandy wasn't following. She sighed in frustration.

"Yeah, practice kissing," Jeannie suggested again. Her heart pounded in anticipation of Sandy's answer, and her mouth grew so dry she didn't think she could speak again.

Her eyes had adjusted to the darkness and Jeannie studied the silhouette beside her, waiting for a response. Hoping that Sandy didn't laugh or, worse yet, kick her out of bed, Jeannie held her breath.

"You want me to kiss you?" Sandy rolled over toward her as she spoke.

She fought to keep her voice from cracking and managed to answer. Jeannie reached for Sandy's hand, which was beside her face on the pillow, and squeezed it softly. "Please?"

Sandy didn't seem to think, just to react, for the word was barely past Jeannie's lips when she felt Sandy's lips against hers.

That first touch—soft, tender, tentative—set off an explosion of sensations, and Jeannie fought to control her breathing even as she heard the sounds that indicated Sandy was struggling with the same difficulty. Jeannie edged closer and Sandy met her, and they began a more thorough investigation of each other's mouths, with lips and tongues sucking and probing and leaving Jeannie dizzy and panting and wet. So wet and hot.

Jeannie circled Sandy's waist with an arm and pulled her closer still, only to be enveloped as Sandy wrapped herself around Jeannie.

When did she begin the grinding of her hips against Sandy's that was sending shocks of pleasure through her body? When had Sandy reached inside her shirt to caress her breast? Time was lost as they kissed and sucked and rubbed and moaned, until suddenly Sandy pulled herself away and jumped from the bed. Crossing the room, she sat on the bench that matched the vanity, her body folded over, cradling her head in her open palms.

Jeannie wanted to scream in frustration. She wanted to cry in anguish. A few minutes in Sandy's arms proved what she had known, that she loved her and wanted to make love with her. The silk of her mouth, the weight of her breast, the curves of her body had driven Jeannie mad in just the short time they had touched. How could she ever not want her? Now that she had tasted her and felt her, how could she live without her?

Jeannie cried out. "What's wrong? Why did you stop?"

"This is wrong," Sandy cried, her voice barely more than a whisper. That was all she could manage as tears choked her voice.

Oh, fuck! Jeannie thought, running her fingers through her hair. She had really miscalculated! She had been wrong to do this. Sandy wasn't homosexual at all, and Jeannie only hoped she wouldn't be really disgusted and allow the kisses they had shared and this reckless plan to ruin their friendship.

Jeannie could hear sniffling from across the room. She pulled herself up and approached Sandy, but stopped at the hand Sandy held in front, keeping her at bay.

Not wanting their kisses to end and at the same time fearing Sandy would suspect the truth about Jeannie's sexuality and hate her for it, Jeannie pleaded with her. "I need more practice," Jeannie begged. "Please."

Sandy looked up and met Jeannie's eyes, and Jeannie saw the answer there before Sandy could voice her feelings. She wasn't going to kiss her again. "I don't want you to practice so you can kiss someone else, Jeannie. I only want you to kiss me."

"What?" Jeannie couldn't believe Sandy's words. That was all she wanted to hear; it sounded too good to be true.

"I love you, Jeannie."

How her knees held her, she wasn't sure, but she made it the few steps to the bench where Sandy rested and sat beside her. She placed a hand on Sandy's trembling knee and leaned into Sandy, resting her head against her shoulder. "I lied," she confessed.

"Huh?"

"I lied. About the prom. About practicing kissing. I don't have a date. I just didn't know any other way to get you to kiss me. And I've been going out of my mind with wanting you to kiss me for ages!"

Now they looked at each other and both laughed as they realized the irony of their situation.

"Really?" Sandy appeared incredulous. "Since when?"

Jeannie stood and pulled Sandy by the hand, leading her back to the bed. "It all started when we were three. But it's been especially awful for the past few years."

"That sounds about right," Sandy answered as she followed closely.

When they reached the edge, Jeannie stood before Sandy and caressed her face with gentle fingertips. "Now, where were we?"

Neither of them could be aroused for church services the next morning.

"What are you smiling about?" Sandy asked, pulling Jeannie back to the present.

"I was just thinking about our first kiss."

"I believe it should be in the record books for great kisses."

"I agree."

They kissed—slowly, deeply, tenderly.

"It's a good thing I saved you from boys," Sandy told her.

"I can't wait for you to save me from my parents!"

They were planning their escape, and Jeannie was anxious, counting the days until they graduated high school and went away to college. While Sandy's grandmother loved her a great deal, she allowed Sandy certain freedoms that Jeannie's overprotective parents didn't. Jeannie was constantly critiqued on everything from her hair and makeup and clothing to her choice of music and decisions about school activities. Even her plans for a career in medicine, which might have elated most parents, caused Jeannie's mom concern. Helen Bennett would have derived considerably more pleasure from her daughter marrying a doctor than studying to become one.

Sandy realized the result of this general atmosphere of conflict was Jeannie's desire to leave home and never return. Yet while she wanted more than anything to be with Jeannie, she loved her grandmother and knew in her heart of hearts she would never break those ties. As they did with every debate, Sandy knew they'd work it out and find a compromise. It would be her way in the end, she suspected. Once Jeannie was away from her parents and began to miss home, she'd be more tolerant of the minutiae that now drove her insane.

"What time are we leaving?" Sandy asked. Today was a big day for them, the wedding day of the Grabowski sisters. Carol, the older sister by thirteen months, worked with Jeannie at Jimmy the Jeweler across the river in Nanticoke. Linda twirled cones beside Sandy at Farrell's Ice Cream. The sisters and their siblings had moved to this side of the Susquehanna six years earlier when their mom remarried, and all five Grabowskis rode the school bus with Sandy and Jeannie. Although natives of Honey Pot, the family was welcomed into the West Nanticoke gang and fit in like they'd lived in town their whole lives.

Like the big sister she never had, Linda had taken Sandy under her wing when she began working at Farrell's three years earlier. She was sassy and fun and loved to break the rules. They were total opposites yet got along famously. Linda gave Sandy her first cigarette, a habit she quickly passed along to Jeannie. In the storeroom at Farrell's Sandy enjoyed her first beer, compliments of Linda's brother Chaz, and she and Linda had the best shift ever. Linda was blissfully happy with her fiancé Jim, and everyone anticipated having the time of their lives at the wedding.

"The ceremony starts at one. Twelve?"

"Your dad's driving us?" Sandy inquired. Neither she nor Jeannie had cars. They didn't really need them, and they were saving every cent for their life in New York. Secretly they had opened an account at the Nanticoke National Bank and saved over a thousand dollars toward their future. Even with scholarships they'd need spending money.

"My mom. We'll have to bum a ride home."

Sandy nodded in agreement. With half of the town at the reception, they'd have no trouble finding a ride.

Sandy leaned closer, resting her head on Jeannie's pillow. They kissed, savoring the last moment of bliss, knowing they had to get out of their bed and dress for the wedding. They wouldn't be able to hold hands like other couples, or dance close together, or show each other any affection in the presence of the wedding guests.

Soon, though, that would change. Their life together would be just as they dreamed it.

As they curled up together, blissfully in love, silently anticipating the promise life held for them, they were completely connected to each other, completely oblivious of the world around them.

They were unaware that a few hours earlier, two hundred miles to the south, a burglary had occurred at the Democratic National Committee headquarters at the Watergate Complex in Washington, D.C. The investigation into that break-in would lead to the eventual resignation of President Richard Nixon.

They were similarly unaware of meteorological events unfolding fifteen hundred miles away, near the Gulf of Mexico. They hadn't yet heard the name Agnes.

Three days earlier, a tropical depression had developed in the Caribbean Sea, and the day before, it had been upgraded to a tropical storm. Agnes was crawling through the Yucatan Channel east of Mexico, but in the coming days she would morph into the first Atlantic hurricane of the season, growing ever stronger as she thrashed along the eastern seaboard of the United States. In these dark days, the skies would pour more than seventeen inches of rain over the state of Pennsylvania. By the time she had unfurled all of her fury and faded out to sea, Agnes would become the costliest hurricane in the history of the United States.

In less than a week, the swollen Susquehanna would rise from its own bed, and the bed in which Sandy and Jeannie were daydreaming would be washed away, along with half the town and all their dreams.

CHAPTER THREE
THE FUNERAL, MAY 25, 2011

West Nanticoke, Pennsylvania

The cemetery was much as Sandy remembered it. A formidable stone wall lined the approach to a majestic stone archway. A wrought-iron gate (which had never been closed during all her trips here) guarded the entrance. Stone walkways allowed access between rows and rows of ancient grave markers. The trees were in full, vibrant bloom, surrounding three corners of the graveyard. On the bottom perimeter, beyond the road, was a cliff that fell hundreds of feet to the Susquehanna below.

Sitting on the freshly mowed lawn, with the sounds and smells of spring overwhelming her senses, Sandy wished she could feel the joy this season was meant to bring. As she stared into the distance, eyes unfocused, she couldn't help feeling just a little sad. Nellie had been a special woman. She had been graceful and elegant, tough and decisive, loving and compassionate. She had loved Sandy unconditionally, taught her values like honesty and integrity, showed her how to laugh at herself and the world. Her grandmother had really been more like a mother to her, and even though Sandy had known this day would come, she wasn't quite prepared for it. She had suffered loss before—her parents, her grandfather, the two great loves of her life—but this one somehow felt different. Nellie represented the past, and with her death, the final link to Sandy's history was broken.

Nellie had been the epitome of strength, up until her final days. She ruled three brothers during her formative years. She stole the heart of Sandy's grandfather, a man from one of the wealthiest families in Northeastern Pennsylvania, one who broke ranks and followed his dream of practicing medicine instead of working in his family's businesses. This man of steel was putty in his wife's hands. And though

Sandy never knew her father, she had come to learn that he was equally enamored of his mother.

As a child growing up in her grandparents' house, Sandy witnessed epic battles of will played out at the dinner table on a nightly basis. There was no topic David and Nellie Parker didn't discuss, often heatedly. As much as her grandparents adored each other, they didn't necessarily share the same views on the Vietnam War and politics, religion, and money. Sandy knew these were the same conversations all couples inevitably had and had chuckled when she found herself debating with Diane for the first time over dinner so long ago.

When she lived in Nellie's house, Sandy often sat and watched the drama unfold before her, a witness to the events rather than an active participant. And just that had been exciting. There were always sick patients, always business activities, always repairs and issues with their rental properties. Sandy's role in her relationship with her first lover had been similar—the quiet sounding board for Jeannie's myriad ideas and opinions.

After Nellie lost her husband and Sandy lost Jeannie, both women evolved in their relationship into a compromise that suited both of them. Realizing that Sandy wasn't the debater her husband had been, Nellie learned to coax opinions and conversations from her. And Sandy learned to open up and share more, growing more comfortable expressing her ideas and opinions. The growth period was one of discovery about themselves and each other and brought them even closer. As a result, when Sandy left for New York—and she had needed to go—her relationship with Nellie didn't suffer. Through the years she had visited often, eventually building a home in the Poconos, and often included Nellie in her travels.

This woman had been so vital in her life! While Sandy had so much to celebrate about her grandmother's long and fruitful life, she couldn't shake the sadness. She would miss her grandmother terribly. She would miss Nellie's wisdom and love, her laughter, and, most especially, their debates.

"It's beautiful here, Mom."

Startled from her reverie, Sandy nearly jumped. She looked up from her seat on the grass and smiled at her daughter, who took a seat beside her and grabbed her hand, squeezing it lovingly. Petite and with coloring that suggested an African ancestry, her daughter couldn't have looked more dissimilar to her. Yet their manners were so similar that they did in fact seem much the same. They sat silently, erect, with laced fingers pulling on bent knees, enjoying the vista before them as well as the calming reassurance of each other's company.

Sandy marveled that four decades had passed since her last visit here. She had lived an entire life in the interim between visits. Passing by so quickly, the days and months and years vanished as she attended college classes and played basketball games, dated women and fell in love again, worked on Wall Street and managed her own firm, traveled the world.

Adopting Angela had been the greatest decision she'd ever made, for her daughter had kept her busy and kept her young, filling Sandy's life with love and joy. Now Angie had given her a most precious gift—a grandson.

Life had come full circle for her as she found herself back in the place she'd spent her life avoiding. In all those years, Sandy had been here only once, but not to this place she'd so often visited as a child. Traveling abroad, studying art and antiquities in museums and exploring glacier bays and river canyons, she'd never felt whole. She now understood she'd been avoiding the very balm for her angst. She'd run from here and bandaged her wounds, but she'd never really tended to them and allowed them to heal.

It was time to do just that. She took in the view of the mountains, breathed in the fragrant air, and felt a tiny bit of peace. It was hard to not feel peaceful here, and even with the sadness the cemetery could invoke, the memories it could stir, it was still a comforting place for her.

Miles upstream, the foothills of the Pocono Mountains faded into the Wyoming Valley and into the depths of the Susquehanna River. On the west side of the river the Endless Mountains of the Appalachian chain formed the valley wall. Between those two ridges lay acres of fertile farmland and towns with businesses and homes and parks, but here just the mountains faced off, the river standing between them as if protecting them from each other. On the east bank, just south of Nanticoke, there was enough clearance to build a railroad bed, but not much else. On this side, the mountain dove so sharply into the river it had to be blasted with dynamite to create enough space to accommodate Route 11. Indeed, at certain points of the journey, if you looked up from the road you would see the mountain looming overhead rather than the sky above.

Why had she and Jeannie spent so much time up here at Riverview, among the dead? Her young mind had never analyzed the reasons, and even as an adult she would have argued it was a desire to be close to her father, whom she'd never met. He was buried on the hillside here, resting beneath the shade of a splendid maple that seemed as old as the mountain itself. She'd come back on this beautiful, sunny day to lay his mother to rest beside him.

Sharing the beauty of this place with her daughter, Sandy now realized she might have had no other motive for her childhood trips here than the simple desire for peace. The cemetery, set so high on the mountainside, was still and quiet. No random cars passed. No ambient noise filtered from nearby homes or schools. As a child who was always under the watchful eye and tutelage of her grandparents, visiting the cemetery let her escape from that adult universe.

She had never ventured here alone, and never with her grandparents, whose only child perpetually slept beneath the trees here. When her father, David Parker, Jr., died in a car accident, his parents were in such a state of shock they didn't consider planting him in the Poconos, where his maternal ancestors were buried, or in Wilkes-Barre, where the Parkers had been laid to rest. Riverview was close to their home, so into the ground of Riverview he went.

Her father had been in his third year of study at the University of Scranton when his car hit an icy patch of road as he was driving back to school one early morning. He was killed instantly. His parents never knew for sure why he'd made the thirty-mile trip home the night before he was killed, but after his college sweetheart informed the Parkers that she was carrying David's child, they suspected he'd planned to tell them the news. Why he didn't, they never knew. They didn't ask questions that no longer mattered; they simply buried their son and tried to vent their grief.

David might as well have been at the South Pole. His parents never visited their son's grave. The Parkers were spiritual people, and they believed their son hadn't died but was granted eternal life in Heaven with God. Bringing flowers to the cemetery, crying over an "empty" grave were just not on their agenda. Her grandparents insisted that the greatest respect they could pay their son's memory was to love and cherish his daughter. That they did.

Even still, the spiritual peace they felt was something that eluded their small granddaughter, who didn't have memories of a father or a child of his to cherish. All curiosity and unanswered questions (Why didn't her parents marry? Where did her mother go? Why did her dad come home that night?), Sandy found she could create answers that were to her liking very easily, explanations that eased the concerns of a child's conscience. Those answers didn't really satisfy her heart's longings. To her small mind, her father existed only in pictures and in his grave. So she went to the cemetery and spent time with him.

Her family plot was small, with just the three graves and two headstones, one that already bore her grandmother's name. She would have to make arrangements to have the date after the dash engraved. Unlike so many families here, including the Bennetts, who had large family markers, it would be easy to miss the three simple graves where her family was buried. Sandy knew where they were, though—she'd been to her dad's grave a million times.

She and Jeanie had hiked and explored the woods, picnicked, biked the roads, and pilfered flowers from fresh graves to adorn her father's site. Riverview was a busy place and never wanted for a fresh grave to target.

Sandy studied the grave markers of the people who were her only family for the first thirty years of her life. Her father had been dead for nearly sixty years, her pop for more than forty. Her grandmother had finally given up the fight and passed peacefully in her sleep, ninety-eight years after taking her first breath. As Sandy looked at the dates, it occurred to her that her grandmother had gone to the ground loving a man who had been dead longer than they'd been married. In all those years after his death, Nellie had never stopped loving her husband and never would have even considered keeping company with another man.

Sandy could understand her grandmother's feelings for her grandfather. God knew, she herself had lived a lifetime in love with the ghost of Jeannie Bennett. Even though she'd found love again after Jeannie's death, no one had ever owned her heart except the beautiful girl she'd first loved. Their love affair was sacred, a secret she'd carried her entire life.

Her partner, Diane, who'd shared Sandy's life for twenty years, had never known. Breast cancer had stolen Diane at the age of fifty-two, and since then Sandy had dated again, many women, in fact, but she knew she'd never love again. She'd been blessed, not once but twice, so how could she possibly hope for lightning to strike a third time? A more-than-adequate supply of single women had been happy to share Sandy's company for the past few years. During the last few months, she'd found herself spending more and more time in the company of one woman in particular. A passion for golf and trips to the theater were two strong ties; they shared fun days and were quite compatible at night as well. But as far as her heart went, the storms of life had washed out that access road.

As much as she enjoyed her time with this new lover, Pat, Sandy would never consider the relationship anything more than casual. And that was okay, because she had everything she needed.

With the sun shining on the beautiful face of her daughter, Sandy thought of those two other women she loved. Jeannie and Diane had been the same in so many ways, yet so different in others. Jeannie was quite feminine, always dressed in the latest fashion and never a hair out of place. Diane was somewhat frumpy but would have been adorable wearing a grocery bag. Jeannie was stubborn, Diane compliant and the peacekeeper. Jeannie could and would play with anything that could be ridden, bounced, or thrown. Diane, a professor of mathematics at Columbia, was interested in how far balls flew in relationship to their weight and volume, but didn't know the difference between a golf ball and a football. Yet they both loved music and food and travel, hiking and camping. They were two very different women, but they had both loved her passionately, and she had loved them both right back.

The time was long overdue to pay that first woman a visit. After the flood, after learning that Jeannie had been killed, Sandy had never returned here. The need to believe in God, to believe that Jeannie was not really dead but given to a higher power, had compelled Sandy to adopt her grandparents' stance on cemeteries. She had never visited, even for Jeannie's funeral. She had never said a proper good-bye. After a lifetime of holding Jeannie in her heart, the time was right to let her go.

During the past few weeks as she had anticipated her grandmother's interment, Sandy had thought of little else but those two women—Nellie and Jeannie. She knew she would have to come to Riverview and see Jeannie's grave. It had taken forty years and many tears, but now she finally felt ready to say that good-bye.

While the cemetery hadn't changed much, Sandy had. Those nimble knees were gone, the victims of too many rebounds and jump shots. "Give me a lift, would you?" she asked Angela, and when they were both standing, Sandy nodded her head uphill. It was time to tell the secret. "Come with me. There's someone I'd like you to meet.

"Jeannie Bennett was the first girl I ever loved," she explained to her daughter. "She was killed in an accident when her family was evacuating during Agnes."

If Angela was shocked to hear her mother's words, she didn't show it. Instead, eyes filled with love met Sandy's, and a sentimental frown turned down the corners of her mouth. "Oh, Mama! How awful! What happened?"

Holding hands, Sandy led her daughter toward the Bennett family plot, not far from her own family site, and told Angie the story of her life in West Nanticoke. She had never spoken much about her early years. In the beginning it was too painful for her, and later it would have been difficult for Diane to hear. Yet Sandy knew her daughter had always been curious, in the same way she was curious about her own mysterious beginnings. Sandy knew this was a story her daughter would like to hear, and she was pleased for them both that she was finally able to tell it.

Sandy carried a single flower with her, taken from her grandmother's spray. As she thought of Jeannie the smile that formed on her face was automatic, as reflexive as her rising pulse when Jeannie had kissed her. She could almost hear her laughter as they walked among the gravestones, among their ancestors and their neighbors' and friends' ancestors, studying a piece of history. On Memorial Day, flags honored those who had died in service of our country. Cherubs on children's stones noted their tragic deaths. Large family stones in the center of their plots commemorated the wealthiest of their neighbors. Those were perfect for climbing on, and one stone was large enough to host a picnic. Jeannie and Sandy had often dined there, eating peanut butter and grapes, then lying on their backs searched for shapes in the clouds, pondering the mysteries of life and death and the unknown beyond.

The Bennetts had been fruitful and multiplied, and locating their plot even after all these years was not a difficult task. Finding the marker for Jeanne Marie Bennett proved to be more challenging. Sandy noted Jeannie's parents' stone and read with sadness the date her on her father's. Paul Bennett had died the night they had evacuated Canal Street—June 22, 1972. The accident had happened just a few minutes after the Bennetts left their house for what would be the last time.

Sandy had stood on her porch watching them go, thinking all the while they'd be back in a few days, hauling mud and muck from their cellars and scrubbing walls with bleach to kill the river germs. She would work with Jeannie, side by side, helping their families through another flood, and when their task was completed they'd steal a beer and share it along the riverbank.

How wrong she'd been!

She brought herself back to the present, not wanting to think too much about the flood. She could tell herself she was ready and mentally steel herself, but traveling back in time was still not a pleasant journey. She shook the sadness threatening to overcome her and resumed her search.

Helen Bennett, Jeannie's mother, had died almost a decade earlier, in 2003. Even though Mrs. Bennett had always been kind to her, in all these forty years Sandy could never bring herself to reach out to the woman. To do so would have been to out Jeannie, for Sandy couldn't have spoken of Jeannie without acknowledging their love. And while she was sure Jeannie would eventually have declared her love for Sandy and told her parents they were lovers, she hadn't yet done it. Sandy thought it best to leave the secret of their love buried with Jeannie, and so she'd never contacted her family. Besides, what would have been the point? The girl she knew and loved was a very different one than her mother knew. Better to talk to old friends, like Linda Grabowski—but Sandy hadn't done that either. She'd simply run away. Away from the pain and the people who would remind her of what she'd lost during Hurricane Agnes.

Jeannie had died from injuries she suffered in the same car crash that killed her father. Always a fighter, she'd hung on for days before her body finally gave out. It had all been such a mess with the flood that Sandy had never even gotten to see her. Flooding forced the closure of the Wilkes-Barre hospitals, causing them to transfer Jeannie out of town. Sandy had never even heard all the details about the accident. It had never mattered to her, though, and it still didn't. Jeannie was dead. No matter how it had happened, dead was still dead. That Jeannie had been unconscious for a week and hadn't suffered gave Sandy one small measure of comfort.

Although she hadn't been to Riverview to visit, Sandy remembered Jeannie through the years in a million little ways. Random acts of kindness. Charitable donations. Volunteering her time at the AIDS clinic in the Village. Adopting a child. She'd visited all the places around the world that they'd dreamed of together, and at each place she'd spoken the name Jeannie in a reverent whisper. She'd carved Jeannie's initials in Alaskan glaciers and in the Berlin Wall, and written them on sandy beaches throughout the Caribbean. She'd lit a candle at the cathedral of Notre Dame in Paris, not because she was religious but because it was something she and Jeannie had done when they were twelve and had vowed to do again. She'd named a star after Jeannie, and somewhere on a preserve in Africa a giraffe named Jeannie was munching on the leaves of the tallest trees.

"This is so strange," Sandy muttered almost to herself, but Angie had heard and agreed with her mother. For fifteen minutes, Sandy and Angela walked back and forth among the gravestones, wiping away blades of freshly mowed grass as they methodically scoured every inch of the Bennett plot for some sign of Jeannie. They hadn't found her stone.

"Do you think she might be somewhere else?"

Blowing a frustrated sigh, Sandy shrugged. Although all of the Bennetts were buried at Riverview, she supposed it was possible they had interred Jeannie elsewhere. She couldn't begin to understand why they would do that. She sat and pursed her lips, looking around, thinking. Closing her eyes and shaking her head in sorrow, she suddenly realized why they couldn't find the stone. "Son of a bitch!" she muttered. "There's no stone. They didn't give her a fucking headstone." Sandy bit her lip and her shoulders sagged. She'd finally found the courage to come to this place, and now she couldn't find Jeannie!

Angie crossed the few feet of grass with quick strides, worry evident on her beautiful face. "What is it, Mom?"

Sandy turned into her daughter's arms and held her, crying for the first time in many years, for her first, lost love. An amazing girl, one who had meant the world to her, hadn't meant enough to her parents to be remembered with a grave marker. It shouldn't have surprised Sandy. Not long after Sandy's arrival on Canal Street, Mrs. Bennett gave birth to a stillborn son. Though he was buried in the family plot, a marker was never placed. It was if he'd never existed. During their trips to the cemetery, Jeannie would spread flowers all around the Bennett graves, hoping to mark the site of the little brother she never had the opportunity to love.

Remembering Jeannie's whimsical but sweet gesture, Sandy rose to her feet and did what Jeannie did so long ago. Plucking petals from her flower, she tossed them into the air to land where they would. Angie scampered back to her grandmother's freshly dug site and returned bearing an entire bouquet of flowers. She handed a few to her mother and then mimicked her actions, wandering between the rows of gravestones marked Bennett. Before long, the entire Bennett family plot was sprinkled with red and pink and white confetti. Wherever she was planted, Sandy thought happily, Jeannie had a flower.

"Still love you," she whispered to the wind.

When they had finished, Angie sat back and admired their work. "It's sort of a beautiful look, Mom."

Sandy had to agree. The sun was shining brightly, the grass neat and trimmed and covered with vibrantly colored flower petals. She fought more tears and took a deep breath. Her daughter didn't need to see her crying over a woman who wasn't the one who'd raised her. What would that say of Sandy's love for Diane?

Turning toward her car, she said, "Modern abstract. I think that style fits Ms. Bennett quite well. Now let's get out of here." At long last, Sandy had made her peace with Jeannie.

As they walked hand in hand toward the car, they didn't feel the prying eyes focused on them. They'd been so caught up in their search and then their frolicking that they didn't notice the gravedigger. Why would they? No one ever noticed him, a detail that really didn't bother him. In fact, it often worked in his favor. He was dressed as a cemetery worker in overalls and boots, and stood shoveling mulch a hundred yards away from the Parkers' plot. They were too far away to notice that he hadn't really done anything except push the pile around in circles—and watch them.

He'd waited forty years for Nellie Parker to be laid to rest, and now he hoped, at last, he could rest, too. She was the only living soul who knew the secrets that could get him into trouble, and he'd hoped for her demise for all those years. If he'd known her precise whereabouts just after the flood, he might have even decided to kill her. As long as she stayed away, though, he felt safe. He'd allowed her to live.

Sandy and Angie continued talking as they climbed into her car and drove away, and still the gravedigger watched, wondering. He'd never really given the old lady's granddaughter a second thought. She was so young when Agnes came, and busy being a teenager, had she had time to notice what was going on around her? It had never occurred to him that she could be a threat. Seeing her, though, made him start thinking. Was it possible Sandy knew the secret?

CHAPTER FOUR
HOME AGAIN

While it had taken over an hour to reach the cemetery in West Nanticoke from the funeral home in Tannersville, the next leg of Sandy's journey took just a few minutes. As she drove down the mountainside from Riverview, she marveled that she'd been there a thousand times, but never behind the wheel of a car. She'd walked up and down that hill what seemed like a million times and had thrilling rides on her bike. She could picture Jeannie beside her, long hair flying behind her as they raced to the bottom. They were reckless, with no helmets, and it was a wonder one of them hadn't been killed. But it had been fun. The speed of the bike and the wind in their hair brought a feeling of pure joy. Definitely not the same in the car. Maybe she should trade in the SUV for a sporty little convertible. She smiled at the thought. Maybe.

She had insisted on limiting the visitors to the ceremony for her grandmother's interment, sparing the distant relatives and her own friends a weary and dreary day. Only Angie sat beside her in the car on the long journey from the Poconos, following the hearse bearing her grandmother's remains. After a service at the funeral home and a celebratory breakfast, she and her daughter laid her grandmother to rest.

Sandy turned off Poplar Street and onto Houseman, marveling at the empty tracts of land that had once borne the homes of her friends and neighbors. Hudak's Bus Terminal had been there, and dozens of school buses lined the street every day before they were put to bed in the underground garage. It was now an empty field. Everything that had been there was gone, destroyed by Agnes and removed by bulldozers. At the intersection of Route 11, just to her right, had been Farrell's, where she'd first earned a paycheck. Now, only an empty patch of grass and weeds remained. She drove south a short distance and then made a left toward the river.

It was difficult to find her bearings, for trees had been washed away and cut down and grown up. The ten-foot-tall vanilla ice-cream cone on the roof of Farrell's could no longer guide her. It hadn't survived the flood. Unlike Poplar Street, where the damage was scattered like the pellets of a shotgun, Canal Street had been blasted by an assault rifle. The houses were all gone, every last one of them.

The mansion built by her ancestors in the mid nineteenth century had withstood a dozen floods over the years, as it was designed to, but couldn't hold ground against the force of Agnes. The Bennetts' home, nearly as big as the Parkers', had been washed down to the Chesapeake Bay as well. As she remembered it, the Roberts' house had been washed down the street and left on its side on the road. The dozen others on this quiet cobblestone street beside the river had met similar fates, their foundations crumbling and nails popping until only heaps of wood and stone remained of her neighborhood.

Hers had been the last house on Canal Street, or the first, depending on the direction you were facing. It was the southern-most dwelling on the street, set back on a small hill where the road bent away from the Susquehanna back toward Route 11. She used that bend in the road now to guide her as she tried to map out in her mind where her house had been.

She supposed all communities changed over time, evolving like living creatures in order to survive. A bank closed and a shop opened. A shop closed and a café took its place. The process continued, the town fulfilling the needs of the citizens. Like people, some lingered long after they'd fulfilled their purpose while others closed suddenly, leaving everyone wondering why. Sandy had seen this happen over the years in the Poconos and also in her little neighborhood in Greenwich Village.

The changes on Canal Street, though, weren't part of an evolution. This was annihilation. The wise men who governed the township had sacrificed an entire street. Deeming this ground too vulnerable to flooding, the redevelopment authority had claimed all of it by purchasing every property on the street. The homes that had survived Agnes were victims of the wrecking ball. The foundations of the homes washed into the river were filled in and leveled. Even the cobblestones that had formed the street were gone, replaced by gravel.

A park had been built in what was once her backyard. A field of green, dotted with swings and slides and a fitness trail, wound from the Parkers' to the Bennetts' and all the way to the Simons' property at the other end of the road. There were all the expected things—trees, picnic tables, a ball field—yet Sandy hadn't expected them and needed to take a deep breath to calm herself.

A family with a dog was playing a game of fetch. The mother had watched as Sandy's Mercedes pulled to a stop in the grass and they exited the car. The woman studied Sandy and Angie for a moment, making no effort to hide her surveillance. No doubt two women in an expensive car was an unusual sight in this modest neighborhood, but the woman assessed the new arrivals and must have deemed them harmless, for she quickly turned her attention back to her family.

"This was my backyard." She motioned to Angie. "The house was here, and I could sit on my front-porch swing and watch the mountain and the river right here at my feet. Over there was the basketball hoop my grandfather built for me. The court was made of fieldstone because Gram wanted it to match the walkways. Created a lot of bad bounces but improved my ball-handling skills!"

Sandy leaned against the car and just stared, from the railroad bed that had bordered their property in the back to the river across the canal in front, to the luscious foliage on the trees and up to the clear blue sky. It was a beautiful scene, but devoid of the children and flowerbeds and cobblestones and beautiful homes that had once made it grand. Absolutely nothing was left of the block she'd called home. Every single house was gone, along with the wonderful people who had lived there. For the first time, Sandy wondered what had become of them all.

The pain over losing Jeannie had been so intense that she'd found it necessary to just walk away from her life here and never look back. And walking away had been so easy, because there was nothing left to come back to after Agnes. She had unleashed her greatest wrath here. The Wyoming Valley had been decimated. Agnes had ruined twenty-five thousand homes and claimed the lives of fifty Pennsylvanians, two of them who had lived just a few feet from where she was standing.

Suddenly the memories Sandy had buried were floating free and flooding her brain. Being back in town made her regret her decision to leave it all behind her. These had been good people, and Sandy hoped they'd been able to pick up the pieces, as she and her grandmother had, and move on.

Angie walked around the car and put an arm around her shoulders.

"It's hard to imagine that river," she nodded to where a glimpse of the Susquehanna could be had through the trees, "doing this much damage. How did you manage to go on?"

Sandy pursed her lips and reflected before answering. On this calm, clear day, with the river resting peacefully in its bed, it was indeed hard to imagine the violence that had done such damage. Yet Sandy had witnessed it, and she would never forget what she'd seen. She blocked her emotions, something she'd gotten good at over the years, and tried to just focus on the facts. "All that rain has to go somewhere, and this is where all of the little streams and sewer pipes drain. It doesn't take much to make a flood. We were fortunate, Angie. We had money. My grandfather had been in college when the stock market crashed, and while his family survived, they had some losses. But they learned and became even more diversified. They invested in land and real estate, and a few businesses that brought in money. My grandfather never really trusted the banks and the market after 1929. He used to joke that he invested in the Canal Street Bank."

"You had a bank here on Canal Street?"

Laughing, Sandy shook her head. "Buster Brown shoe boxes in the attic."

Angie's jaw dropped. "You've got to be kidding me!"

"It was a different time, Ang. There were no credit cards then, and people did everything with cash. For years, my grandfather took all of his rental collections and the cash he brought in from his medical practice and put it in the attic. Not to mention the money from the various Parker enterprises. If he needed a new car, he went upstairs for money. If Gram wanted something for the house, he'd pull out a shoe box. After he died, my grandmother started using the bank more, because she preferred to write checks. Less driving around that way—she could just drop a check in the mail."

"So what happened to the money in the attic? Did you spend it all?"

Sandy laughed again. "Oh, no. I think we could have purchased a few cars and a new house with the cash Grandpop had up there, but unfortunately it all washed away."

"You're kidding me, right?"

Shaking her head, Sandy gave her a sad smile. "I'm not, Ang. No one knew it was going to be as bad as it was. We thought we'd get water on the first floor, so we moved everything to the second. We thought we'd be back in a few days, so we weren't really worried about leaving everything. No one expected the house to get washed down the river."

"So you took nothing with you when you left?"

"Clothes, a book, my toothbrush."

"Our entire family history, washed away. There must have been so many treasures, Mom. Antiques, huh?"

Sandy sighed. "All the furniture was beautiful. Finely constructed, real wood. Of course the household things like the silver and china were special, gifts to my grandparents on their wedding. My grandfather had a coin collection, with Indian-head pennies and buffalo nickels, that was quite valuable. He owned an original Wyeth that he bought when he was in med school. That painting would be worth millions today. My grandmother had a Norman Rockwell painting—not a print, an original painting—over the buffet in the dining room. Also worth a small fortune. And from my great-grandfather Parker, we had an array of old American West art and artifacts. A Remington bronze of a cowboy—like the one I own and some old guns and a poster promoting the Buffalo Bill show with Annie Oakley."

Ang smiled, biting her lower lip, as was her habit. "That must have been cool, growing up with all that stuff."

Sandy smiled in memory. It had brought her grandfather such joy to talk about his treasures, and she'd played Wild West with him so many times she couldn't count them. With real guns. "I did have a great childhood," she admitted.

"I'm sorry you lost all that stuff, Mom."

Sighing, Sandy shrugged. "We lost a lot, but we had a lot. We did okay after the flood. The redevelopment authority bought our properties for a fair price. And my grandfather's family had owned heavy equipment since the days of the mines. His brother was running the company then, but my grandmother was still a partner. They made millions cleaning up after Agnes. Some people were too poor to rebuild their homes and ended up living in low-income housing complexes until they died years later. Others were moved into trailer parks. Agnes destroyed those people. Us, she just kicked our knees out from under us. We got back up."

She again thought reverently of her neighbors, this time recalling their personal treasures. Mr. Babcock, who'd lived just a few doors away, had still proudly displayed the medals he'd earned serving America during World War II. As a young man he'd been part of Operation

Overlord, one of the brave soldiers who landed on Normandy Beach on that bloody June day so long ago. Another neighbor had been a member of the Nanticoke boys' basketball team that won the Pennsylvania State Championship in 1961. Sitting proudly upon the mantel, his trophy had been one of his prized possessions. Had he taken it with him? The china in Mrs. Bennett's closet had come from her family in Ireland. It was an irreplaceable treasure, and Sandy knew it hadn't gone with the Bennett family to higher ground. She'd helped them move it to the second floor just hours before they fled their home.

Everyone had lost something. Some lost everything. The value of their loss could sometimes be measured in dollars—her grandmother's Rockwell, for instance—but other treasures, like trophies and pictures, were far more valuable and equally irreplaceable.

"Everyone lost something," she said again, this time out loud, for Angie's benefit. She was speaking of family fortunes, of course, but also of her very personal loss. *I lost everything.*

"Do you want to see the river?" Angie asked.

Wearing low heels had seemed like a good idea in the morning when she was heading to the funeral home, but now they gave Sandy pause. They complemented her skirt, but she'd sink to her ankles if this grassy plot was wet. Because it was so close to the river and the water table so high, the ground beneath their home had never drained properly, and every good rain left their yard a soggy mess. She tested the ground before putting her full weight down. It was dry. She laughed to herself as she thought about that fact and about the last time she'd been in this very spot. On that occasion, she'd stood in six inches of mud.

CHAPTER FIVE
TOTAL DEVASTATION, JUNE 30, 1972

A week.
　　Seven interminable days of waiting for the river to recede and the roads to be cleared. One hundred sixty-eight hours, give or take, of watching television accounts of the flooding on the news, wondering what blows the river had dealt to their home, what had become of their friends and neighbors. From the safety of her grandmother's childhood home in the mountains they watched the devastation that Agnes brought to the Wyoming Valley. The city of Wilkes-Barre was buried, with eighteen feet of water on Public Square. Sandy had been there with Jeannie just a few days earlier to see *A Clockwork Orange*. They had snuck into the Paramount Theater and then treated themselves to a slice of pizza at the lunch counter at Kresge. Across the river in a cemetery in Forty Fort, two thousand coffins had been unearthed and bodies were seen floating, coming to rest on rooftops and inside homes. It was thought these bodies would never be identified again, for if dental records had existed before the flood, there was a good chance they had been washed away, too. Bridges were washed out, their massive steel frames twisted and bent like toy models. Up and down the valley, from Pittston to Shickshinny, the destruction was unimaginable.

　　On the news they saw helicopter footage of the flooding and knew what they would find upon their return home would be awful. Just how awful remained to be seen. Congressman Dan Flood promised help to the citizens whose homes and businesses were destroyed, and President Nixon toured the area, avoiding questions about the break-in at the Watergate Hotel as he focused on his mission to help the two hundred thousand homeless people Agnes had left behind.

　　While Sandy watched the television constantly, she kept her ear on the phone. Jeannie hadn't called. Many phone lines were down and the calls she'd placed to Jeannie's aunt's house hadn't gone through. Pacing and pulling her hair, Sandy thought the waiting would drive her mad.

For days after the water receded, they had been warned to keep out. The safety of bridges had to be verified, debris blocked roadways, power and phone lines were down. Spilled oil and gas and sewage created further trouble. There was concern for disease from typhus and tetanus and whatever grew in the blanket of mud that cloaked the Wyoming Valley. Finally, after days of worry, sleeping and eating just enough to survive, they received a call from Joe Sneck, West Nanticoke's fire chief. Her grandparents had both been active in the community, and raising money for the local fire and ambulance squad had forged a friendship between the elder Parkers and the chief. He'd promised to call Nellie when it was okay to return home.

Sandy was frantic to speak with Mr. Sneck. Perhaps he had some news of the Bennetts. The fear that something was wrong had taken hold of Sandy, and with each tick of the clock her anguish intensified.

Watching closely as her grandmother listened to the chief, Sandy could tell the news was bad. Even so, she couldn't have imagined the devastation that had occurred in her hometown. She took the phone from her grandmother when it was proffered and introduced herself. "How's our house?" she asked.

"It's gone. Your house is gone," the chief responded. He sounded indifferent, but Sandy later realized that he was in shock from all he'd seen. Even though she'd been watching news of the flood on their television, Sandy couldn't comprehend what he was telling her. "What are you talking about?"

"The house was torn from the foundation and washed away. There's nothing left."

"You're joking, right? That can't really happen."

"I wish I was, young lady. This is something the likes of which I've never seen."

"What about the Bennetts' house?"

"Gone. I don't know how Helen will get through this without Paul."

Her heart seemed to stop and Sandy felt light-headed. She slumped to the floor, for the phone in the farmhouse was on a wall in the kitchen a good distance from the table. His words rang in Sandy's ears. *Without Paul.*

"What happened to Mr. Bennett, Chief?" Sandy knew instinctively that the answer to that question would solve the mystery of why she hadn't heard from Jeannie.

"A car accident. The rain, I guess. They hit another car head-on. Paul was killed instantly."

"Chief, what about Jeannie?"

"One of the girls was hurt pretty bad, I'm not sure which one." He might not have known, but Sandy did. It was the only explanation for Jeannie not calling her. She pressed him for more details, but he didn't have any.

Three hours later, Sandy was standing in a foot of mud next to a hole in the ground that was once the cellar of her home. She had pleaded hysterically for her uncle Arthur to take her home, and when he refused, she'd grabbed his car keys from the hook by the door and essentially stolen his car.

She didn't have a driver's license, and she'd never driven on a road, but she understood the principles since Chaz Grabowski had let her drive his car in the church parking lot a few times. She had no money, no purse, no wallet. None of that mattered. She needed to get information, and for that, she needed to get home.

The children in the backseat don't have to memorize the route the driver takes, but luckily Sandy had. The drive from Arthur's house to her own home seemed to take hours under normal circumstances, and today was even worse. She had no map but knew enough to wind her way south through the mountains, staying high up above the area where flooding had occurred. News reports warned of blocked roads, washed-out bridges, and treacherous driving conditions. They had warned all unnecessary persons to stay out of the flood zone.

Sandy felt it was necessary for her to be there. She drove Route 904 through Lake Ariel and followed it all the way to White Haven. She weaved through Mountaintop, down Alden Mountain, and into Nanticoke before she found any signs that Agnes had been there. Concentrating on driving gave her a headache, and her grip on the steering wheel caused her hands to cramp so badly she was forced to pull over to rest for a few minutes. This driving wasn't as easy as she thought it would be.

She didn't notice the traffic or the roads or the trees, but when she reached Nanticoke, she couldn't help notice. The road was covered with mud and debris, and was nearly impassable. Lower Broadway was in chaos, with homes knocked off their foundations and toppled. Sandy's grandmother owned a dozen houses here, and since her grandfather's death it had been Sandy's job to collect the rent. During the warm weather, she would ride her bicycle, knocking on doors and walking away with the rent money—all in cash. It was a wonder no one had ever robbed her. Now all of these families would be without homes, and from the destruction she witnessed, it would be a long time—if ever—before Lower Broadway was restored.

Mud was everywhere, with national guardsmen walking along roadsides piled with the debris they'd cleared so cars could squeak through. People scurried around, talking to neighbors and guardsmen, beginning the impossible task of getting their homes and lives back in order.

Allen's Scrapyard didn't look so bad—it always looked muddy to her. Spencer's Junkyard was filled with muddy cars, and the windowpane at Swither's Gas Station served as a marker for the floodwater. Three-quarters of the way up, the glass was coated in mud, and then the glass became clear. She was afraid of what she'd see if she looked inside.

Across the bridge, it was even worse. West Nanticoke, once a beautiful town of quaint houses beside the Susquehanna, was destroyed. From one end to the other, houses had been knocked off their foundations. The ones that still stood were without windows, doors pulled from their hinges, awnings and porches swept from the dwellings by the swift current of river water. In the heart of town, water had reached the second story of these homes and businesses. Norm Faux's service station was still standing, but with windows and doors knocked out. The Parembas' and Grabowskis' and Deemers' and Starks' homes were still standing, but in filth. Bevan's Furniture Store no longer had windows, and inside gas ranges were piled upon soggy sofas, the ceiling hanging down on top of it all. Across the street, the huge Victorian that overlooked Harvey's Creek had burned from the roof to the waterline above the first-floor windows. Price's Gas Station pumps were ripped from the ground. A huge plastic tire, at least ten feet tall, once beckoning customers into the garage for car repair, had been washed through the plate-glass window of the office.

The entrance to Canal Street was barricaded at the north end, and as she drove farther to approach from the south she couldn't believe her eyes. The giant ice-cream cone that had beckoned customers from the roof of Farrell's had been been washed away and was caught in the branches of a tree. The ice-cream shop itself was a pile of rubble. She pulled over next to it and parked, for the southern entrance of Canal Street, across Route 11 from Farrell's, was closed as well.

She ran from her car, across Route 11 and up the bank of the railroad tracks that shielded Canal Street from the main road. That bank and the trees lining it obstructed her view. Sandy labored up the muddy incline, slipping near the top, and looked up as she regained her balance. Then she dropped to her knees.

The chief wasn't lying. Her house was gone. So was Jeannie's. Someone else's house was on the road near where hers once sat, collapsed on itself with such force that the chimney had disintegrated into a pile of bricks. Despite the fact that she'd lived on this street for fourteen years, she couldn't tell whose house it was. It was white, but so were half the houses on the block. Trees were uprooted and lay broken in yards and on porches. Sitting on the railroad tracks she surveyed the street where she had spent most of her life and began to cry.

It looked like a crazy person had gone berserk and begun throwing things all over. Here clothing and a bicycle in the branches of a tree. There an overturned car. A sofa sat in a swimming pool of mud. Mud, mud, mud everywhere, with strange things sprouting from beneath, like warped plants in a horror film. Toys, furniture, appliances, books, unidentifiable debris—in some places scattered, and in others arranged in piles.

Sandy sighed. No way could she let her grandmother see this. Her grandmother couldn't get through it. Yes, she was spirited. She was a hard worker. She had an unyielding faith in God. But she was approaching sixty years old, and she didn't have the strength to clean up and start over, to rebuild a house that would be empty in a year when Sandy left for New York. Nellie would have been fine living here without Sandy, in the home she loved, with the memories of her son and her husband to keep her company. She had once owned a beautiful home, had nice neighbors, on a quiet, tree-lined cobblestone street along the river. And now it was gone.

The vision before her was so devastating that for a moment Sandy forgot why she'd come here. Then she wiped her eyes on her shirtsleeve and stood up. She needed to find Jeannie.

She saw people down the road, where homes still stood, and walked along the railroad tracks until she reached them. She paid no mind to the shoes on her feet that would be ruined as she made her way across the Hannahs' yard. Mr. Hannah was there with some men who Sandy didn't recognize. She greeted him and although she had known him her entire life, it appeared he didn't recognize her. He, too, was in shock.

She had to introduce herself. "Have you heard about the Bennetts?"

He shook his head. "I can't believe it. On top of this," he said, gesturing at the destruction surrounding him. He confirmed Paul Bennett's death, but knew no other details. He didn't know how Jeannie had fared in the car crash that claimed her father's life, or even what hospital she should check. Nor did anyone else who Sandy met.

She walked through the yards of her neighbors, back toward the place where her own house once stood. She asked everyone she met, from neighbors crying in anguish to strangers just there to gawk, but no one could help her to find Jeannie. Pausing at the hole in the ground that had been Jeannie's house, she began to cry again. This was so very awful, and she was so very sad for all the people whose lives this flood had changed forever. She cried for all the things she knew Jeannie would miss in this place—the front-porch swing and the tree house, the widow's walk along the front, the bedroom that afforded a view of the river and mountains. Jeannie's quilt had been sewn by her grandmother, and together she and Jeannie had painted the room to match it. It was somewhat loud, but perfect for her. The court where they once played basketball in the backyard by the tracks wasn't visible under the mud. The flowerbed where their friendship had blossomed so long ago was washed away with everything else.

With difficulty, picking up shoes and pants weighted down by mud, careful not to fall in this wasteland, Sandy walked another hundred yards to her own backyard and looked around. The debris she saw didn't look familiar. A milk jug might have been theirs, but she didn't recognize the coffee can or the toaster oven, the box of cereal or the record player.

Nothing else was there. Everything was gone. She thought of the furniture, some of it older than Nellie, given to her by her parents and grandparents. The brass bed that her father had slept in. The four-poster bed that had been hers, where she and Jeannie had explored their passion. The cuckoo clock that hung in the stairwell, driving Sandy crazy with its hourly cries. The hardwood floors and crown molding, pocket doors and the built-in ironing board in the kitchen. And the photographs. Her grandparents' wedding photo, sitting proudly on the piano beside her dad's graduation picture. The albums of photos chronicling not just her life, but the lives of generations of her family. She thought of the rooms of the house—the big kitchen and the formal dining room, the grand family room with a view of the river, where her grandfather had played the piano and her grandmother had sat beside him, singing songs they both loved.

How she would miss this house, but it would be so much worse for Nellie. For Sandy this had only been a stop on her journey, but for Nellie it had been the final destination. Her grandmother's heart would be broken, and Sandy didn't know what she could do to help her. The only thing she knew now was that she had to find Jeannie.

CHAPTER SIX
THE HOSPITAL

Stopping at the bank looking like she did seemed inappropriate, but Sandy had no choice. Her upper half was okay, but her pants were splattered with mud and caked from the knees down. She felt uncomfortable until she saw the other patrons in the lobby. Half of them were in the same shape, and a line of them extended through the great marble-lined common area and nearly out the big glass doors. The manager, Mr. Kimble, was walking through the crowd, patting some customers on the back and nodding sympathetically as he listened to their tales of tragedy.

After Sandy explained about losing her passbook in the flood, the teller helped her fill out the necessary paperwork to withdraw her money. Apparently many other customers were experiencing the same problem and, having lost all proof of their savings, had come to the bank in fear that their money would be lost in addition to their homes and businesses. Verifying her identity was easy—Sandy knew everyone at the bank. Since her grandfather had passed away, she had not only been responsible for collecting the rent payments, but she had also been the one depositing them into her grandmother's checking account at the bank. Her signature on the form was all the formality necessary to withdraw money. She took all of it, every penny she and Jeannie had been saving for their life in New York. Right now, New York was a long way away. She thought of her grandmother's needs as well. A good amount of her cash was in this bank. How easy would it be for Nellie to get back here? Since Sandy's name had been added to the accounts after her grandfather's death, she had access to that money as well. After a moment's debate, Sandy withdrew a thousand dollars for her grandmother.

She'd seen piles of money before—stored in boxes in her attic— but she'd never felt the weight of it in her hands. That she was carrying over two thousand dollars—practically the cost of a new car, and enough to pay her first year's college tuition—was dizzying. How much more had been washed, in Buster Brown shoe boxes, down the river? The number was staggering.

Immediately upon exiting the bank she entered the building that stood beside it. The Leader Store was a small general store where she knew she'd find something suitable to wear. She dumped her dirty shoes and picked up a new pair, as well as a change of clothing. She couldn't very well go traipsing about the local hospitals in search of Jeannie looking like she'd been playing in the mud. She cleaned up nicely in the restroom and tossed the dirty clothing into the trash can. Not looking good, but at least improved, she climbed into Arthur's car and began the search for her lover.

Nanticoke Hospital was the first stop, the closest. They had been born there, but now the hospital had no record of Jeannie. The operator on duty was sympathetic and helpful. Two local hospitals had been closed, but Wyoming Valley and Wilkes-Barre General were filling the gap, and it was likely Jeannie had been taken to one or the other.

Staying on the high ground on the east side of the Susquehanna, Sandy found passable but congested roads. The entire valley was forced to travel this route. The logical first stop was at Wyoming Valley Hospital, since it was closer. The solitary building sat atop a hill in the Heights section of Wilkes-Barre, far above the flood zone, and it had been used as an evacuation center. Cars were double-parked all along the streets surrounding the hospital, and people milled about, talking, smoking, some just staring ahead, their blank eyes holding no focus.

She bummed a cigarette off two men talking on the sidewalk. She didn't smoke often, and never would in front of Nellie, but she was feeling the need. The meter measuring her stress was about to blow.

"The mannequins from the Boston Store were bobbing in the water, like dead bodies. It was eerie," one man said.

"Did you hear about the cemetery in Forty Fort?" His companion nodded in response.

"One of the nurses here told me they set up a makeshift delivery room at College Misericordia and they're worried they may have switched some babies in the chaos. Apparently they gave one lady her little girl to take home and she started screaming. She'd delivered a boy."

"Where are you from?" they asked Sandy as one of them used his cigarette to light hers. Shaking her head, she sighed and told them some of what she'd seen in the Nanticokes.

"My grandmother's in her eighties. She's lived here her whole life and she's never seen anything like this," the first man commented.

Indeed, there never had been anything like Agnes.

So many patients had flocked to the hospital that the operator couldn't verify if Jeannie Bennett was a patient there or not. They were having trouble keeping the records up to date. She was forced to visit every floor in the hospital, and in the end her search was fruitless.

Up the road a few miles, at Wilkes-Barre General Hospital, the scene was even more chaotic. Army tents had been erected in the parking lot, and medical personel were taking care of patients right there. Everywhere she looked she saw people walking in different directions, all kinds of people—some well-dressed, some half-dressed, soldiers and doctors and nurses all scurrying about like ants on a sandhill.

Here, though, Sandy had better luck. Although Jeannie hadn't been admitted to General Hospital, an orderly chatting with the operator in the lobby offered a tip. He was a volunteer ambulance aide, and he'd heard about the fatal accident on the night of the flood. It had happened on Route 309 in Mountaintop, and he suspected the victims had been taken to Hazleton. He was also kind enough to give Sandy directions to Hazleton General Hospital.

She was getting the hang of driving, yet it seemed that the trip to Hazleton was interminable. Though she'd been through Mountaintop just a few hours earlier, it seemed like days had passed since she'd been there. Sandy was anxious—would this be a dead end, too? She was nervous—was Jeannie badly hurt? She shook off the worry and told herself it didn't matter. She would find Jeannie if she had to drive to Florida, and her love would be the balm to nurse Jeannie through any injuries, no matter how grave.

Compared to the others, the hospital lobby seemed eerily quiet as Sandy entered. Here in the mountains they were geographically far removed from the chaos Agnes had created, and it was evident from the empty parking lot to the barren lobby.

As she approached the information desk, ready to make her well-practiced inquiry, a hand touched her arm. Startled, she jumped back and turned to face a woman she barely recognized as Helen Bennett. Jeannie's mother looked ten years older than Sandy remembered. The puffy, red eyes told Sandy she'd been crying, and her skin was frighteningly pale. Before Sandy could speak, she was pulled into a hug and felt sobs of anguish that petrified her. Sandy couldn't speak, couldn't pull away, couldn't collapse to the floor, although her legs wanted to. She could only stand there in Mrs. Bennett's arms as they comforted each other. For what, Sandy didn't yet know.

An eternity later, Mrs. Bennett pulled back. Taking Sandy's hand, she led her to a group of chairs nestled discreetly in the lobby's corner and sat down. Sandy copied her movements, leaning forward in the chair as she stared at the woman, unable to find her voice. Her heart was pounding so loud it seemed to choke her vocal cords.

Grief marred Mrs. Bennett's lovely face, and as she stared at Sandy her lip trembled, but she didn't speak.

Trying not to show her anguish and anxiety, Sandy finally cleared her throat and asked, "Is Jeannie here?"

Mrs. Bennett dropped her head and her shoulders shook with sobs.

Sandy moved farther forward, all hesitation now gone. "Where is she, Mrs. Bennett? Where is Jeannie?"

Finally Mrs. Bennett raised her eyes to look at Sandy, although she couldn't seem to find the strength to lift her shoulders or her head. "She died an hour ago."

Sandy howled in anguish, mortally wounded, and just then Jane Bennett walked into the lobby. Jeannie's older sister looked as awful as her mother. Relieved that there was someone to console Mrs. Bennett— for Sandy knew she couldn't possibly be up for the task—she stood on rubbery legs and found her balance with a hand placed on the back of the chair.

She needed to get out of there. She needed to scream or punch something or bang her head against the wall. She needed to find a place where the oxygen in the air hadn't been replaced by lead. "I have to go," she bravely announced, and she used all of her strength to hold her body erect and make her legs move.

She didn't remember the drive to Mount Pocono, but she would never forget the comfort of her grandmother's arms around her as she refused to get out of bed for the next two months.

Chapter Seven
Cleaning House, May 26, 2011

Escorting her daughter and her family to their car, Sandy tried not to cry. Again. As much as she would have loved it, she didn't want Angie to feel it necessary to stay and keep her company. Angie had spent the week before Nellie's death with her in the Poconos, and Sandy suspected she needed to spend some time in her own house, with her husband Tom and their sleeping son. On the day after the funeral, Sandy evicted them.

"When's Pat arriving, Mama?" Angie asked.

"Not sure. Juries are unpredictable. Maybe tonight, though." A Brooklyn lawyer, Pat had been going into closing arguments when Nellie died and wasn't able to make it earlier. Although Sandy hadn't minded, now that Angie was leaving she found herself looking forward to a visit from her lover.

She hugged her daughter and son-in-law, kissed their sleeping child, and stood watching as their car disappeared around the bend in the drive. She was exhausted, and she didn't want to think, but her mind found it hard to rest when unsettled matters were rattling around in there.

Nellie had left an unsettled matter of enormous magnitude.

As a young girl growing up on a farm near the vast expanse of Pocono Manor, Nellie Davis had loved the outdoors. She explored the woods and inspected the farm, reporting back to her father the news of broken fence boards and fallen trees. On one such mission she'd met her future husband, whose family had purchased the farm adjacent to her own.

As Nellie told it, her grandfather was hopelessly trying to catch a fish in a fast-moving stream when she first spotted him. David had claimed to be not fishing at all, just resting in the woods beside a babbling brook.

Both families had understood the value of the land. The Davises were farmers, the Parkers investors. Both sides had done what they could to keep the land in their families. They witnessed the gradual disappearance of farms in favor of other enterprises. Both tried to keep their land safe from their descendants by making complex decisions regarding the disposition of their property upon their deaths. On the Parker side, it was easy. A few generations of Parkers had only one or two children, and a few tragic deaths occurred, leaving only a few descendants of the coal baron Daniel Parker to do battle over his estate. One of her grandfather's two brothers died during the influenza epidemic in 1918, leaving the estate to be split between only her grandfather, his brother, and a few cousins. The Pocono land had been given to her grandfather and was now in Sandy's hands. On the Davis side, things were a bit more complicated.

Seeking to help provide for their children, and wanting to keep them close, her grandparents had offered each of their four children parcels of land on which all but her grandmother had built their homes. The land remained deeded to the parents. The terms of their will set up a winner-takes-all contest in which the last man (or woman) standing inherited the land. Two of the children had died years earlier, and in the end Nellie had outlived her beloved brother Arthur by just a few months, leaving the Davis property to Sandy as well.

On the real-estate market, nearly a thousand consecutive acres of farmland would fetch quite an asking price, but that wasn't what had the Davis descendants foaming at the mouth. Arthur had multiplied by four, and those by four, and now there were over fifty great-grandchildren in their twenties and thirties, some of them creating even more children. Divided, had Arthur outlived Nellie, the grand total wouldn't have amounted to much for any one of them—perhaps thirty or forty thousand dollars each. A new variable had been thrown in, though, calling into question the true value of the land and the identity of the rightful heirs.

One of the husbands of one of the descendants of the House of Arthur had informed Sandy just a few days after Arthur's death that his side was contesting the will. The swiftness of their action told Sandy that their plan had long been in the making. Their argument was simple: the intention of the will was always to keep the property whole, never to deny any of their children what was rightfully theirs. Now, the Arthurs weren't debating the division of the land—they didn't want the land—so the spirit of the will would be upheld. They wanted the mineral rights, which the will had never specifically addressed.

The value of soil in Northeastern Pennsylvania had skyrocked since it had been determined that gas trapped within the Marcellus Shale beneath it could be extracted by hydraulic fracturing. The process known as fracking was creating instant millionaires out of those who had been struggling farmers. And while it wasn't known how much gas was beneath the Davis farm or what it was worth, the House of Arthur was taking no chances. They had lawyered up and were fighting for the right to drill for gas in the event there happened to be any there. Gas drilling would keep the parcel of land intact yet benefit all of the Davis descendants, and had they known about hydraulic fracturing in their lifetime (argued the House of Arthur), their great-great-grandparents would surely have split the mineral rights equitably among all of their children.

The filing of the lawsuit had forced Sandy to obtain legal counsel of her own. Fortunately, she was sleeping with a lawyer who was admitted to the bar in Pennsylvania. While it wasn't her specialty, and Sandy knew she was going to have to find a representative with more expertise in wills and trusts and mineral rights, Pat offered sage advice to guide her through the preliminary battles of this war.

Sandy knew she needed to attend to another piece of unfinished business as well. The unpleasant responsibility of disposing of her grandmother's effects rested on her shoulders. Wandering through the house, Sandy found it amazing that her grandmother had accumulated so little stuff in the time since Agnes. It was as though the loss of all material possessions—and her survival through it—had taught her how little value they held.

The clothing was donated, which was the easy part. There were documents that might be of importance, but then again how important could deeds and articles of incorporation from businesses started in the early 1900s really be? She figured she would keep the paperwork just for its historical importance. What to do with the rest of it? Furniture and appliances and artwork would need new homes. The fate of the house and the farm was in her hands.

Should she fight the Arthurs or just let them have the farm? She could walk away from this parcel, and they could hash it out while she enjoyed a cocktail on the deck of her cabin just a short drive away on the neighboring Parker land. It would be so easy! Her heart held no desire to fight them, and they had the biggest motivator of all on their side: money. Sandy didn't need the money; she would be fighting for honor or justice or some theoretical ideal, or just to have more money.

And deep down inside, she wasn't so sure the House of Arthur was wrong.

A decisive woman of conviction, Sandy found this indecisive state unsettling. She wished she had the fortune of her grandmother's wise counsel, but in the months preceding her death, Nellie hadn't been in possession of the mental faculties that had been so keen in her younger days. In fact, her health at the end had been so poor that Sandy was certain Nellie would die first and she wouldn't have had this headache to contend with.

She knew her grandmother didn't really care what happened to the old homestead. Nellie had always lived a privileged life, yet her needs were simple. As easily as she attended balls with the governor, she cared for the sick, and she could enjoy a cocktail after a round of golf or a beer after working in the garden. Compared to the excitement she'd known in Nanticoke, Nellie lived an arguably boring life after the death of her husband. Yet she was happy on this farm where she was raised, and after her great losses, material things had ceased to matter to her.

Sandy once again found her grandmother's lack of sentimentality at odds with her own feelings. Understanding over the past few weeks that Nellie's end was near, Sandy had spent time thinking and decided that she didn't want to empty the house until she'd determined the farm's fate. There was no need to. She would leave the furniture and appliances and take the personal items such as jewelry and a few knickknacks, as well as the pictures.

After the flood, the greatest gift anyone gave either of them was pictures. They had lost all of them to the Susquehanna, but fortunately there were copies. As a child, Sandy always wondered why her grandmother bothered to send a picture of her to Aunt Claire and Uncle Bill in New York or to Uncle Arthur in Mount Pocono. Who really cared what she looked like in third grade? Fortunately, Nellie had done just that, and after the flood, Sandy understood why. The relatives had delivered so many treasures—her grandparents' wedding photo and her father's baptism portrait, pictures of him as a boy playing with his cousins. There was a photo Sandy had never seen, of her parents at their high-school prom. All the photos of Sandy's mother had disappeared after she left Sandy on the Parkers' doorstep, and Sandy knew virtually nothing about her, so the prom picture was a treasure. Having lost so much of her history in the flood, she was thrilled for the little pieces of her past, captured by the camera so she could preserve her memories long after she began to forget.

Now looking back, Sandy again felt so fortunate that these memories had been salvaged.

She walked through the farmhouse that had been her grandmother's home, but never her own. Leaning against the door frame of what had once been her bedroom, Sandy stared across the room. Tucked into the frame of a mirror that had grown foggy with age was the only photo she had of Jeannie. It was taken at a photo booth at the Bloomsburg Fair, and the black-and-white images were a bit blurred, but even from across the room Sandy could see the big smiles on their faces. The photo had escaped the fate of her other possessions by sheer luck. Jeannie had stuck it as a bookmark into the paperback novel she had been reading and left it there. Sandy had borrowed the book from her in the days before the flood, intending to read it, and when they were packing she threw the book into her suitcase, thinking it would help her pass the time as she waited for the waters of the river to recede.

Sandy had found this hidden treasure in the book months later, when she finally had the energy to raise her arms and hold the book to read it. She'd been keeping it safe here ever since.

She surveyed the room. The furniture had been there before Sandy's arrival and remained still. That had been a dark year and she'd done little to improve upon her barren quarters, and the room seemed almost the same as it was when she arrived, with only that one memory from her past added. The furniture was old and solid, just four pieces. There were no personal effects other than the picture, and if she decided to give up the farm, it would be easy to clear out this room. She could easily find one of Arthur's grandchildren to take the furniture. Lord knew they'd take any handout she'd give them.

She walked back into the kitchen and poured herself a glass of iced tea, then got down to work. A few hours later, the honking of a car horn surprised her. The time had been well spent, and just about everything that would be donated was organized and ready to go—the trash cornered in one room and the personal effects packed for transfer to Sandy's house. She walked to the window in time to see Pat climbing out of her Jeep.

"What's the verdict?" Sandy asked by way of greeting.

A cocky grin spread across Pat's face as she reached for her duffel. "In favor of yours truly."

"Congratulations! Can I buy you a drink to celebrate?"

Dropping her bag at Sandy's feet, Pat wrapped her arms around Sandy's waist and placed a chaste kiss upon her cheek. "I can think of many ways to celebrate, but a drink's a good start!"

Sandy encircled Pat's waist and cringed, as she always did when she discovered Pat's weapon. A former cop, Pat was never far from her gun. "I think you're safe here in the mountains."

"You never know. I might run into a bear."

Smirking, she said, "You're going to need a bigger gun, honey."

Still dressed in a business suit, Pat had apparently made the trip directly from court. "You look very handsome. And formidable." At nearly six feet tall, Pat was indeed a striking image, and Sandy knew she worked hard in the gym to maintain the firm body hidden beneath the tailored suit.

"Would you be terribly disappointed if I change into something more comfortable? I don't want to intimidate you."

Sandy roared, and it felt good.

"Come on, I'll take you home." She closed up the house and hopped into her car, leading Pat to her cabin just a few miles away.

Shortly before her birth, a fire had destroyed the Parkers' Pocono home. They never rebuilt. Perhaps if their son hadn't died so suddenly they would have come back to the mountains, but as it was, their life changed dramatically. Soon after David's death they were given the responsibility of caring for his three-year-old little girl, and in their late forties at the time, it was an exhausting task. They settled Sandy into their home on Canal Street, and though they still traveled and enjoyed the local culture, their life didn't include the outdoor activities they'd enjoyed in their younger days when they were raising their son.

When Sandy and her grandmother came to live with Arthur, he'd taken over their parents' home. It was the original house on the property, and though quite grand in its day, it was showing its age. It had been Nellie's childhood home, and she seemed to slip easily back into this farm life. Sandy, however, did not. Her final year of high school involved studying and playing basketball, and not much time at the farm. Just a short year after arriving there, she left for college, not giving her much time to grow attached to the place.

During her collegiate years, she found the trips "home" very difficult. New York offered her nightlife and culture and sports, and of course women, and Mount Pocono just couldn't compete. She continued her sexual explorations at Queens College, finding—as she and Jeannie had expected—quite a few lesbians in the Big Apple. Though she dated extensively, she never contemplated bringing any of her sexual partners home to meet her grandmother. She was left choosing which way to spend her holidays, and the choice of a beautiful young woman often won out over the aging one who had raised her.

She did miss her grandmother, though, and she did come home. And Arthur drove her crazy. He was miserly and obsessively neat, and how he and Nellie could have been related puzzled Sandy. Nellie didn't seem to mind him, though, so Sandy tried her best to tolerate the man.

Using money from the Parker trust, Sandy supported herself in New York. Had she understood the details of the trust—which became available to her in small allotments when she reached her eighteenth birthday—Sandy and Jeannie would have had no worries. The trust covered her tuition and gave her plenty of spending money. It would have been enough to support them both for the duration of their college days. Hell, it would have supported them for the rest of their lives.

Sandy used a sum of her money for the purchase of a pop-up camper, which she permanently installed on her land. It had no heat, so served its purpose only from April to October, but during those months Sandy enjoyed the Poconos. She could spend an entire day with her grandmother, then escape to the camper for a bit of quiet. She built fires and stargazed and read by the light of a kerosene lamp. When the winter came, she worked harder and longer on Wall Street and felt justified in avoiding the mountains, but she still came home for Christmas. For those few days, Arthur seemed to be more cheerful and Sandy could tolerate him a little more easily. Spring followed winter and the snow eventually melted and once again it became warm enough to visit the camper.

The mid-1980s were a busy time for Sandy. She had opened her own investment firm and routinely spent seventy-hour workweeks, and still found time to camp on her Pocono property. Then one day she met Diane and her life changed. Their relationship quickly became serious and she found herself, for the second time in her life, in love. Within months of their first date, Diane had moved into Sandy's Greenwich Village apartment.

Diane was the first woman she brought home to meet her grandmother, and after taking one look at the accommodations she promptly informed Sandy that she needed to build a house. Literally.

Diane's mind was of the analytical type, stimulated by equations and spatial relationships, and she loved building things. She wanted to build Sandy a house, and she did. Sandy—who loved working with her hands and had all the skills to build the house herself—helped on weekends, but during the week, Diane stayed in the Poconos and built. With the help of some of Arthur's strong grandsons, all week long Diane supervised the construction. Her day began at dawn and she worked all day beside her crew of teenage boys, and at night she rested her head on a pillow at Arthur's house.

Both Nellie and Arthur loved Diane, and if they ever questioned the nature of her relationship with Sandy, they didn't speak of it.

They began digging a foundation at this time of year, just before Memorial Day, when Diane's semester at Columbia concluded. By Labor Day, Sandy and Diane spent their first night in their cabin. During the twenty-three years they had been together, they had spent just about every holiday, and most summers, in the peace and quiet of the cabin in the mountains.

Sandy reached the cabin via a dirt and gravel road snaking through the forest, with Pat not far behind. A few women had been guests at Sandy's apartment since Diane's death, but Pat was the first to visit the cabin, a detail that hadn't escaped Angie's attention. Teasing her mom—just a little—she'd told her it was about time.

Pat settled in while Sandy fixed drinks. She very seldom drank alone, and she spent a good deal of time alone, so she seldom drank. With Pat, the cocktails went down easily. Pouring Ketel One and tonic into a glass pitcher, Sandy perfected the drink with a whole lime, sectioned. She took two short glasses of ice and waited for Pat on the porch swing. It was only three in the afternoon, but Sandy figured, as the saying goes, it truly was five o'clock somewhere.

Pat joined her on the porch. Looking incredibly sexy in faded jeans and a Mets tank top, with no socks or shoes, she sat beside Sandy and raised a glass. "Cheers." The glasses clinked in midair.

It had been a sad and lonely few weeks for Sandy here, watching her grandmother fade and die, going through the funeral ritual, and finally sorting through her personal effects. She was blown away by her visit to the Bennetts' gravesite, where the love of her life was hidden in an unmarked grave. She missed Nellie. She missed Jeannie. She missed Diane. But they were all dead, and Sandy knew it was okay for her to move on, again. For this next segment in the journey of life, perhaps Pat would walk beside her. Smiling at the handsome woman who had put a twinkle back in her eye, she raised her glass. "Cheers."

CHAPTER EIGHT
THE BIG APPLE

Sandy had read that the latest technological innovations would soon enable cars to drive themselves. She suspected her car already could, for she often found herself arriving at one home or the other without remembering the details of the drive. As she pulled into her parking space near her apartment on Washington Square, she wondered if this was a sign of early senility.

The commute had been a part of her agenda for nearly thirty years, since she and Diane had built their cabin and spent huge blocks of time in the Poconos. During the sweltering days of summer, Diane never inhaled a breath of heavy New York air. Instead, at the close of school in May they headed for the mountains. Sandy shortened her workweek and drove westward on Thursday evening, making the return trip every Monday morning.

In the early mornings before September 11, Sandy could easily make the trip back to Greenwich Village in ninety minutes. The road was dark at five a.m., and she hardly saw another set of headlights until she approached Stroudsburg. As she progressed east on Interstate 80, the volume of traffic exploded, with commuters from North Jersey adding to the mix. As long as she was out of Mount Pocono by five, though, her commute was tolerable.

Fast-forward a decade and the interstate in New Jersey had become a parking lot. The terrorists had put fear into the hearts of many, and hoping that the sprawling Pocono Mountains would be a less likely target, thousands moved west. New developments popped up everywhere, businesses flourished, schools were built, and the roads were a mess. No one thought of adding an extra lane to accommodate traffic, and these days if Sandy wanted to be in New York for an eight o'clock appointment she needed to see Mount Pocono in her rearview mirror by four.

It was nearly a month since she'd received the call from Nellie and with an ever-growing sense of panic left her apartment and headed for the Poconos. Nellie had been coughing for a few days, but as was typical she didn't complain and even minimized her symptoms when Sandy pressed for details. On that morning, though, as they talked, Sandy could hear her grandmother's breathing. Pausing after just a few words, she'd inhale audibly before she could speak again. As soon as the call ended, Sandy threw her essentials into a bag and, since the traffic was heading her way, was in Mount Pocono an hour and a half later. From that point Nellie's health rapidly declined, and she never recovered from the pneumonia that had invaded her lungs.

Always prone to order and organization, Sandy had left the apartment in an impeccable state. Opening the front door, though, she inhaled the smell of neglect, part dust and unidentified odor. Episodic visits by Angie for the purpose of emptying the trash and bringing in the mail had done little to combat the dreary conditions. The rhythmic beeping of her security system warned her to deactivate the alarm before a piercing siren sounded, shattering neighborhood windows. She keyed in her code and flipped the light switch.

Making her way through the spacious loft, she opened blinds and windows, allowing the sunshine and fresh air to wash out the decay. The building was nearly a hundred years old, but the only thing left of the original construction was the exterior. It had been in dilapidated condition when she made the purchase and had to gut it and completely start over. The result was much more spacious apartments and a modern look that she thought suited the cosmopolitan city she called home. With the radio on for company, she sorted the mail and filed 90 percent of it directly into the trash. She had no messages on her voice mail and questioned again the utility of a home phone. Everyone called her cell phone if they needed to reach her, and more and more lately she'd been texting.

It was so simple to contact her friends and family en masse. Communication that once took hours could be completed in seconds. If she needed a date for the theater, she sent a text to her group of friends and, within minutes, she could choose whatever companion she wanted. She could arrange a lunch date similarly. Her text function had been very helpful in keeping those who cared abreast of her grandmother's condition during her final days.

As she held the cordless handset to her ear, she marveled at the slim form of her current smart phone, and at how far phones had evolved.

Remembering her grandmother's kitchen on Canal Street, she could still see Jeannie across the yard, the old rotary phone cord stretched to the limit as she stood at the window waving to Sandy in the house next door while they talked.

What had they talked about? Conversations were hard to remember after all these years, but Sandy knew the answer to her question. Everything. She rarely if ever voiced her opinion to her grandparents, but with Jeannie she miraculously overcame that hesitation. They had talked and debated and argued about everything. They agreed on most, but embraced even the topics that caused them dissent, for the debates were stimulating, and on those occasions when they truly became angry with each other, the making up was fabulous.

Sandy surveyed the room as she wiped down the kitchen countertops and table. Needing a change, she had updated the kitchen a few months after Diane's death and was pleased with the stainless-steel appliances and the sleek look they gave the kitchen. She featured the rustic and traditional look at the log cabin, but here in the city she preferred sleek and sophisticated. With the combination of marble and glass complementing the appliances, and walls painted a bright purple, she had achieved the look she'd sought.

An hour later, after she'd wiped the dust clean and banished the dead food to the trash, she poured a Stewart's Crème Soda, propped her feet up on the coffee table, and thought of what she might do next. The sheets tumbling in the dryer were now competing with the radio for her attention, but otherwise Sandy was alone with her thoughts.

A week had passed since she'd buried her grandmother, and this was the first significant alone time she'd had. Pat hadn't left until late on Labor Day. Her friends Colleen and Jody made their appearance that day, a break from their journey from Maine to their home in Rehoboth Beach. When they'd left in their motor home that morning, Sandy was just behind them.

Her apartment was much like her, she thought as she looked around. Quiet and uncomplicated, with a calm and comforting color scheme throughout, spiced up here and there by an extravagant piece of artwork. Her life was orderly and predictable, her calendar dominated these days by charitable events and theatrical productions, and of course by her family obligations. For the past few years family obligations had mostly meant caring for the people she loved—first Diane, and then Nellie. Now she hoped to spend more time with Leo.

Would that be enough for her? She had worked hard during her youth, and she didn't need to anymore. The Parker Trust had secured her fortune, and all the work she did over the years had helped her amass considerable wealth. In those days, managing money had been thrilling to her, but now the thought of entering that arena for more bullfighting held no appeal. She needed to find a new passion to occupy her time.

A small Picasso adorned the wall above the fireplace, the museum lighting drawing the eye immediately to the canvas that was the focal point of the room. She looked lovingly at it before closing her eyes. It had been a gift, really. Although she had paid for it, bought it from a man who was dying from AIDS, the check she'd written him was for a fraction of the painting's value. She had helped him, though, in setting up a trust and orchestrating the disposition of his assets that would fund it, keeping his money from the hands of greedy relatives who had turned their backs on him but would have been all too eager to embrace his considerable estate. Sandy helped make sure they'd have no claim to the tens of millions of dollars he'd made in the fashion industry.

A glance at the Picasso naturally caused her to glance at the only other notable piece of art she owned—the Remington bronze. Spotting the piece at a gallery fund-raiser, she'd thought the masculine statue of a cowboy on his horse would be perfect for the lobby of her investment office. The problem was, at the time she didn't have an office. She'd bid on the statue and was thrilled to win it, thinking as she brought it home of the piece her grandfather had owned, inherited from his father. And then a few years later, when she finally hung her own shingle in the financial district, the bronze stood proud and welcoming to all the clients who trusted her with their money.

After officially retiring and selling her firm, she had brought the Marlboro Man home with her. He didn't necessarily fit into the décor of the apartment, but he belonged in her life.

This expansive room was cozy and comfortable, with warm colors and conversational seating, the television off to the side and not dominating the room, but accessible for popcorn and a movie. Sitting here, where she could see her art—the two masterpieces and dozens of equally beautiful pieces by lesser-known artists—she had always felt at peace. Now, though, she was restless.

Today is the first day of the rest of your life, she told herself. *How do you want to spend it?* It was just after noon, leaving only eleven plus hours to this day. How many days were left in this life? She could figure out how to pass the eleven hours, but how was she going to pass the days?

Working those crazy hours all those years ago, making her fortune, she didn't dream of a future. She'd focused solely on the plan she'd laid out as a teen—college, a career on Wall Street—and never dreamed beyond that. Had Jeannie lived, Sandy would have shared more dreams with her, but without her, life was quite empty. It was exciting, and rewarding, and she was wildly successful, but at the end of the day, her bed was empty. None of her sexual partners ever had come home with her because she never extended the invitation, and she never extended the invitation because no one had interested her.

Feeling restless in her life and frightened by the number of her friends and neighbors who were succumbing to AIDS, she'd found a purpose at an HIV clinic. They offered what little information there was and helped arrange for medical care and social services for all of those men—and a few women—who were heading to what was at that time the inevitable conclusion of the disease.

There, while doing something that gave her more sense of purpose than she'd had since Agnes, she met a young professor of mathematics who had just been granted tenure at Columbia University. Diane was raised on a farm in the Midwest, and she understood hard work. Her energy at the clinic was tireless, and Sandy secretly watched her during her daily shifts, admiring her spirit and the gentle kindness with which Diane cared for their clients. She treated everyone with equal respect—from the successful gay men who had been leaders in the arts and business of the Village to the drug addicts who stole for their next meal. They were all suffering human beings who needed her kindness and not her judgment.

It took time to collect her courage, but a few weeks after Sandy started volunteering, she finally spoke to Diane, just a few cheerful words. Then they met on the street, and they both stopped, smiling in recognition. A brief conversation followed, which led to more conversation when they again met at the clinic. They shared enough common threads to cause Sandy to suddenly reevaluate her life. She wanted someone to share her evenings, and her mornings, too. She wanted someone to think about during a boring conference, someone whose image could bring a secret smile to her face.

She asked Diane to dinner, and before long, they were sharing breakfast as well. Shortly thereafter, Diane moved into Sandy's

Greenwich Village apartment. Sandy had been wildly successful in the stock market and used the profits to invest in an apartment complex, where she had taken over the top floor. After the move, they continued their good work taking care of the patients with AIDS.

On a day that changed their lives, a young woman came into the clinic with her three-year-old daughter in tow. Angela was a cheerful break from the sometimes-gloomy mood that struck when a new patient was diagnosed or an old one died. After months of visits to the clinic and no good news from her doctors, Maria asked Diane and Sandy to care for her daughter.

They hadn't been together long enough to have weathered any significant storms, and raising children together wasn't one of the conversations they'd had. The only women they knew with kids were those that had previously been married before coming to their senses. Yet Sandy and Diane didn't have to debate, for they both adored the little girl who they knew would soon be an orphan in foster care. Using some favors from people in high places, they were able to adopt Angie before her mother had even passed away.

Their love helped her through that awful time, and it didn't take long for her to become the love of their lives. Angie adjusted quite well from one realm to the other. Apparently three short years with a heroin addict had prepared her for the chaotic schedule of two career women. Even so, they rearranged their lives to care for Angie. Diane had flexibility in her schedule and was home often; still, Angie spent more time in the math department at Columbia than some of the students. Sandy was able to arrange meetings around Diane's agenda, and she paid a small fortune for a primitive model VCR when she saw one playing a children's video. Angie's two moms put that electronic babysitter to good use when they absolutely had to get some work done.

The early days of their relationship were filled not with a passion that burned bright and faded over time, but rather with one that constantly smoldered, exploding only in narrow corridors of time when their daughter was asleep or otherwise engaged. Sandy found that her schedule as a parent and the limitations it imposed on her love life caused her to appreciate her partner even more. Angie wasn't a strain but rather the cement that solidified their union.

Never a sports fan, Diane was happy to surrender her seat for Knicks and Mets games to Angie. For the outdoor sports, though— skiing, hiking, boating—they became a threesome. Angie traveled the world with them, filling in all the pages on her junior passport before it expired.

Work and casual sexual liaisons had consumed the days and nights of Sandy's twenties. When her family came together, nearly overnight, her heart and, subsequently, her priorities had changed. She worked her tail off, still, but now for a reason. She wanted the best for Angie, whether it was the Strawberry Shortcake dollhouse or a Schwinn tricycle. And she dreamed that one day, when she had made enough money and had enough of Wall Street, she and Diane would watch sunsets from their porch swing and grow old together.

She'd made the fortune. She'd left the job. She just didn't have the girl whose love and friendship would give her life meaning. She liked Pat, she really did, but she supposed one reason she was sitting alone in her apartment and feeling a bit sad was because of the time she'd spent with her over the Memorial Day weekend. It was exhausting. A few hours with the woman completely drained her battery. Sandy did enjoy her company, but the price was high. Maybe that would change as they grew more comfortable together. She hoped so.

Hoping to fight the melancholy that threatened to ruin the eleven hours remaining in the day, she picked up the phone and speed-dialed Angie. She'd left the Poconos, where she could play thirty-six holes of golf and tinker in her garden, to spend time with Leo and Angie. Mostly, though, Leo had brought her back to her winter home in the late spring.

Angie had given birth to her son at Halloween the year before, and right now he behaved more like a puppy than a plant. He was beginning to crawl and loved exploring, and was fascinated by everything in his world, which he investigated first by tasting. He loved the Baby Einstein videos, a plastic bee that vibrated and buzzed, and his grandmother.

"I'm back," she announced when Angie answered. "How about a stroll?"

"Leo's hungry for French fries. Do you want to have lunch?"

"Of course. How can a grandmother refuse such a request?"

When she arrived at Angie's apartment a few blocks away, she and Leo were awaiting her arrival. Bouncing on his mother's knee, watching the traffic pass from his perch on the steps, he grinned when he saw his grandmother, a sign of recognition or gas, Sandy wasn't sure which. Pulling him from his mother's arms, she showered him with kisses. Angie had been three years old when she came to live with her and Diane (the same age she had been when she moved in with her grandparents) so Sandy had missed the wonders of a newborn.

She had tried to be an unobtrusive grandmother, not wanting to crowd Angie and her husband Tom, but her daughter and son-in-law's constant invitations to visit and babysit had quickly dispelled any fears she might have had.

The resultant time she had spent with Leo had forged a marvelous bond between them, and his presence in their lives strengthened the ties between mother and daughter as well. These walks were a near-daily occurrence, and they met for lunch a few times a week. After enjoying a maternity leave that now stretched to eight months, Angie was looking forward to returning to her job teaching high-school students in September. Even so, she often said she would miss these afternoons with her mother. Leo, however, would be blessed to have Sandy as his sitter.

They walked in silence for a little while, enjoying the day and Leo's cooing, until his added weight caught up with her and the pain in her knees told her it was time to put him into the empty stroller his mother had been pushing. He easily made the transition. "I'm old," Sandy complained, rolling the tension out of her shoulders. Carrying the added weight of the baby did a number on her knees, as well, but she didn't mention that to Angie.

"If you take after the Parkers, you're just a babe," Angie observed.

Sandy laughed. "I've actually been thinking about that over the past few weeks. Isn't it inevitable to ponder your own demise when you're watching someone you love die before your eyes? I don't think I want to live as long as Nellie and Arthur."

"Why? They were happy, and very independent, right until the end."

"Yes, but they had each other. It would have been a different story for the surviving sibling if one of them had died twenty years ago."

Angie stopped and grabbed her arm. "Mama, you're going to meet someone again. Someone who makes you as happy as Mommy did."

Startled, Sandy was momentarily speechless. How had she let that slip out? She'd never wanted to burden Angie about her loneliness, and letting her know that little bit of truth was likely to give her cause to worry. She waved her hands, dismissing Angie's statement. "That's sweet of you to say, honey. But I'm not thinking about that. I…" She looked at Angie, who was studying her through eyes filled with love, and decided the truth might be best after all. "Ah, who am I kidding? Right now I miss your mom. With Nellie gone, I feel sort of lonely."

The constant worry about Nellie, especially since Arthur's death, had driven Sandy to the Poconos even more often to check on her aging grandmother. When she wasn't with her, they shared twice-daily phone calls. These past months had been filled with caring for Nellie, and now that she was gone, Sandy felt a grief beyond the loss of a loved one. She'd lost her purpose as well.

"And Pat doesn't fill that void?"

There was no big void, she wanted to explain. A dozen little voids existed instead. The companionship void. The theater void. The sexual void. The golf void. The "reading the *Times* together" void. She had the privilege of many wonderful friends, some she'd known for years, like the ladies she golfed with in the Poconos, and some who had come into her life relatively recently, like Pat. She never lacked for conversation or, especially in New York, ways to pass the time. Yet it was difficult to transition between friends with their various personalities and ideas, and she found it tiring. A performer at the theater, rushing between scenes or numbers for a quick change before reappearing on stage as a new persona—that's how it seemed she'd been living her life since Diane had died. The problem, it seemed, wasn't that she didn't have enough friends to pass the time. She had too many. Too many people to talk to and do things with, and no one with whom she could be silent and still.

"Maybe you should find someone in the Poconos," Angie suggested. "I think you enjoy your time there more than here. Or you can have someone in both places!"

"A girl in every port, eh?" Sandy chuckled. Although she wouldn't share the information with her daughter, that was actually how she'd lived her life during the swinging '70s. The Village had been a wild place in the days before HIV taught them that casual sex could be deadly. "What would you and Leo do without me?" she asked, poking a tickling finger at Leo's belly, feigning interest in him while waiting for Angie to respond.

"We'd miss you like crazy, Mom. But we'd be happy for you. You're too young to give up your life and play granny."

The image of an old woman in a rocking chair came to mind, and as much as she wanted to help Angie with her son, as much as she loved him, Sandy somehow sensed that the role of babysitter wouldn't fulfill her needs. She didn't know what she wanted, or what she needed, though, and she didn't want to talk about it until she had a stronger grasp of her own feelings. Changing the subject, Sandy said, "I think I've taken care of just about everything for Nellie."

"Is the headstone engraved?"

"I spoke with the man at the monument company. He should be doing it soon, and he'll call me when he's finished so I can go inspect it before issuing payment."

The gravestone that *wasn't* at Riverview was something else that had been weighing on Sandy, adding an additional element to her bag of mixed emotions. Why hadn't the Bennetts given Jeannie a marker? The question had been weighing on her and really pissing her off! Since sharing her secret about Jeannie for the first time with Angie, they hadn't spoken her name again, but Sandy felt comfortable enough to voice her concerns.

"Is it possible for you to buy one, Mom? I mean, is there a law that says it has to be the family who puts a stone on a grave?"

Sandy stopped and faced Angie. What a great idea! Smiling, she contemplated the possibility. She was planning a trip back to Riverview to see Nellie's gravestone, so why not make some inquiries while she was there? It didn't seem possible she could do this without Jeannie's sister Jane's permission, but why would Jane mind? She'd check at the cemetery office for a contact number for Jane and reach out to her. The worst that could happen would be for Jane to deny Sandy's request. Maybe, though, she'd allow Sandy to do this for Jeannie.

"You are brilliant! What a great idea."

Angie smiled in response and Sandy could actually feel a weight lifting from her shoulders as the plan formed in her head. She would get Jeannie a gravestone. It was something she deserved, and it would make Sandy feel good to do it. It was so nice to have a purpose.

CHAPTER NINE
A GRAVESTONE

A pathologically early riser, Sandy had been up and began the hour-long trip from her mountain home to the Wyoming Valley before most of the continent was awake. This habit had served her well on Wall Street, where she could analyze the foreign markets' operating hours ahead of the New York Stock Exchange. She often thought it good to be up early no matter what sort of worm you were hoping to catch.

The monument company had called informing her that the engraving on her grandmother's gravestone had been completed. She had driven back to Pennsylvania the day before in time to play in the ladies' golf league she enjoyed, and had spent a quiet evening at home. No alarm was necessary to wake her, but as she slipped into the morning sunlight from her cabin a family of chirping birds who had nested in the trees surrounding her house greeted her. She had watched the forecast on the news, but even if she hadn't she'd have known this would be a magnificent day. The sun had just risen and was busy burning the dew from her grass and flowers, and the sky was clear as far as she could see.

Her golf round yesterday had the benefit of perfect, early June Pocono weather—a high in the mid-seventies. When spring turned into summer, she wouldn't relish an afternoon round of golf. Temperatures in the high eighties and nineties were the rule in July and August, and the morning sun would find her teeing off on the first hole, watching the track of her ball on the dew-covered fairways.

She anticipated finishing her business in the Wyoming Valley early enough on this day to play eighteen holes before the sun set again. Pat would be visiting her later in the afternoon and spending a few free days in the Poconos. Sandy was anxious to see how she'd feel this time with Pat. Perhaps some of her angst was the aftermath of a funeral. Perhaps she just needed more time.

En route to the cemetery, her stomach grumbling, Sandy decided to journey back in time and have breakfast at one of the favorite places of her youth, Austie's Drive-In. She and her grandfather had often shared breakfast there on those days when he chose to stop in and visit Parker Lumber, which was just north on the San Souci Highway.

The diner had expanded but was still quaint, its décor fifties chic. The food was still fantastic, just as she remembered, perfect eggs over light, fried potatoes, and thick, crispy bacon. When she cooked for herself, she tried to keep the menu healthy. But when she went out to restaurants, she kept no regard for her coronary arteries and ordered whatever she wanted. As she sat alone savoring the wonderful diner food, she pondered the fate of the Parker Companies.

The trust set up years earlier protected all the land and mineral rights from sale. A diversified stock portfolio that boasted original blue chips had funded it, but since the flood there had been changes, and now there was essentially no growth to the portfolio other than dividend earnings. Business interests developed over the years by her grandfather's father were kept in common out of mutual agreement, but none of the owners was obligated to hold on to their share of the Parker companies. Her grandmother had sold her interest a few years after the flood. The geographical distance between her new home in the Poconos and her husband's old family companies was too great for her to manage. His brother had been happy to buy Nellie's share, and due to old and deep tensions between them, Sandy had never really had contact with her uncle or cousins since the flood.

When she'd started college, Sandy began to very closely follow the management of the trust fund. What she found didn't please her. The company that her family hired was incompetent, charged high fees, and wasn't achieving the results it should have. When she started at her first job, she hired an attorney and successfully fought to change management, bringing that business in house. The result was higher earnings but more animosity between the branches of the Parker family tree.

When she had once asked her grandfather why they had to take time from their day to visit the lumberyard and the excavating company, the quarry and brickyard, he'd smiled and patted her hand. "My brother is all for himself, Sandy. He thinks because I went to medical school and he went to business school, the family businesses should be all his. So I check everything he tells me twice, and then I have my accountant check it three times."

Sandy remembered her grandfather's words when her uncle Dale showed up at Arthur's house a month after Agnes. Sandy sat at the kitchen table with him and her grandmother. "Nellie," he said, patting her hand, "I've come to do you a favor. I'm going to buy you out of the businesses so you don't have to worry about this stuff anymore. And I'll buy all of your rental properties, too."

Regarding him thoughtfully, Nellie stared for a moment, then pulled her hand from beneath his and patted his. "I would imagine the thousands of homeless people in the valley would be happy to rent my properties, even pay premium prices for them, Dale. But they're already rented, and I have no intention of chasing my tenants from their homes, now or ever. And why would I want to sell my share of a demolition company that's working round the clock on flood cleanup, making hundreds of thousands of dollars? Or sell the companies that will furnish the raw materials for rebuilding?"

Ashen, Dale leaned back, his eyes slanted as he stared down a woman who was clearly his match. "I would pay you a fair dollar," he insisted.

"And how would you arrive at that sum?"

"I'd use earnings for the past years, of course."

She laughed. "This year's earnings will be ten times that, thanks to Agnes."

He drove away, angry and humiliated, and they'd never seen him since. When Nellie did decide to sell, a few years later, her attorney handled all the transactions. By that time, the Agnes boom and profits had died down and she had vastly increased her fortune. Time had healed some wounds as well, and she was then psychologically ready to walk away. She sold all of the businesses to Dale, but the rentals she offered to her old handyman, Bill Burns.

Many of the homes and apartments were aging and beginning to show the signs. They needed the attention of someone close by, not an absentee landlord. With nearly twenty rental units—thirty had been lost to Agnes—it was a rare day without a call from a tenant complaining about something or another. Since the beginning, Mr. Burns—and later his sons—were the ones to take care of those problems. He had done financially well in the post-Agnes demolition and reconstruction, and when Nellie offered him the properties he hadn't hesitated to buy. He could afford them, and they were a sound investment for someone with the skills to manage and maintain them.

Leaving the restaurant, Sandy turned left and headed toward Wilkes-Barre, curious to know if Parker Lumber was still in business there. With Home Depot and Lowe's in every town, she wasn't sure the old company could survive. Yet, there it was, and it seemed to be bustling, as large as any Home Depot she'd ever seen. An impressive marquee stood near the road, boasting a hundred years of service to the community. The generous parking lot held dozens of vehicles, most of them trucks and contractor vans. She pulled in next to one and headed inside. The smell of sawdust welcomed her.

A young man at the service desk, no more than a boy really, greeted her with a smile. The resemblance to her grandfather was startling. Like most Parkers he was tall, with fair skin, blue eyes, and blond hair. His was cut rather short. His massive chest and shoulder muscles stretched the fabric of his T-shirt. A big smile lit up his face when he greeted her.

Glancing at the nametag on his shirt, Sandy grinned. Danny. Since arriving in this country from England two hundred years earlier, Daniel Parker had spawned about a dozen generations of Dannys. Her grandfather's brother Daniel had died of the flu, and from that point Dale's descendants adopted the name. A miserable brat of a boy named Daniel was just a year or two older than Sandy, and she guessed this was his son or grandson.

Offering her hand, she introduced herself. His young face brightened as she explained their blood connection, and when she revealed the reason for her visit he offered condolences for her grandmother. This Danny was actually the son of the cousin she'd played with as a child. That one had either changed dramatically to have raised such a charming young man, or he'd married exceptionally well.

"So all the businesses are still running?"

"Yep, and Parkers are managing all of them. My uncle runs the excavating company and the landfill, and my dad is here and at the quarry. He actually overseees everything. But there are still Parkers in every one of the family companies."

"I'm glad you survived Home Depot."

"Yeah, me, too! People know us, and they trust us, so we hang in there. And we give good prices to the contractors, plus we're in a convenient spot, so it works out. Hey, do you wanna look around? We have some pictures hanging in the office I'll bet you'd like to see."

Sure enough, a book of her family history written in pictures hung on the wall of the lumberyard office. She remembered some of the photos. They'd been there even when she was a child, and she told him so. Their rediscovery was like opening a gift on Chrismas. Smiling, she took a journey back in time. There was her grandfather and his brothers as boys, and again as young men, with mayors and governors and other stately looking people whose importance had faded with the ink on the paper. She noticed new photos as well, and newspaper clippings of Dale and Governor Shapp touring after Agnes, others with Congressman Dan Flood and the mayors and councilmen of the towns where the Parkers were helping to rebuild.

Trying not to show her emotions, Sandy cleared her throat and took a moment to collect herself before speaking. "These are amazing, Danny. Thanks for inviting me back here."

Business had grown, and even though she had no connection to this branch of the Parker tree, a sense of pride filled her that they were still going strong. The grandfather who had climbed out of a coal mine in England with barely enough money to buy passage on the boat to this country had definitely left his mark.

"I'll make copies for you," he offered.

Sandy grinned in response. "Wow. That would be great."

She dictated her contact information to Danny, and noted that he wrote with his left hand."Another lefty," she observed. She was also left-hand dominant, and her grandfather had been as well. In his day, it had been more of a challenge. Laughing, he'd told stories of trying to do things the "right" way for many years, trying to be just like his two older brothers before finally accepting that he was just a little different. He had tried so fervently to use his right hand that even as he grew older he still did some things with his non-dominant hand. As a young golfer, he'd never had much power off the tee until his father gave him custom-made left-handed clubs. With the proper equipment he went from shooting the highest scores in the family to shooting the lowest. As Sandy shared that story with her newfound cousin, she experienced great memories of her grandfather.

Danny shared some of his information with Sandy as well. The seventh man in the family named Daniel Trevor Parker, he was the only one in generations who was called Danny. The others had interesting monikers such as Cowboy and Bear, and his own father had always been known as Dan. He was a college student but had been working at the lumber yard since he was a kid. Since summer was the busiest building season, he worked full-time during breaks from school.

Impressed, Sandy was elated that she had made this spur-of-the-moment decision to stop in. As they bid farewell, Danny promised to personally copy every picture on the walls of the office and send them to her. And he refused to accept the money she offered in payment. He glanced at the note he'd written and confirmed the address.

"This address is in the Village, isn't it?" he asked when he glanced at it. He looked up and studied her more carefully, clearly more curious about this long-lost cousin.

Studying him right back, Sandy nodded. How did a twenty-year-old from Nanticoke know the Village?

"I spend some time in the Village," he confessed, and a knowing look passed between them. "I'm a senior at NYU. Well, I will be in a few months, anyway." He told her where he lived and both suggested good places to eat in their respective neighborhoods.

Sandy smiled. "It's a good place to live. You have culture, great restaurants, interesting people. Please call me if you venture downtown. I'd love to talk to you some more. You can even stay with me, if you'd like. I have a spare room."

"I just might take you up on that. I usually need a place to crash when the bars close." He glanced again at the paper Sandy had given him. "It's just easier than trying to find a cab."

Sandy tried not to sound too motherly. She'd been his age once, and she'd been as adventurous as anyone. "Spoken like a true kid. Are you even old enough to drink?"

"I'm almost twenty-two!"

"Practically ready for retirement. The bar scene grows old when you can afford to buy a whole bottle of your own booze."

"Maybe, but I'll probably never have a dance floor or a DJ in my house."

Laughing, Sandy shook her head. "You're not like the Parkers I remember, Danny. In fact, if you didn't so strongly resemble them, I might wonder where you came from."

Rolling his eyes, he sighed dramatically. "I wonder that all the time."

❖

After avoiding West Nanticoke for all those years, Sandy found herself back for the second time in as many weeks. Passing through the grand gate of Riverview, she pulled her car to the curb. Workers were disposing of a fallen tree, cutting it into small logs that would surely become their winter firewood.

"Good morning, gentlemen," she greeted the two workers. "Can either of you tell me who's in charge at Riverview?" The funeral director had handled all of the arrangements for her grandmother and she hadn't spoken to anyone from the cemetery on the day of the funeral.

Wiping his hands on his shirt, the elder of the two men stepped forward and held out his hand in greeting. About her age, he appeared neat and clean despite the job he was doing. "I'm Rob Burns, the superintendent."

Sandy stared at his face for a moment before breaking into a wide grin. "Robbie?" she asked. Robbie's father had managed all of their rental properties, and Robbie had often helped on projects at the house on Canal Street. He had also been her classmate.

"No one has called me Robbie in a long time," he answered, his tone light.

"I'm Sandy Parker."

"It's been a long time, Sandy, hasn't it? You left after Agnes, right? Never came back?"

She nodded. "Haven't been back till a couple of weeks ago." She studied him for a moment. His dark hair was covered by a baseball cap, but showed a touch of gray on the sides. He was never handsome, but his face was gentle and there was still a smile in his eyes. And he was tall! The scrawny boy had filled out into a well-built man with a long, muscular frame.

"I'm sorry about your grandmother. She was always very kind to me. She was a good cook."

Laughing, Sandy didn't betray the well-kept secret that Nellie's cook prepared all the meals she never failed to take credit for. As a youngster she was quite a fussy eater, and Sandy was tortured by the cook's menu. Preferring peanut butter and jelly, she was forced to sample such delicacies as lamb chops with mint jelly and rare prime rib. She had spent mealtimes sweating through the few mandatory bites required to qualify as having eaten dinner before escaping the table. Later, after all the offensive food was put away, she'd eat cereal or a cookie. It wasn't until college that a regular diet of cafeteria food made her realize the error of her ways.

Apparently Robbie Burns's palate had evolved at a more hurried pace than her own. "Oh, God, Robbie. You should have lived there. I'd have killed for a burger for dinner once in a while."

He gazed off into the mountains across the Susquehanna, the expression on his face reflecting the sweet memory. "Well, the grass is always greener, isn't it? Anyway, how can I help you today?"

"I need some information. I want to put a gravestone on Jeannie Bennett's grave, and I don't know how to go about doing that. Do I need to contact the family to get permission? How does this sort of thing work?"

Robbie was silent, apparently thinking. "I don't believe I know the answer to that question. I'd start by just asking the family."

"Okay, I can do that. Do you happen to have contact information?"

"How about meeting me in the office in about fifteen minutes?" He pointed in the direction of an unpainted cinder-block structure off in the woods to the left of the main cemetery road.

She agreed and climbed back into her car, then headed toward her family plot. She was able to see the stone from the car, but climbed out anyway. It was beautiful, with a delicate latticework of flowers bordering it on the left and top. Her grandmother's date of departure had been carved into the granite, completing the work that had been started when her grandfather passed away so many years earlier.

As was her habit, she sat and enjoyed the quiet beauty that was Riverview. After a while, she spoke. "I'm probably going to be back here again soon, but don't worry—I won't make a habit of it. I'm buying Jeannie a headstone. Can you believe the Bennetts? I don't even know what to say. You of course probably wouldn't care, but I do. She was an amazing girl, and there should be a little piece of rock over there that says so."

Sitting in silence, she studied some of the stones in her sight. A few were emblazoned with flowers, like her grandparents'. There were quite a few crosses and cherubs. Lute Grabowski, her old fishing buddy, had died in 1978. A true outdoorsman, his stone was a piece of art, adorned with a hunting cabin and a pond, and a twelve-point buck looking off in the distance. Sandy wiped away a silent tear. Lute was two years younger than her and only twenty years old when he died. Sandy never even knew he was gone. Just like Jeannie, he was someone of such great potential, cut down when he was just a baby.

Preoccupied with finding the protocol to obtain a stone, she had given little thought to what she would actually put on it. At a glance it was obvious that she couldn't go wrong with flowers. Or cherubs. The cross was out. At the time of her death, like many of her generation, Jeannie had been vacillating between atheism and agnosticism. This while she attended the weekly church services required by her parents in exchange for such privileges as spending the night at Sandy's house.

The carving Sandy chose was quite literally going to be set in stone, so she realized she would need more time to ponder her options. Jeannie deserved something special. She wanted it to be perfect.

Wrapping up her thoughts she walked toward the building Robbie had specified. It wasn't much of an office, more of a garage with a desk tucked neatly into a corner, but it was well organized and clean. She accepted the proffered seat in a busted office chair. She crossed her ankles and leaned back, trying to relax. Just thinking about the topic agitated her.

"Now tell me what you're looking to do, Sandy?" he said.

Sandy offered the abridged story.

"I can check with the attorney, but like I said, it might be best to just ask the Bennetts about it."

Robbie turned and removed a primitive file box from a corner, and as he rooted through the *B*s Sandy marveled that so many dead bodies could be linked to so few filing cards. It was because of people like the Bennetts, who were buried by the dozen in the family plot. All of them shared one card.

"Here it is," he said. "Helen Bennett." He read the phone number.

Sandy tried to keep the chuckle out of her voice as she pointed over his shoulder through the wall of the garage and into the cemetery. "Robbie, Helen Bennett was planted over there almost ten years ago."

Looking contrite, he offered an apology. "Someone just forgot to make the change on the card. It's not a big deal, really—we don't usually have to call families. Once in a while if there's a storm and damage to a headstone. Usually people are the ones calling us."

"Does that card tell you which grave is Jeannie's?" she asked, nodding to the paper in his hand.

"No, but the blueprints do. No need, though—I can tell you she's buried right next to her father."

Swallowing a lump that formed unexpectedly in her throat, Sandy nodded. "Oh. Okay." That was fitting, it seemed. They had been close.

Robbie pulled something from his pocket and began rubbing

it between his fingers of his left hand as he wrote with his right. He suddenly seemed nervous, moving in his chair and glancing over her shoulder and out into the sunshine. He handed Sandy a scrap of paper that he had inscribed with Helen Bennett's number.

"This is Mountaintop, isn't it?" she asked, glancing at his writing.

He nodded in agreement and Sandy probed further. "Is there anything at all you might have written down? How about the name of the funeral home they used, or maybe an address?"

Frowning, he shook his head and shrugged. "I wish I could do more to help you."

As Sandy studied him, Robbie moved the object in his left hand to his right and she caught a glimpse as his thumb began rubbing circles around what appeared to be a watch face.

"Whatcha got there?" she inquired. It looked like a pocket watch, an old model from what she could see.

Nervously, Robbie chewed his lip and contemplated for a moment before he lifted the watch to show her. "My grandfather's watch. I inherited it when my father died."

Her jaw dropped and her eyes opened wide as she sat forward in her chair, focusing on the watch in his hand. Then she gave a peaceful smile as she remembered a similar watch once worn by her own grandfather. "Wow, Robbie, it's amazing that you still have this. May I?" she asked, and held out her hand.

Gingerly, he placed the watch in her palm. Bringing it closer, she studied the piece. It was a replica of her grandfather's, a side-winding, stem-wound model popular during an era when men wore three-piece suits and the pocket on the vest wasn't sewn closed. The gold face was carved into the image of one of the collieries that processed the coal from the Parker mines. The glass had suffered minor scratches over the years, and the gold was worn, but the face was still perfect. As she held it in her hands she listened to the rhythmic ticking that hadn't been audible from just a few feet away. For the second time in an hour, Sandy journeyed back in time, and for the second time it felt good to make the trip. After spending a lifetime avoiding her childhood because of the memories of Jeannie Bennett, she was glad she'd finally come home.

"I remember your dad talking to my grandfather about the mines. They were just about closed by the time I was born, but your dad still remembered when they were running. Your grandfather was a miner?"

"They gave him this watch for saving some miners in a collapse. He drug seven men to safety, risking his own life. Right after he rescued the last one, the mine flooded. If it wasn't for my grandfather, they all would have drowned."

Sandy leaned back into the creaking chair and smiled at him. "Wow, Robbie, what a great story. He was a hero."

"Yes, he was." Rummaging through a file he pulled from a drawer, Robbie located an ancient newspaper article depicting the tragedy at the Parker mine. There was a picture of her great-great-grandfather, who was still in charge then, and a young Bill Burns, the hero who had saved his co-workers. Sandy read the article with a sense of both pride and sadness. It mentioned the outstanding safety record of the Parker mines, yet she knew many men had died in them over the years, enabling her family to make their fortune. Even though the mines had given her family their start, she was happy they had closed and men no longer had to crawl in the dark earth to earn their keep.

Handing the watch back to him, she wished for a moment her own grandfather's timepiece had survived Agnes. Just like everything else, it had been lost in the flood.

Sandy shook his hand and wished him well, thanking him for his troubles. She was just about to turn and walk away when she spotted a battered tome atop a filing cabinet. The spine was facing opposite her, so she couldn't be sure what the book was.

"Is that a phone book?"

Robbie glanced over his shoulder. It was indeed. A ten-year-old issue. "But you already have the phone number."

"But not the address. If I find the address, I can show up at her house. Maybe the new owner will have some information for me."

Handing her the battered book, he congratulated her on her great luck and good idea. It would have been a huge effort to track down a phone book from the years before Helen Bennett died.

"Cross your fingers, Robbie," she said as she flipped through the *B*s. Then she sighed, and Robbie did as well. While hundreds of people were named Bennett, none were listed as H. or Helen Bennett.

"I guess it was too good to be true."

With nothing else to say, Sandy agreed. "Yes, I guess it was."

❖

Robbie Burns stood watching, silent and still, as Sandy Parker drove away. If appearances meant anything, Sandy Parker still had money. One could never be sure, Robbie knew—many people splurged on fancy cars and expensive clothing, but at the end of the month they couldn't pay their bills. He still owned the apartments his father had purchased from the Parkers years earlier, and he often walked past brand-new cars to knock on tenant doors in search of the rent they owed him. It wasn't unusual to be turned away until payday, or to be handed a check dated a few days ahead.

Sandy's loafers would probably have paid his cable-television bill for the month, and that included high-speed Internet access. She'd driven away in an expensive foreign car, her diamond earrings glittering in the morning sun. More than that, though—she still carried herself with a confidence that gave a legitimacy to all the props. He knew the purse was authentic Coach and rocks were not cubic zirconium. Sandy Parker still had money.

It shouldn't have surprised him that she was doing well. Unlike his people, everything had always come easily to the Parkers. His ancestors had toiled in the mines, contracting diseases like cancer and black lung that sent them to early graves. Nellie Parker had lived to be ninety-eight! With the exception of this generation, no Burns family member had ever lived to their seventh decade. For their sacrifice they were paid a pittance. And while the Parker mines were known to pay a more generous wage to their laborers than the others, it was nothing compared to the fortune the owners brought home. The Parker mines claimed the best safety record of any mine in Pennsylvania, but that meant nothing to the families of the men who were killed in the explosions and drowned when the mines flooded. They gave their lives, and the Parkers took the profits.

His racing heart was pounding in his ears, and he took some deep breaths, all the way into his stomach, like he'd seen on the television yoga program. An inner conflict was now weighing on him, for he truly liked Sandy Parker. They were the same age and had always been in the same class at school. While some kids picked on him for being the son of the gravedigger, Sandy had always shown him kindness. It was nothing special—she was kind to everyone—but he always appreciated that about her.

As youngsters, before his father had put him to work at the cemetery, he'd enjoyed picnics with Sandy and Jeannie Bennett, and they'd climbed trees and chased each other through the maze of stones adorning the mountainside. His beat-up old bicycle couldn't compare to the shiny new one she rode, but she always allowed him a ride on hers, without his even having to ask.

Working beside Sandy at her grandparents' house, painting and doing home repairs, working in the garden and landscaping, Robbie had felt a sense of companionship he'd never really known before. The meals her grandmother prepared were the only home-cooked ones he could ever remember, and she was generous with the tips she gave him for the work he'd done. Yet, she could afford to be generous, with all the money she had.

So even though it gave him some pause, in the end, he decided that he owed nothing to Sandy Parker. Someone was going to owe him something, though. Just how big a something, he wasn't sure, but he was about to find out. He pulled the Bennett card out of his file and flipped it over to the back, the side he hadn't shown Sandy. He dialed the number he'd scribbled on it years before.

Leaning back in his desk chair, he stared out through the double garage door into the thick forest behind the office. He paused dramatically for a moment after the phone was answered, just like he'd seen on television, before responding. "This is Rob, from the cemetery."

There was another pause, this time from the woman on the other end of the conversation. Rob could sense apprehension coming over the line as he waited. Finally, she spoke. "Yes, Rob, how can I help you?" Jane Bennett's voice was strained.

"I thought I should let you know that Sandy Parker visited the cemetery today."

He could hear a sigh. Impatience? Annoyance? It was hard to tell. She had always been snobbish, looking down her nose at him because of his father's job. The Burns family lived in an old house by the cemetery, not a mansion on Canal Street like the Bennetts. And even though he now had as much money as the Bennetts, Jane still thought he was nothing. Her sister Jeannie had been a nice girl, but Jane had never had a kind bone in her body. It would give him great pleasure to torment her.

Then a calmer voice responded, breaking his thoughts. "Okay, so?"

"She wants to buy Jeannie Bennett a headstone, and she's trying to find the next of kin to get permission."

The gasp was audible at the other end of the phone, and Rob smiled. That was the effect he'd hoped for when he'd called.

"What did you tell her?" Now, Jane's voice was clearly laced with fear.

"I had to tell her something, we were friends when we were kids, you know, so I gave her the contact information for Helen Bennett."

A sigh of relief escaped. "Thank you."

He paused again, feeling quite powerful. "I'm not so sure I did the right thing."

"What do you mean?"

"Maybe I should call her back. After all, we used to be friends."

A moment of silence followed.

"Rob, there must be some way I can convince you that you made the right decision."

He had no idea what was going on, or how much this information was worth. How much his silence was worth. He took a guess. "Five thousand dollars—that would convince me."

"Now, Rob," Jane said softly, "that's an awful lot of money."

Too calm, he thought. It wasn't too much money at all. He just wondered how much *would* be too much?

CHAPTER TEN
DIGGING AROUND

As Sandy expected, the phone number listed for Helen Bennett wasn't a viable lead. The man with the heavy New York accent answering the phone had offered her an Italian special with free delivery on a twenty-dollar purchase. Having just moved here from Brooklyn and opened his business the year before, he couldn't offer any information on the woman who had used the same phone number before him. Furthermore, he didn't know any Bennetts and couldn't talk because he was in the middle of processing a large order for a lunch meeting.

It might have been time to prepare lunch, but it was too early to eat it, and Sandy wasn't sure of her next move, so she just drove. North on Route 11 she wound through West Nanticoke and then Plymouth, the birthplace of the Parker Coal Company. Pulling to the curb, she shifted the car into park and sat and stared for a moment at the building that still served as the company headquarters. Great care had been taken to maintain the exterior, and it was still the most prestigious building on this stretch of Main Street. She'd spent many hours in there as a child, but she had no desire to go inside now. The people she'd known back then were her grandfather's age and likely dead. At the very least, they were retired. Danny's father, Daniel number six, was likely in the office overseeing his empire, and Sandy had no desire to see him. They'd never been on good terms, but after locking horns when she took control of the trust fund, there was outright animosity between them.

Exiting into the northbound traffic, she followed the flow into Edwardsville and finally Kingston. No longer shocked by the changed landscape, she just looked around and took it all in. Old homes and businesses were gone, and the modern franchises that dotted every city's landscape were here now too: McDonald's, Subway, Starbucks. There was empty space, too, land reclaimed by the government to prevent a repeat of the destruction of Agnes. Nothing except parks and athletic fields would ever be built on those tracts of land again.

Finding a Dunkin' Donuts in Kingston, she pulled into the lot and walked into the lobby, ordered, and then took a seat in a quiet corner. She nursed a cup of coffee while her brain worked out a plan. Something was bothering her, but she wasn't sure what. Was it something she'd seen at the lumberyard, in one of the pictures perhaps? Or was it something Danny or Robbie had said? She wasn't sure, but something was irritating her brain like a grain of sand between her foot and her flip-flop, and she knew it wouldn't go away. It would churn in the back of her mind and pop to the surface eventually. She let go of the thought and sighed, ponderering how to find the family of a long-dead woman. She decided to list the possible relatives, to see if that would give her some direction. Utilizing a napkin, she made a flow chart of the people she could remember from Jeannie's family.

The immediate family was small, and both her parents were now at Riverview, so they couldn't help. Her sister Jane, if still alive, would be sixty. She had been in nursing school at the time of the flood, and with that degree she would have had the ability to move virtually anywhere in the country. Knowing what she did of her, though, Sandy thought Jane wouldn't have ventured too far from the umbilical cord, especially after Paul died. She was spoiled and manipulative as a child and hadn't outgrown those traits as of their last parting, and Sandy wasn't sure she ever would have. Jane was likely to stay close to her mother and all the monetary benefits that relationship could bring.

Jeannie's dad had several siblings, all scattered to the winds, and as a child Sandy could remember their periodic visits to West Nanticoke with their children in tow. After Paul Bennett's parents died, though, so did the visits. Instead, they would travel in large groups every summer to places like Niagara Falls and Nantucket, allowing the siblings to connect and their children to form friendships. None of them had ever called Northeastern Pennsylvania home, and she wasn't sure how she could ever hope to contact any of them. She wasn't even sure what states they had been from. Indeed, no new graves had been dug in the Bennett family plot in the interim between Paul's and his wife's.

Helen's family was much larger, as Sandy remembered, but she had no idea who those people were. An aunt Elsie had lived at Lake Nuangola forty years ago, and while Sandy was sure the woman had a surname she sure didn't know it. Evelyn and Lucy sounded like familiar names of aunts, but, again, the first names weren't very helpful.

Jane was the one she needed to find, the only relative Sandy could be sure of. She had no last name, no address, and no certainty that Jeannie's sister was still alive. Yet it was important to her that she try anyway. Swirling her coffee, she stared into its depths as if the answers she sought were hidden there and careful study would bring them forth.

Charities? They would keep donor records. But probably not records of next of kin. She tried to remember who the Bennetts' lawyer had been. Even if he was now dead, it was possible a son or daughter had taken over an established firm and was the party who'd handled the Bennett estate when Helen had passed. She knew a handful of lawyers, but she'd need a phone book for that job. It would be too big a task for her old eyes on a smart phone. Mentally she filed that idea for later. Church? Another possibility. The Bennetts had attended services in West Nanticoke, but it was unlikely they were still there all those years later. It was at least a twenty-minute drive from Mountaintop to West Nanticoke. But Mrs. Bennett had been a devout Christian, and she would have found a new church, probably one in Mountaintop. Sandy could scour the phone book for churches on the mountain if the lawyer idea didn't pan out. As a last resort, she figured a modest contribution to College Miserecordia would gain her access to an alumni directory. Knowing Jane, though, it was possible she never even graduated. If Mr. Right had come along, Sandy was certain Jane would have rushed him to the altar before he could escape her clutches.

Then another idea came to her—the newspaper! Wilkes-Barre had two dailies, and Helen's obituary would have been printed in one or the other of them. The obituary would be a gold mine of information about the next of kin. One of her relatives was bound to be listed in a phone book!

Her phone rang and, reading the caller ID, she sat back in her chair and answered. "Hey." She greeted J.R., her contact at the monument company.

"Did you make it to the cemetery yet?" he inquired.

"I did, and it looks great. Thank you very much. Just send me the bill and I'll get a check right out to you."

He verified her contact information, and as she was saying good-bye, an idea occurred to her. His company was located just across the Susquehanna in Nanticoke. That's how her grandmother had chosen them years ago for her grandfather's stone. Was it possible Mrs. Bennett had chosen the local company as well? "Did you by any chance take care of the Bennett stone, just down the hill from my grandmother's? It was about ten years ago when Helen Bennett passed away."

After pausing for a moment, J.R. answered. "I don't remember offhand. I'm on my cell phone, but I'll be happy to check when I get back to the office. May I ask why?"

Again Sandy explained her idea.

"Hey, if you promise to buy the monument from me, I'll find you the phone number for her senior-prom date."

Sandy chuckled, a real belly laugh, and she was still smiling a minute later when she pulled her car onto Market Street and headed across the Susquehanna to the headquarters of the *Citizen's Voice*, one of the Wilkes-Barre newpapers.

At the traffic light on the Market Street bridge, a thought occurred to her, and while she was so close, she decided to do a little more investigating. While she didn't have Helen Bennett's address, she did have her name. An attorney would have handled any transfer of property from her estate, with the paperwork subsequently filed at the courthouse. With any infinitesimally small bit of luck, that attorney would still be breathing and would point Sandy in the direction of Jeannie's family.

The Luzerne County Courthouse stood just a block away, in the northern section of town, at the end of a beautiful tree-lined commons often used as the setting for wedding photos, wedged between River Street and the Susquehanna. While the courthouse wasn't spared the wrath of Agnes, the century-old structure had survived and still stood witness to the history of this great valley that had produced so much of the coal that fueled the growth of the nation.

Parking across the street, she dodged two lanes of traffic in both directions before she could pass through security and enter the building. Once she was there, it was a remarkably simple feat to find the information she sought. Helen Bennett's property in Mountaintop had indeed been sold upon her death, and an attorney named Glen Franklin had handled the affair. Less than an hour after she'd parked, Sandy was again behind the wheel of her car, this time tapping away on her smart phone. In another minute she had a phone number for Mr. Franklin. Not surprising, just as Helen Bennett's had been, it was a Mountaintop exchange.

Electing to just show up at his office and hope for the best, Sandy pointed her car up the mountain and drove. It was still early, and with any luck she'd catch him before lunch. Within twenty minutes she was parked in front of an older ranch home that had been converted into Mr. Franklin's office. His business, or his clients, was doing well, because the other cars in the lot made hers seem modest by comparison.

"May I tell him what this is about?" his secretary inquired when Sandy asked if she could speak with him. When Sandy explained, the woman looked snobbishly doubtful that Mr. Franklin would be of help, so Sandy decided to use a trick one of her college teammates had taught her. It was called the talk tactic. Sandy began talking to the woman about everything she could think of, hoping to stumble onto something of common interest. After talking for half an hour, she mentioned her relationship to the Bennetts and how she'd moved after losing her house in the flood.

Eureka! Marsha, the secretary, had lived in Kingston, and her family was one of thousands to relocate to the mountain in 1972. Her sympathy at the loss of Sandy's home was genuine, and she suddenly seemed eager to help her reconnect with her childhood friend. "I'll see if I can hurry him along," she said with a conspiratorial wink.

The interior of the office was lavishly furnished in leather and wood, with a few choice pieces of art on the walls and in the corners. There were no plants, no radio, and no television. Fortunately Sandy's smart phone kept her entertained, for she waited nearly another hour before she was able to see the man. Marsha was busy with other work and couldn't chat, but she promised he would see her, and just after another client exited Sandy was ushered into the lawyer's office.

In his early fifties, Glen Franklin was a ruggedly handsome man with a handshake meant to crush his opponents from the first bell. Sandy countered with one of her own. It was something she had worked to develop to announce to her peers and her clients that she was a force to be reckoned with, not ignored. Glen Franklin looked down to assess his hand for bruising before reclaiming the seat behind a large, carved mahogany desk.

Quick about her business, Sandy sat opposite him and explained the purpose of her visit.

"I did handle that estate," he admitted, telling Sandy nothing she didn't already know. "But of course, I can't tell you anything, Ms. Parker. You surely understand that?"

Sandy gave him a sugary sweet smile that displayed all thirty-two teeth. "Of course. But if you would be so kind as to pass along my contact information to Jane, or whoever was in charge, perhaps they might contact me."

He nodded his agreement and rose, offering his hand and signaling the end of their brief minute. Sandy wondered why she'd bothered to sit down.

Back in the lobby, she was hugged by Marsha before she was allowed to leave.

As she turned her car back toward home, she felt a great sense of accomplishment. She had met a distant cousin and seen family photos she'd forgotten about, ones that made her smile. She'd met an old friend, Robbie Burns. And she thought she had a decent lead on finding Jeannie's next of kin through the family lawyer. When she arrived back home, with the cooperation of her temperamental Internet service, she would try to find Helen's obituary. The lunch hour had just about arrived, and she'd already had a complete day. Just when she thought it couldn't have gone much better, her phone rang.

Glancing at the caller ID, she pulled off Route 309 near the entrance to Interstate 80. For the second time this day, her contact at the monument company was phoning. "Hi, J.R.," she said in greeting, glancing with horror at the traffic zooming by.

"Hello, again, Ms. Parker."

"That was a quick response." It had been less than three hours since they'd last spoken.

"It's amazing what a good filing system can do. I found your information. We did in fact do the work on the Bennett stone."

This day was getting better by the minute! "Do you have contact information for me?"

"I certainly do. I'm surprised I didn't remember this, because the guy I dealt with was a King's student. He's Mrs. Bennett's grandson, and he handled all the arrangements. I remember him because I'm a King's alum and I was very impressed with his maturity."

"They had a college kid making these kinds of arrangements?" It shouldn't have surprised Sandy. Knowing Jane, she would have passed on the menial work to someone like her college-age son. But perhaps she was a bit judgmental—maybe Jane was dead or sick, and there was no one else to do the job. Sandy hadn't seen her gravestone at Riverview, though. Maybe she was buried somewhere else? Or maybe, like Jeannie, there was no stone at all.

"Yeah, as I said, he was quite mature and handled himself very well."

"That's nice to know, J.R. The Bennetts were good people. What's the boy's name?" Sandy thought Jane must have hired a nanny to raise her child.

"It's Bobby Berkavich. I think the spelling is B-E-R-K-A-V-I-C-H, but I'm not sure. An Irish guy like me is at a loss when it comes to Polish names."

Sandy had to agree with him on that one. "Do you have a phone number?"

"I do. Remember, this is going back a few years, but it's worth a shot." He gave her the phone number he had on record. It began with a Philadelphia area code. So Jane had fled town after all.

"Remember me when you're buying the headstone," J.R. said.

Sandy promised to do just that. Disconnecting the call and not missing a beat, she dialed the phone number he'd given her. She could hardly contain her excitement! In only a few hours she'd been able to make contact with one of the Bennetts. She just knew this was going to work out! She'd obtain the necessary permission and settle this once and for all.

The phone didn't even ring. Instead, it immediately went to voice mail. Damn! Sandy left a simple message. "Hi, Bobby. My name is Sandy Parker, and I was a friend of your aunt. We grew up together in West Nanticoke. Anyway, I'd like to speak to you when you have a moment. Can you please call me?" She left the number and, after thanking him, said good-bye.

❖

Traveling always excited Bobby Percavage. Throughout his parents' dysfunctional marriage, the one thing they did well was travel. As a child and teenager he'd visited most of the capitals of Europe and some in Asia. Attending the Olympics in Seoul had been one of his greatest life experiences. He was looking forward to Rio for the next Summer Games. He hadn't been to Antarctica but was doing well on the other continents. It made his pulse race, thinking of the people he'd meet—their accents, their dress, the way they carried themselves. Over the years he'd gotten great with accents and enjoyed playing detective when he met foreigners, trying to figure out their origins from their names and the particular way they expressed themselves.

He loved food, and eating in foreign countries was such an awesome experience for his palate. Whether in a gourmet restaurant with hundred-dollar wine when he was with one of his parents, or from a street vendor with whom he could share a little conversation, it was all so flavorful and decadent and different.

His heart had been beating at a rapid pace for the past week as he prepared for this trip to Paris. As a marketing expert for a pharmaceutical company, he often traveled internationally, and the travel was one of the reasons he had sought this job. When he was older and settled he would opt for something more conventional, but for now, this was perfect. He was seeing the world and it didn't cost him a cent.

Clearing security at the Philadelphia airport's international terminal, Bobby slipped back into his shoes and repacked his electronic devices before heading toward his gate. En route, he powered up the smart phone he'd turned off at the security checkpoint and called his mother. He'd been playing phone tag with her all morning, and the game was still on.

"Hey, Mom, sorry I missed you again. I'll e-mail you when I check in at the hotel. Love you."

Before he could turn the phone off again, it beeped, indicating he had a message. He punched the appropriate keys on the phone and within seconds was listening to Sandy Parker's voice. He jotted down the number and then dialed. After a few unanswered rings, he was directed to voice mail. A sweet and trusting young man by nature, he didn't question why someone would reach out to him about his aunt after forty years with no contact. He simply left a message and followed the signs for his gate.

❖

On her end, Sandy had just hit the send button on her phone, and within seconds, Pat answered. "Hello, there. Where are you? Getting close?" she asked.

"Delaware Water Gap." Pat had just passed through that breathtaking wedge in the mountains where the Delaware River cut through, separating Pennsylvania from New Jersey.

"We'll get there at the same time," she said as she entered the stream of trucks traveling east on Interstate 80. They spent the next twenty minutes talking. When Sandy rounded the bend of her long driveway and her house came into view, she was delighted to see Pat's car parked in front. Pat was on the front-porch swing, looking quite appetizing in tan shorts and a sleeveless golf shirt that showed off the arm muscles she developed with twice-weekly gym sessions.

They exchanged a sultry kiss, but knowing they had a tee time, Sandy pulled back playfully. "Save that thought," she commanded.

She quickly changed into golf clothes, and they left the house again within half an hour, wanting to squeeze in lunch before their round of golf. It wasn't until the round was completed, six hours later, that Sandy noticed she had a message.

A deep voice that she didn't recognize greeted her. "Hi, Sandy. Bobby Percavage returning your call. I'm actually in the departure lounge at the airport at this very minute, and I'll be here for about two more hours. After that, I'm out of the country for the next week. So call me back soon, or next week. Okay, bye for now."

"Damn," Sandy said softly. She'd just missed his call. Now she'd have to wait another week! At least, though, she'd made contact.

"What's up?" Pat asked.

She hadn't shared her mission with Pat. Jeannie had always held a special, almost sacred place in Sandy's heart, and this wasn't a topic she would share easily with anyone, most especially with her lover. Putting a smile on her face she eased Pat's concerns. "Nothing to worry about. I just missed a call."

She'd waited forty years, Sandy figured. How hard could it be to wait another week?

CHAPTER ELEVEN
NEXT OF KIN

After Sandy Parker left his office, Glen Franklin leaned back in his leather desk chair and lifted his feet up on the desk. His loafers needed polishing. Or maybe he should just buy a new pair? Business was good. He could afford the expense of four-hundred-dollar shoes, and looking good was essential to continued good business. If one wanted to be a successful attorney, one had to look the part of a successful attorney.

Sandy Parker's inquiry had been laughable. Of course he remembered the Bennett family! He had had an affair with Jane years ago, and it was only because of that he'd gotten her mother's business when her old lawyer passed away. They were no longer exactly on good terms, though. Apparently, she'd expected him to cheat on his wife with *only* her, but had never conveyed that to him. Discovering him with another woman had brought about a rapid end to the passionate interludes that had delighted him for several years.

He wasn't particularly eager to rekindle a romance with Jane. He had younger and more attractive women at his disposal. Yet Jane Bennett had been a valuable asset to him during their time together—outside of the bedroom as well as between the sheets. Both members of the Valley Country Club, she always seemed to have the scoop on everyone. She was active with various charities and organizations, and her list of contacts was endless. Information is power, and Jane was a high-voltage transformer.

He would be foolish to not take advantage of this opportunity to reconnect with her.

It was the grandson, Bobby Percavage, who had acted as the executor for Helen's estate. Bobby had been a college student at King's when his grandmother passed away and had done an admirable job in sorting things through. The old lady had chosen well.

He should have dialed Bobby's number with this request from Sandy Parker. As executor, he was the contact person for the Bennett family. Glen didn't dial Bobby's number, though. Pressing a number on his speed dial, he called Jane Bennett.

Apparently his contact information was stored in the memory bank of her phone as well, for her greeting was very suggestive. "How may I help you, Counselor?" she asked. Apparently time had healed her wounds, he thought with a smirk.

He wasn't sure why, but he suspected her mood would be different after he revealed the reason for his call. And although she didn't say anything specific, just thanked him for passing along the message and promised to keep in touch, Glen could tell that the message wasn't welcome.

Remembering the awful day when she read Nellie Parker's obituary, Jane decided it was too early in the day for a cocktail. On that occasion, she'd spent the rest of the day in a stupor, stumbling through the house before finally passing out on her couch. Instead of a drink, she popped open the lid on her Xanax bottle and washed a tablet down with water. Zero calories and no hangover. Sixty was looming just ahead, so her metabolism was on the sluggish side and she couldn't afford to put on weight. Obesity was unattractive, and with the remarkable job her aesthetic surgeon had done on her face, she was looking quite good. She wanted to stay that way.

She opened the door to the storage closet adjacent to her kitchen, reached into the dark depths, and retrieved a pack of cigarettes and the disposable lighter she had hidden there.

She didn't light up until she was seated on her deck. No longer a smoker, Jane only chose to enjoy a cigarette under circumstances of extreme duress, and this certainly qualified. She inhaled and felt the supreme pleasure of smoke filling her lungs, the nicotine instantly reaching equally dark depths of her brain and calming her. Her eyes closed, for a moment she felt just fine.

Opening her eyes, staring into the expanse of forest that bordered her property, she barely registered the natural beauty that surrounded her. It was a luxurious townhouse, if a townhouse was the type of home you were interested in. If, however, you'd spent most of your life in the grandeur of magnificent estates, spreading your many things around five thousand square feet of marble and hardwood, staring out from your courtyard to a manicured garden, with no neighbors in sight—well then, this was hardly a residence to brag about.

How had her life gone so far astray? She couldn't unravel the mystery no matter how often she thought it through. She'd become a nurse. She'd married the doctor. She'd borne him a son. Not wanting to be left alone at home, she'd enjoyed her career—not the actual hands-on patient care, but the administrative position she'd held until her hospital merged and she was let go. She'd been the wife who volunteered and chaired committees, the PTA mom who knew her son's friends and their parents. She was active at the country club and in the church. She thought she was happy. She *was* happy. Her husband wasn't.

Having come from a modest background, he'd worked his way through college and worked his tail off in the early days of his medical career to repay the school loans and the mortgage on the house and the country-club membership he never used. A workaholic, he missed the evenings at home and the weekends with his family. He missed much of his son's childhood. In truth, he never felt he was missing much because he'd so loved doing surgery and delivering babies and making rounds in the hospital.

But medicine changed from those early days of his career, when doctors were kings and they were given free rein over hospitals and patients, and rewarded handsomely for their efforts. Paperwork and regulations, quality assurance, sexual-harassment seminars, and malpractice premiums had wrung all the fun out of medicine. Upon his only child's graduation from college, and with no plans for graduate school, the last obstacle to his freedom was cleared.

He left Jane with two hundred thousand dollars of debt on the home they'd shared. He left her with a fifteen-hundred-dollar-a-month car payment and a five-hundred-dollar-a-month country-club fee. He left her with no job.

The landscaping and the security system and the electricity and the household expenses all added up to more money than her investments brought in. She'd exhausted unemployment and wouldn't even consider a bank loan. The bankers would laugh her out the door, and then she'd have to face them at the club with the shame of her poverty known to one and all.

As she inhaled deeply, she could hear her mother's mocking voice telling her she had to cut back her spending. Her mother had never been critical of Jane's lifestyle, and for as long as Jane could afford to live that life, her mother didn't voice any objections. But Helen was from another era and was inherently different from her daughter. She was frugal. She was cautious. She was conservative. She just didn't understand what it was like to be Jane, who had friends to keep up with and men to impress!

Although she had the means to bail her daughter out, she chose not to. Helen Bennett could see no utility in Jane keeping a house she couldn't afford, or a country-club membership either. She gladly offered her daughter food, but not the money to go out for dinner.

Most reasonably, the house was the first thing that had to go. And miraculously, a buyer had turned up as soon as it was listed, a wealthy New Yorker anxious to escape the city after September 11. After fees and taxes, satisfying the mortgage and splitting the proceeds, she had been able to afford the townhouse she now called home and still had close to two hundred thousand dollars in her accounts. Bad financial markets and bad spending habits had eroded that nest egg, and now Jane was nearly broke. Even the money her mother had left her couldn't cover her expenses. A crisis was looming, unless something happened soon to change her cash flow.

And, as luck would have it, a solution was on the horizon. It was imminent. In just another couple of weeks, all of her problems would be solved. She wouldn't have to give up the club and the car and the lifestyle. Unless something, or someone like Sandy Parker, came back into her life and fucked everything up.

Taking another long drag on her cigarette, Jane cursed her luck. The old lady had lived for nearly a century; why couldn't she just hold out for another few weeks? Then this would all be over and Jane wouldn't give a shit about Sandy reappearing in her life. She had shown up, though, and seemed to be working quickly to disrupt Jane's very existence. Her grandmother had been dead only a few weeks, and already she was beating a path to Jane's door. Robbie Burns might not have given Sandy Jane's name, but still Sandy had discovered where she was and was one step away from ruining everything.

Jane had too much to lose to let Sandy Parker interfere with her plans. Snuffing out her cigarette, she released a deep breath and vowed to be strong. She could do this. She could hold it all together. She'd been strong before—when her father was killed, for example. She had driven her mother to the hospital and held her hand through the entire ordeal while Jeannie was there fighting for her life. And after, she'd helped to settle the affairs in West Nanticoke and even picked out her mother's new house in Mountaintop. This crisis was gaining momentum and was almost as bad as that had been, and she'd done so well back then, hadn't she? She would have to act quickly to divert an absolute disaster, but with what was at stake, she could pull herself together and do what she had to. And at this point, she'd do just about anything to keep Sandy quiet.

❖

Not so very far away, a man unknown to Jane Bennett sat pondering the same questions about Sandy Parker. Why the hell had she had to come back? Nosing around at the lumberyard, plying his young son for information—what was she up to?

Daniel Parker VI didn't feel it was too early in the day for a cocktail. The one he sipped was, in fact, his second of this young day. He would probably be topping it off with yet a third.

If a biographer were describing him, the word *powerful* would have been at the top of the list of adjectives. *Controlling* would have been equally accurate. He wielded power and control over his brothers, his children, everyone in his family. His employees feared him. Competitors feared him. Politicians feared him.

Only two realms of his kingdom were out of his control: the Parker trust fund and his uncle David's family.

His personal attorney had told him the trust was unbreakable. Harvard lawyers had reviewed the terms and found no way to bust it. Over ten million dollars sat in that fund and he, the head of the family, received an annual dividend of fifty thousand. It was the same amount all the heirs of Dale Parker received, and with the birth of each new child, the number dropped yet again. His ancestor had probably thought he was protecting his family in setting up the trust, but as he saw it, the trust did nothing but generate revenue for the stockbrokers and the lawyers. Yet he couldn't change a thing. And just as he couldn't control the trust, he had no influence over his second cousin.

The reappearance of Sandy Parker in town was indeed troubling. He'd been monitoring her and her grandmother over the years, tracking their movements and finances. He was happy for them to stay where they were, out of his graying hair, far away from the Parker Companies. The more geographical distance between them, the less likely they were to learn something that could be damaging to him. He couldn't control these two women, but he could keep them on his radar, and he had. It infuriated him to know that Sandy's last check from the Parker trust totaled nearly half a million dollars. It infuriated him that the commission for managing the trust gave her another hundred grand.

He hadn't opposed his father's decision all those years ago. On the contrary, he'd fully supported Dale. The covert move they made had proved to be quite profitable to the family, but like most ventures, it wasn't without risk. For years he'd avoided discovery, and now he wondered what the cost of exposure would be? He feared his cousin Sandy could bankrupt the Parker Companies or, even worse, walk away with control of all of them.

Without the handsome salary he pulled as CEO of the Parker Companies, living only on the pittance from his trust, Dan would be virtually destitute. The inheritance his father had left to him and his brothers wasn't growing enough to keep up with inflation. The money he could throw around had always been a powerful weapon. Like the mines that had spawned the Parker fortune, though, that money was drying up. With it would go his lifestyle, his power, his identity.

He was in this situation for several reasons. His divorce had cost him an oceanfront house on Kiawah Island and an apartment in Manhattan. Several pieces of art, whose value had only appreciated, had left with his wife. These were crippling losses, but only a part of the problem. Just as his growing family had split the trust, they split the revenue from the Parker Companies. The stock market had been most unkind to him, like it had to everyone else on the planet. Competition in their various ventures took a cut out of their business. And while they still made a profit, with so many more ways to divide that revenue, none of them were really doing very well. It was simple math. Dale's half of the company had been split by his three sons, who had children, who were now beginning to have children of their own.

His cousin Sandy, the only child of the only child, was sharing just with her only child. Like all the children, her grandson wouldn't be eligible for his share until the age of eighteen.

Sandy didn't need anything from him, but what did she *want*? She had no reason to come after him, and as far as he knew she had no reason to suspect what he and his father had done. Yet for forty years she and her grandmother had stayed away. Why was she coming back now? As he poured another bourbon and water, Dan vowed that he wouldn't allow her to harm his family in any way. He was a fighter, and a winner, and if Sandy was coming for a fight he would be ready for her.

❖

The gravedigger was restless. As was his habit, he silently strolled through the grave markers at Riverview. He knew every marker, the names and the dates and the associations between family members buried in the ground here. He walked to his parents' grave and sat with them, talking aloud as he often did. They couldn't answer his questions or offer any advice.

Since spotting her at her grandmother's funeral, the gravedigger had been wondering if Sandy Parker would return to the cemetery, and hoping she wouldn't. As he thought about it, he decided she was a potential threat—to his financial security, and freedom, and way of life. He was tired of the burden of the Parker family. Waiting out her grandmother had been enough; he couldn't sit around waiting for Sandy to die, too. They were the same age. He might have to spend the rest of his days waiting. Besides, he was getting too old for this kind of stress.

That damn watch! It was filled with too much sentiment and was far too fancy to wear for work at the cemetery, not really appropriate at all without a nice suit with a vest and a watch pocket. The man who'd helped his father all those years ago had been wearing such a suit when he died. The gravedigger had the watch in mind when he thought of taking the man's suit. Then he had to go and soil it with urine. Shit, shit, shit. Just like then, things weren't going his way now, either.

Sandy Parker had seen the watch and read the newspaper article about his grandfather. How long would it take for her to figure out his secret? This whole Parker family was nothing but trouble and intrigue, from the doctor and his brother right down to this little punk who worked at the lumberyard, all friendly and full of questions.

The gravedigger thought back to when the intrigue all began. Money had started arriving just after Agnes, sent from a "concerned friend." A note accompanied the first installment, but thereafter it was simply money wrapped in loose-leaf paper and mailed in a plain white envelope. Initially, it had been addressed to his father, and then, after his father's death, to him. The note stated that a friend had lost contact with Nellie Parker and wanted to be informed if the woman died. It was that simple. If Mrs. Parker died, obviously the cemetery would be notified to prepare the grave. And the gravedigger's father would dial a phone number and inform the friend of the sad news.

In the first year after Agnes, the friend had sent five dollars weekly. A total of two hundred and sixty dollars a year for doing nothing except waiting for Nellie Parker to die. Although the gravedigger's father didn't need the money, he didn't refuse the terms of the note. His father had been smart and cunning, and he was one of the few who came out of Agnes better than before, but for some reason he'd never called the phone number on the note to turn down the deal. Each year, on the anniversary of Agnes, the fee increased by a single dollar, until, breaking the pattern, the year before the fee was bumped from thirty-eight to fifty dollars, and the increase came in the late fall, not the beginning of the spring.

Years ago, the gravedigger's father had figured out the identity of the friend. A phone number had been left, after all, and he'd used a contact in the police department to link that phone number to a name. When his father told him the identity of the friend, he'd found the information interesting, because it turned out that he knew both Mrs. Parker and her friend, and he couldn't figure out why in the hell the friend was sending them good money to find out something she should have been able to find out on her own.

If his father was worried about the friend, that concern never showed. His father had been worried about Mrs. Parker, though, because of what she knew, so he had watched out for Nellie Parker almost until the day he died, until he was too confused from liver failure to care about anything. If she'd had shown up after Agnes asking questions, his father would have killed the old woman. His father had killed two men because of the secret. What would one more soul on his conscience matter?

The first man his father had killed was the man with the boat. His father had drowned him, because he knew enough to cause trouble. In the driving rain, after their job was done, his father had hit the man over the head with a wrench and then held his head under the murky water. At first the man with the boat had struggled, but not for long. Soon his body grew still, and then he'd helped his father push the body out into the current of the river, and it was washed away.

The gravedigger knew the man's body was never found. The man's parents were buried at Riverview, and years later, so was his wife, but he and his father had never dug a grave there for the man. His boat was found, so everyone understood that the Susquehanna had claimed him, and no one ever suspected foul play. Had anyone ever asked why the man had been out in his boat that night?

The second man his father had killed was the man who helped them. That man had to die because he'd become greedy. After he and his father and the man with the boat had risked their lives for their fortune, the man who helped them tried to cheat his father. His father had strangled the man, squeezed his throat until his eyes were bulging and his face turned blue. The man who helped them peed in his pants when his father choked him, and the gravedigger was angry because he would have liked to keep his suit, but it was ruined. They buried the man who helped them atop a coffin in a freshly dug grave at Riverview. He wanted to keep the man's car, since he couldn't have the suit. It was a new Cadillac finished in white with leather so soft you could sink in it. His father wouldn't let him, though, and he'd felt very sad when they set fire to that car out on the Parkers' land in Hunlock Creek.

As far as he knew, those were the only people his father had murdered, other than enemies of the United States of America whom he'd killed in Europe during World War II. His father wasn't a killer, after all. He'd just been trying to recover what was rightfully his, and those two men had gotten in the way.

Sandy Parker's return wasn't good; he understood that now. He'd watched her on the day of the funeral, and she'd seemed to be at peace. She didn't seem like a woman who was angry, or even curious. He'd been hopeful he didn't have to worry. Now that she was snooping around, he knew he did.

CHAPTER TWELVE
CHAMPAGNE AND TWO SHOTS

The cabin was still blanketed under the cloak of darkness when Sandy slipped silently from bed and headed for the kitchen. She hadn't slept well, with the nagging thought that she'd overlooked something the day before still rattling around in her brain. As much as she focused, the elusive detail hadn't come to her, and she was relieved when the hands on the clock told her it was finally a suitable time to start the day. She was going to start it out well.

Creaks from aging planks of hardwood were the only sounds in the quiet night. With no neighbors, no roads, and nothing but woods surrounding it, the house was always peaceful, but at night with the sense of sight muted, the silence was even more profound.

After growing up on the bucolic Susquehanna, then spending a year here before moving away for college, Sandy at first had had difficulty in adjusting to the city that never sleeps. New York was noisy. It took her months to develop the ability to tune out all the stimulation so she could relax and drift off at night. Once that happened, though, it amazed her that she could ever readjust to the mountains. She seemed to have two mental settings, one for city and one for country, reflecting the two lives she'd lived for nearly forty years. A flip of the switch brought a change in scenery, activity, wardrobe, diet, and attitude. Though seemingly opposite, both homes gave her something she needed, and Sandy loved them equally.

She was beginning to suspect that the Brooklyn girl asleep in her bed might have a bit of country in her, too. Pat really seemed to enjoy her time in the mountains. From hiking to golfing to sunning on the deck with a book in her hands, she adjusted from her fast-pace lawyer mode to relaxed tourist rather easily. Sandy could sense the energy always flowing through Pat's veins and had come to understand that Pat could never truly relax. But here in the mountains, she came pretty close.

Sandy wasn't sure how she felt about that. After their last weekend together, Sandy had needed a break from Pat. Then she'd thought her reaction to their time together might have been too harsh. Now with Pat back again, Sandy didn't know what to think.

The cabin had been her refuge from the world, first with Diane and Angie and then by herself. It was small, with only five rooms and a bath. The small kitchen was separated from the large living room by just a small island of cabinets, and the small, open design created an intimate atmosphere. She was never far from Diane or her guests, and that was why they came here—to be together. There were two bedrooms on the first floor, off the kitchen and living room. A loft looking over the first floor served as the third bedroom. There was only one, well-used bathroom. The cabin had been built from a kit and the log walls had been left unfinished, giving a rustic and warm look to the rooms. It was truly a wilderness retreat, and her property here was a perfect setting for it. She was surrounded by woods, with no neighbors for miles.

She enjoyed the solitude of the mountains and always found herself refreshed within hours of her arrival here. She forgot board meetings, and audits, and clients as she shifted into mountain mode, checking the cabin for problems, bringing in wood for the fire, wiping down counters and tables, refreshing the linens. All of this mindless work calmed her, and just as it had all those years ago when she worked on the house on Canal Street, the work formed a bond to the cabin that anchored and soothed her.

At the first expectation of company, her mood changed. Alone, it didn't matter if she ate cheese and crackers and washed it down with beer. For company, though, she needed food. Real food, prepared and cooked and cleaned-up-after food, and while she could manage the cleanup part easily, it was in the preparation skills that she was lacking. Cooking had been Diane's forte.

Company also created a need to clean her house. She needed to at least think of an agenda so she was ready with suggestions when people seemed in need of a distraction. She didn't relax with company; rather, she felt a need to take care of her guests and tend to their needs so that her own needs went neglected.

Having Pat as a playmate was fun, but she wasn't comfortable enough with her to make her a part of her regular routine. She still needed to pay attention to Pat and cater to her. If that feeling ever changed, if she ever felt the urge to tell Pat to just get something herself, it would be a sign that the relationship might make it. She wasn't there yet, though, and now Sandy was questioning her wisdom in inviting the woman for a second consecutive long weekend.

Feeling a bit lonely, she'd thought it a good idea when Pat called and asked if she wanted company. Now, Sandy wasn't so sure, and she wasn't so sure why. On paper, she should have been falling madly in love with the woman. In her heart, though, it just wasn't happening.

She was, however, developing a wonderful friendship and had come to know Pat's likes and dislikes. At dinner at a restaurant, Sandy could narrow Pat's choice of entrée down to two or three items from a menu of fifty. For dinner, the woman only ate steak (filet mignon), hamburger, and chicken. Her lunch menu was limited to deli meats and peanut butter. Breakfast was a little more exciting, with occasional eggs, bacon, ham, and pancakes mixed with fruit and yogurt.

It was fruit and yogurt formed the foundation of the breakfast Sandy had begun to put together on the table. A mixture of strawberries, blueberries, and blackberries went into a plastic bowl atop a heap of vanilla yogurt. No granola, though. That wasn't on Pat's list. Sandy packed that into a plastic bag, a serving for one. Next came cheese—a wedge of Havarti and a block of cheddar—along with a bag of bagel chips and jelly. Finally, she retrieved an ancient ice bucket from her closet. It was scratched and dented from many picnics in the mountains, but the stainless steel was thick and unbreakable. After placing a bottle of champagne in the bucket, she poured ice around it, then packed it into her backpack and carefully set all the food and utensils around it.

Although Pat tended to be practical and predicable, she'd shocked Sandy the night before by suggesting a sunrise hike. On her prior trip to the Poconos, Pat had awakened to find Sandy gone on such a hike, and last night, with the prediction of clear skies that promised a beautiful sunrise, they'd agreed to the adventure. The picnic was Sandy's idea, and she'd risen just a few minutes early to pack all the necessary ingredients for a delightful morning on the mountain.

Sneaking back into the bedroom, Sandy paused to take in Pat's naked form on the bed. She was really a startlingly beautiful woman. Her black hair, thick with a hint of curl, was cut short. Her classic features—long nose, full lips, high cheekbones—appeared flawless in the dim light filtering in from the hallway toward the bed. Tall and muscular, her body suggested she could play the part of WNBA center, and Sandy knew she was tough enough to do the job as well. Even though Pat was approaching fifty, nothing about her physique suggested it.

Sandy thought back to the night before. After their golf and their dinner and their shopping they'd spent several hours in this bed exploring each other's bodies, and it had been truly fabulous. She frowned as she studied Pat's still but exquisite form and asked herself, "Why don't I love you?" She had no answer to the question. Nothing held her back, there was no reason she shouldn't.

Maybe she just needed a little more time. Fortunately, she had plenty. Maybe it was just a matter of letting go of the past, and perhaps once this matter of Jeannie's headstone was settled she could do just that. She could move forward and embrace love again, perhaps with this woman sleeping in her bed.

She sat down and gently stroked Pat's cheek. When her eyes fluttered open, Sandy smiled. "The sunrise awaits."

She returned to the kitchen while Pat dressed, and in just a few minutes they were on their way. They both wore jeans and sweatshirts to chase the morning chill, and Pat carried the backpack. "Only if you let me carry it back!" Sandy had argued. In a relationship, you had to share the work, and that's what this was, right? A relationship?

Several hundred yards of clearing around the house in all directions now sported mature fruit trees and landscaping that broke up the expanse. After one too many encounters with bears and snakes, she had built the cabin clear of the woods to stay out of their habitat and hoped they would return the favor. Small hills and valleys at the base of a taller range surrounded the flat on which the house was built. From the house they walked almost due west, where the mountain began to climb out of the forest. About halfway up, a half hour's climb, a clearing afforded a clear view to the east where they could watch the sun rising over the next range.

They talked as they set out in the darkness, and Sandy found the way with a flashlight she splayed over the ground before them, but once on the mountain trail they became quiet as they climbed, all of their breath needed for the effort. The morning chill evaporated as they began to sweat from the hike, and just as the earliest rays of light began to illuminate their path, they reached the clearing.

Shedding the backpack, Pat opened it and handed Sandy the end of the picnic blanket, which was packed on top. Thin and lightweight, it kept the food clean and didn't take up much space. They sat beside each other and looked eagerly to the east. It was like listening to an orchestra warm up—here an oboe, there a harp—one sound and then another, each alone and finding its way, with more instruments joining the duet as each line of music played. In the same fashion, colors of the sun appeared one at a time, pale and muted at first, gray blending into pale yellow into pink and then orange and finally a full magnificent sunrise, a symphony of color and light.

It wouldn't matter if she watched the sun come up every morning of her life; Sandy knew she would never grow tired of the sight. She looked to her right and studied Pat, who seemed mesmerized by its beauty as well. Silently, Sandy reached for the backpack and pulled out the ice bucket, then proceeded to pop the cork on the champagne. The noise caught Pat's attention and she turned and smiled in delight. She hadn't asked about the picnic, and Sandy knew this was a special surprise. As their plastic champagne glasses touched, so did their lips, in a soft and tender kiss.

Sandy was amazed to find her heart pounding, amazed to see the world spinning, amazed to feel the wetness between her legs. How did this woman have such a physical effect on her? They'd made love not once, not twice, but three times the night before, and now Sandy was ready for more. As they set down the champagne and began the seductive stripping of each other's clothes, Sandy wondered if she just might fall in love with this woman yet.

A little while later, as she began to unpack their feast, her head was still spinning from the orgasms Pat's hands and mouth had given her. Feeling the delight that only sex can bring, they laughed as they enjoyed their fruit and cheese, washing each bite down with sips of perfectly chilled champagne. Still feeling her way with Pat, Sandy resisted the impulse to feed her, although she had certainly done that on many occasions with Jeannie and Diane. The intimacy of that act seemed far greater to her than the sexual experience they'd just shared, and Sandy didn't want to open any more doors just yet.

"I like the cheese," Pat confessed, and the surprise in her voice caused Sandy to laugh. It really was an effort to persuade her new lover to try different foods, but at least Pat was willing to consider the prospect.

"Don't sound so shocked!"

Pat tried to appear offended at the reproach, but their overall good humor prevailed. She defended herself. "I like many different kinds of cheese."

"Oh, yeah? Can you even name any different kinds of cheese?"

Pat held up the opened wedge in her hand and peeled the label back into place so she could read it. "Havarti." Then she looked up and held out her hand and began tapping fingers as she counted. "American. Swiss. French. Spanish!"

Sandy leaned back onto the blanket and closed her eyes, a smile forming at the corners of her mouth. "Close enough." She was feeling the effects of the champagne and the sex and marveled at her peace. Her time in the mountains had always been good; just the past few years had strained her. A couple of deaths did that though, didn't they? She hadn't been relaxing at all, and now she felt so relaxed she might fall asleep.

She heard Pat packing the remains of their breakfast, then felt her as she rested on the blanket, nearly touching her but not quite.

"What are you thinking about?" Pat asked.

It had been a long time since Sandy shared her true feelings and thoughts with someone new. Angie had been in her life for twenty-seven years and was the last one Sandy had allowed to get close. With Diane and Nellie now dead, was it time to allow someone else in?

No, Sandy decided before her reply. Not just yet. "Chuckie. You forgot Chuck E. Cheese."

"Well, Grandmother, I don't suppose *you'll* be forgetting him anytime soon."

She was a grandmother, wasn't she? Considering that, she was sure a trip to Chuck E. Cheese would be in her future. Although since Leo was still drinking his meals, she hoped she'd have a year or so to prepare. "You're probably right. Do they have champagne there?" She giggled.

"I think they must serve something. My sister eats most family meals there, and I don't know how she could do it otherwise." Pat had a sister a few years younger than she, who hadn't started having children until she was in her late thirties. Sandy imagined kids that age didn't do well at fine restaurants.

Except for Angie. Angie had adjusted to her moms' lifestyle with ease. Whether going to Knicks games or museums or eating at five-star restaurants or cooking hot dogs over an open fire in the backyard, Angie was always up for an adventure. In that regard, she and Diane had been extremely lucky.

"I think I should teach you how to play golf today," Pat announced.

Sandy snickered. The day before she'd finished the round three over par, twenty shots ahead of Pat. Apparently Pat wasn't intimidated by Sandy's formidable skills on the links. And that was good. She didn't need to compete with anyone on the golf course except herself. "Anytime you wanna give me a lesson, I'm ready."

Pat sat up and stared her down. "Shall we?"

They rose, and while Pat folded the blanket, Sandy carefully repacked the backpack. She spilled the champagne on the ground so it wouldn't spill down her back, then put the bottle into the bucket and back in the bag. She tucked in the cheeseboard and all the leftovers before topping it off with the blanket.

The bag was noticeably lighter as she hauled it onto her shoulders, as promised, and began an effortless descent. Birds chirped in the woods, and they could see the first rays of sun filtering through the trees as they made their way back toward the cabin. With Sandy leading the way on the narrow trail, she pointed out the wildlife she spotted as they walked. When the woods opened into the clearing at the bottom of this rise, Sandy paused for Pat to catch her and they headed back toward the cabin, hand in hand.

Pat, with the longer legs, had shortened her stride to keep pace with Sandy, but she was a step ahead when they reached cabin's front porch. Releasing Sandy's hand, Pat reached for the door handle just as Sandy planted her second foot onto the cabin's porch. The sole of her sneaker had barely made contact with the knotty-pine plank when the deafening blast of a rifle sounded in the clearing and Sandy felt herself thrown forward, crashing into the cabin door. Pain wracked her body and she couldn't breathe as she sank to the wooden porch planks, her arms resting against the door.

She had stumbled past Pat, who immediately turned into a crouch and had her weapon drawn as a second shot hit Sandy. Pat had already turned the doorknob as she fired a shot into the woods to the left of the house, then sprang to her feet and pulled Sandy through the door, kicking it closed behind her.

"Holy fuck," Pat cried as she rolled Sandy over to examine her. She needed to assess the scene. Whoever had fired that shot could be descending on the house at that very moment. She needed to call for backup. But first, she needed to see how badly Sandy was injured.

Their eyes met, and Pat was relieved that Sandy's were still open.

She couldn't be dead if she was making eye contact. "Where are you hit?" she asked as she began to ease the backpack off and look for blood.

Sandy's breath was short. "My back. And my chest. And my neck. And my head." Sandy had broken into a sweat and Pat could see her struggling to breathe.

Her thoughts racing, Pat knew Sandy wasn't making sense. Only two shots had been fired, so she couldn't have been hit in four places. Seeing no blood on her white sweatshirt, Pat examined the backpack and found two large holes in the fabric over the zippered pockets on the front, but no exit holes in back. A sigh of relief escaped her lips as she realized the weighty steel of the ice bucket must have absorbed the bullets.

"Suck it up, you're just bruised. You're going to be all right. I need you to get your phone and call 9-1-1. Then grab that shotgun in the bedroom and all the shells. You watch the back door. I've got the front. And stay low." Pat whispered the orders, and Sandy quickly began to follow her instructions.

Pat rushed the window and carefully peeked through. Quickly sweeping her eyes across the expanse of land in front of the cabin, she detected no movement. Forest bordered the clearing in every direction, and a second, closer look bore no more success in detecting their assailant. A dozen fruit trees were scattered in the clearing, and she focused briefly on those, trying to determine if their broad trunks might be concealing a gunman. It was possible.

To the left, both her car and Sandy's were parked adjacent to the house, offering cover to the assailant if he were approaching the house in that direction. The shots had been fired from left of the front porch, and Pat looked as closely as she dared, trying to figure out where he might have been when he fired. Behind a large apple tree? In the woods themselves? Up in the tree house at the edge of the property?

More important, where might he be now? Without making herself a target in the window, she swept the clearing yet again. It had only been a few seconds since the shots were fired, and she doubted anyone could have made it across the two-hundred-yard clearing from the woods in that short time. Then she realized it didn't matter. From the looks of the holes in Sandy's backpack, the shooter was armed with a powerful, long-range weapon and was a threat no matter where he was positioned.

Her weapon, a Glock 17, had another sixteen rounds, and if the assailant migrated in her range, she'd need only one of them. Past fifteen yards, though, she wasn't likely to hit a moving human target without firing a few rounds from her semiautomatic weapon. The scope she presumed was on his rifle gave him an advantage, and the power of the rifle added to it. She dropped below the window and moved to position herself where she could cover both the door and window.

The cabin wouldn't actually be difficult to defend. One window on the front side, two on the left, and a sliding-glass door on the right were the only entry points except the front door. If the assailant came through the rear of the cabin, through Sandy's bedroom, they would hear him and be easily able to cover the bedroom door.

Pat was convinced they were facing a single assailant. If there had been two, she would be a dead woman now, for she hadn't been wearing the same armor her friend had. But even so, this one was good. He'd reloaded quickly and hit his mark, twice. Pat wasn't eager to face him, even at close range with sixteen rounds in her Glock.

She surveyed Sandy's progress as she went to retrieve the rifle and hoped the gunman hadn't made it around the back of the cabin. Sandy would be a sitting duck in the bedroom.

Every bone in Sandy's body hurt, and she didn't have trouble obeying Pat's command to stay low. She would have had trouble standing even if she'd wanted to. The fall into the door had twisted and bruised every muscle in her body. Her arthritic knees had taken a blow when she landed, and both were throbbing now. Her head had whacked the cabin door and the hard wood hadn't been forgiving, and every movement produced a stabbing pain on the left side of her skull.

Adrenaline carried her, though, and she followed Pat's instructions. Her cell phone was in its charger just a few feet away from the front door, on her countertop. She reached up to grab it, tenuous, expecting a bullet to fly through a window and blast it from her hand. Amazed when that didn't happen, she dialed 911 as she crawled across the living room to her bedroom.

"Don't linger in the bedroom! Just get the gun and get out here," she heard Pat warn as she listened for the sound of the phone ringing.

Years earlier, when Diane had become ill, they had swapped bedrooms with Angie, giving their daughter the loft in exchange for the convenience of the first floor. As she headed that way, she was grateful for both the small size of the cabin they'd built and her decision to switch rooms. In her condition, the stairs would have presented a challenge.

The operator answered and, trying to remain calm, Sandy asked for the police. At the same time, she located the gun in the unlocked cabinet in her room, relieved she hadn't decided to lock it and hide the key where she would never find it during a sniper attack.

"I've just been shot. Twice. I need the police," she explained as she loaded a shell into the shotgun's chamber. The gun was a necessity living where she did, for the occasional rattlesnake wasn't up for debate about who should move from the fieldstone patio behind the cabin. Bears were equally determined to move in on the human territory. She'd never shot a bear, but the gun's blast usually kept them away for a few months between raids on her garbage.

"Do you need an ambulance?" the operator asked. How could he be so fucking calm? "No. I. Need. Police." She paused. "With guns. Someone is shooting at me."

Obviously understanding Sandy's fear and impatience, he sounded reassuring. "I'll dispatch the police, too, ma'am. But you said you've been shot, and I wonder if you need medical attention?"

Sandy had crawled back into the living room and positioned herself against a wall, partially protected by a table but with a clear view of the sliding-glass door that opened to her deck. If the shooter tried to come in that way, she'd have a clear shot. And she wasn't a bad marksman. Her grandfather had owned over a thousand acres in Hunlock Creek, and he'd always loved to hunt. He and her father did it together, and a sense of obligation rather than a love of hunting drove her out with him. Their time together was special, though, and so Sandy always went along when he invited her. Alone in the woods, they were able to talk and he taught her about guns, among other things. Conversations with him one-on-one were intelligent and insightful, not argumentative and boisterous as they were when his wife was around.

David Parker had taught her how to load a weapon and to lock the safety, how to unload and carry it, and how to shoot it as well. Like the specially made golf clubs, his rifle was designed for a lefty, and it was on that weapon that Sandy learned to shoot. The once-perfect vision and depth perception that helped Sandy sink jump shots at twenty feet also had made her an expert marksman. Although she never killed an animal except in defense of her home and her family, she'd shot the labels off her grandfather's beer bottles, and then for fun, poked holes in the caps.

Sitting in her living room almost fifty years after he'd shown her how to use a gun, she hoped she wouldn't have to. Her heart beat wildly and her palms were sweaty. The day promised to be a hot one, and she was inside a warm cabin wearing jeans and a sweatshirt, sitting in the crosshairs of a sniper.

She looked to Pat for comfort as she answered the operator. "I'm not really hurt, just banged up. How long before the police arrive?"

Their barracks were just down the road in Swiftwater, but she didn't think they were just sitting there in their cars awaiting her summons. What if they were in a budget meeting? Or training at the Delaware Water Gap? Or at another shooting?

Then the operator, having identified her by her cell-phone number, asked her address. Jesus, she and Pat would be dead if the police didn't get here soon, and the 911 operator was assuming she was in Washington Square, in the Village. She told him the address, asked him to hurry, and then disconnected the call. She needed two hands and total concentration to manage the shotgun.

It had probably been only two minutes since the first shot was fired, but to Sandy it seemed like a millennium. Sitting there, watching the panes of glass reflecting the sunlight that now bathed the house, she tried to calm her shaking hands and slow her breathing. Neither she nor Pat spoke, but she occasionally glanced in Pat's direction for reassurance that she wasn't alone.

She detected movement a few minutes later and saw Pat out of the corner of her eye, once again surveying the clearing from the cabin's front window. "Police are here. Lots of them, it looks like."

"What should we do?" Sandy asked. "Should we go out there?"

"No, we stay put. We can't be sure the shooter is gone, even if the police are here."

Pat kept her place at the window, though, and when the police were close enough to hear her, she opened the door of the cabin and jumped back, leaving her weapon in plain sight on the counter. She called through the open door, identifying herself and Sandy, and then calmly sat at the kitchen table.

From her vantage point, Sandy saw two officers on her deck, approaching the sliding-glass door. She ejected the round from the shotgun, placed it on the table, and with her hands raised in front of her, she approached the glass door. She slid it open just as two other officers charged into the kitchen.

After frisking and searching revealed no hidden weapons or

gunmen, all but two of the officers retreated to assist with the search of the woods surrounding the cabin. Sandy and Pat seated themselves at the kitchen table with the two officers and began to answer what seemed to be a million questions.

CHAPTER THIRTEEN
RETREAT

It was difficult to focus on the conversation taking place around her. Sandy's head pounded, her heart raced, and her hands trembled.

Someone had shot her. Twice. If it hadn't been for a Guardian Service ice bucket left over from Grandma Davis's lifetime, hers would be over.

They sat at the table—Sandy, Pat and two Pennsylvania State Troopers. Fragments of the conversation filtered into her consciousness. "Retired NYPD. Picnic. Two shots. Expert marksman." She became aware of Pat's hand on her own and then slowly drew her vision into focus and was able to concentrate on the words floating toward her from around her kitchen table.

"Do you know of anyone who would want to harm you, Ms. Parker?" Trooper Carl Beers of the Pennsylvania State Police asked.

Mystified, in total shock, Sandy shook her head. "No," she whispered, "Absolutely not." This attack was unbelievable. To her knowledge, she had no enemies. She had left her firm on Wall Street to take care of Diane well before the crash in 2008. If anything, her former clients would have sung her praises. She'd advised them through the bull market that had made many of them wealthy, and none of them had any reason to want to bring harm to her. From a personal perspective, she couldn't imagine anyone she knew wanting to harm her. Her life was a good one, filled with good friends. She didn't have any family except for Angie and…

"Oh, my God," she said, focusing again on their faces. The unthinkable had just occurred to her. It was awful, too terrible to comprehend, but it did happen. It happened every day, she imagined. Money is the root of all evil. She knew that from the feud in her family and from her career on Wall Street. Was she seeing it yet again?

"What is it? Sandy?" Pat asked, the concern in her voice evident.

"The Davis land. There's a lawsuit over the land. If I was out of the picture…well, I think it would make a few dozen of my distant relatives very happy." Sandy knew Angie wouldn't have fought the Davis descendants. Without Sandy in their way they would have their gas leases and all the millions that came with them. Could it be one of them was *that* desperate that they would have tried to kill her for the money they'd make in the deal?

As the thought took hold in her mind, it grew roots and became stronger. It made perfect sense! Her cousins knew this land, even better than she did. They were hunters. They had motive. Any one of them could have fired the shot that might have ended all of their trouble and then faded back into the woods undetected. Sadly, she realized that was the most plausible explanation for this attack. One of her grandmother's relatives wanted the gas rights to the land and would kill to get it. She'd seen enough of the evil in mankind to know that men had killed for much less.

Sandy gave the trooper the names of her cousins, the older ones. She knew most of the younger ones, too, could recognize them in the grocery store and carry on a conversation, but she didn't know details like addresses and phone numbers and who owned rifles and wanted her dead.

As she buried her head in her hands, Officer Beers asked the same question of Pat. Sandy trembled as she heard the conviction in her voice. "I can get you a list of everyone I've ever arrested, but it would be a waste of your time and mine. This guy was aiming at Sandy and hit her square in the back, twice."

Pat jumped from her chair and retrieved the backpack, showing the officers the bullet holes marring the canvas. When they unzipped it, they found four holes in an ice bucket filled with glass, and two markedly deformed bullets lodged in the cheese board Sandy had used to serve their picnic.

Sandy studied the remains of their picnic as Pat placed them carefully on her table, as if these pieces might help solve the puzzle. But the plastic bags and storage containers held no answers, just the remains of a breakfast that had been the start of a wonderful day. That magnificent morning had certainly taken a very bad turn.

Just then another officer appeared in the doorway. After nodding to acknowledge Sandy and Pat, he addressed Officer Beers. "It looks like he fired from the tree house across the meadow over there." He pointed back out the door. "We didn't find any shell casings, but the dust on the floor has been disturbed. There's a window with a clear line of sight to the front porch." Angie's tree house was visible from the front porch so Sandy and Diane could keep an eye on their daughter. "There's also some brush disturbed in the woods past the tree house. It looks like he probably came that way. It's about a hundred yards from there to the driveway if you cut straight through." Sandy's property was totally wooded on all four sides, and the drive leading to the clearing and the cabin snaked through mature forest to the state road. If the shooter hadn't parked on her drive, he would have had a long hike through the woods to get to the closest road. Or to the Davis land, which bordered her property, coincidently, to the south, the same direction as the road.

Trooper Beers acknowledged his colleague's revelation, and after assuring that proper evidentiary proceedings were under way, he dismissed the man. Clearly, though, the interview with Sandy and Pat was over. After getting contact information and suggesting that they abandon the cabin immediately, the officers readied themselves to leave. Pat asked them to stay for a few minutes longer so she and Sandy could pack. Neither of them welcomed the solitude of the cabin now, and they wanted to be on their way before the police presence was gone.

Not feeling capable of driving but knowing she had to, just ten minutes later Sandy found herself behind the wheel of her Mercedes and heading east.

Without knowing who had fired that shot, the police had suggested that Sandy and Pat not go back to their homes in New York City. Instead Sandy followed Pat, who was leading her to her sister's home in Hazlet, New Jersey. Pat's sister, a teacher, had just left town for her annual family summer vacation, a month-long adventure to Maine. Pat had the keys to a house that was completely off the radar. Unless the CIA was hunting her down, Sandy would be safe in Hazlet. The trauma of the shooting had left her feeling anxious, though, and she worried about having to spend time with Pat. She would have preferred the solitude of her own apartment, but she realized the wisdom in the police officer's advice. She brushed aside her concern about Pat in favor of the pleasant thought of a safe harbor.

Forty-eight hours into her exile, she couldn't brush aside her concern any longer. Stress had frayed her nerves, and her energy was taxed by the attempts to control her anxiety, leaving her little left with which to banter with Pat. And Pat required tons of energy. Constantly in motion—talking, debating, humming—Pat was exhausting to be around. At full strength herself, she could handle Pat, but in her weakened mental condition Sandy found her unbearable. With the diversions of golf and the theater, dinner and shopping, they were able to keep a conversation going that stimulated and entertained both of them. Under the strain of the attack, though, the weak foundation of their relationship was crumbling.

Sandy marveled that Pat seemed so calm. Did her police training allow her to process this attack with negligible evidence of emotional impact? Or did her belief that Sandy was the target allow her to keep her composure? Sandy supposed it would be easier to witness an attack six inches from your nose than to take the bullets yourself, but still— shouldn't Pat feel *something*?

Pat's sister's house was comfortable, a three-bedroom ranch with a spacious deck overlooking a tree-lined backyard. Under normal circumstances Sandy might have found a visit there pleasant. The neighbors were visible but quiet, save for a dog who seemed to be as anxious as Sandy on this early June weekend. Saturday had dragged by, but they filled the time with old movies and then dinner on the grill. By Sunday afternoon, though, Sandy needed a diversion. She had clearly shown her priorities to be in order while packing for the impromptu trip to New Jersey—she forgot her reading glasses and her iPad, but she remembered her golf clubs. The weather was in their favor, and there seemed to be no lingering injuries from the shooting, so in the early afternoon they headed out to the links.

Even whacking a little white ball with a club did nothing to alleviate her stress level. On Monday morning, after Pat left the New Jersey house to return to her apartment and office in Brooklyn, Sandy packed her car and headed back to Washington Square. *Fuck the police warnings*, she thought. She imagined death by bullet more appealing than death by anxiety.

The trip back to the city was easy, and within an hour she found herself pulling her apartment keys from the glove box. What were the odds the gunman would follow her here? If he was truly one of the Davis clan, it would be easy enough to find her address in New York. And it had to be one of them, she reasoned. No one else in the world had a reason for wanting her dead. What were the odds he would try again to kill her, with the police now involved in the shooting incident? Sandy was sure the killer would retreat now that an investigation was under way.

Her physical injuries were nearly resolved, with nothing more than a little stiffness in her neck to prove the ordeal she'd been through.

Her mental status was another story, though. She'd barely slept in the two nights since she'd been attacked, and she'd jumped at every creak and moan of the floorboards and air-conditioning unit. Back in her own house, she wanted nothing more than to set her alarm and crawl into bed with a good book and her heating pad.

As she exited the elevator and approached her door, keys in one hand and her overnight bag in the other, she stopped at a sound coming from within her apartment. Heart racing, she eyed the floor, hoping to detect a shadow moving beneath the door. Her ears strained and she heard the noise again, and then she suddenly grew weak with relief in recognizing the noise. It was the sound of Leo's stuffed giraffe. Angie was probably there checking on things since Sandy hadn't been there in a few days.

Even though she was relieved, Sandy's hands were still trembling when she keyed the lock and opened the door. It wasn't until she hugged her daughter and held her grandson that a calm began to settle into her bones.

During the short commute from Hazlet, Sandy had debated telling Angie about her ordeal. She'd planned to stay in the Poconos through the week, so she'd have to come up with some explanation to appease her daughter's curiosity at her unexpected return. It wasn't until she saw them both, her daughter and grandson, that she decided she couldn't *not* share this trauma with Angie.

At first irate that Sandy hadn't called two days earlier, Angie's anger dissolved into concern, first about her injuries and then about the shooting. "Mom, what are you doing here? What if the guy tries again?"

Sandy rolled her eyes impatiently. She was exhausted. She hadn't slept well in three nights, she'd been shot at and forced to flee one of the only places in the world she felt the most safe, and now her daughter was telling her to leave the other. "At least come stay with us! Leo will love it. And I won't be able to rest if I'm worried about you. You're my mom, I need you, I love you, and I can't lose you." Angie's passionate plea was too much to ignore, and a few minutes later Sandy found herself with yet another suitcase in hand as she locked the door to her apartment and followed Angie and Leo a few blocks to theirs.

As was Sandy's, the building that housed Angie's apartment was owned by Tilbury Realty, the company Sandy had founded in the 1970s to manage her real-estate investments. Years earlier, when their very independent daughter had expressed her desire to move into her own apartment, Sandy and Diane had moved Angie into one in this building. A few years later, when the adjacent apartment's tenant gave up the lease, they took advantage of the opportunity and converted the units into one very spacious apartment they knew Angie would be able to grow into. It was complete with a large kitchen, formal dining area (now used as a playroom), living room, two full baths, and three bedrooms. After navigating the baby's highchair, play yard and toys, Sandy deposited her bag in the room that would be hers for the foreseeable future.

"I have your mail," Angie announced as she returned to the kitchen. An old-fashioned Mr. Coffee was brewing, and the wonderful aroma was comforting as Sandy began to sort mindlessly through the pile her daughter had retrieved from Leo's stroller. Leo was obsessed with a toy and Angie began chopping vegetables in preparation of an omelet. Sandy knew better than to offer assistance. As capable as she was in just about every other sphere of her life, in the kitchen, if it could break, spill, or burn, Sandy would find a way to make it happen. Angie, on the other hand, was a fabulous cook.

After tossing the junk mail aside, she came to a padded mailer. *Photographs: Do Not Bend* was boldly written in red in several places on both sides, with Danny Parker's name and address in the upper left corner. He must have mailed these photos the day after he'd seen Sandy for her to have received them already.

"Hey, in all the excitement, I forgot to tell you about your cousin Danny!" Sandy said, as her eyes met Angie's.

Of course Angie was curious about *any* relatives, having so few. Being adopted, she knew nothing about her birth parents. Not that Sandy and Diane had kept it from her; there just wasn't any information. Her mom had been destitute and living in shelters, with no known family, when she had become too ill to care for her. No father was listed on Angie's birth certificate. Diane's family had disowned her when she came out to them. Angie had never met a single one of those relatives. She knew the Davis side of Sandy's family because she spent so much of her time in the Poconos, and she was close with a few of her cousins who were the same age. They had played together as children and grew up together, and some had even visited in New York. Angie still kept close ties with her favorites.

The Parkers were a big mystery, though. Sandy had shared all of her remote family history with Angie, about the formation of the coal company and the colorful and exciting lives her ancestors had lived. She'd offered no information about herself and why she'd left after Agnes and no longer kept contact with her family. Other than Nellie, Sandy hadn't acknowledged another living relative in all of her conversations with Angie. But Angie knew there were still Parkers in Pennsylvania and was quite curious about them. So it was with eyes wide open that she asked for details. "Another Dan Parker? What number is this? What made you go back there?" she asked.

As they ate, Sandy explained her impulsive decision to stop at Parker Lumber after eating breakfast, just as she had done with her grandfather as a child. Sandy pulled out a pile of 5x7 photographs and a handwritten note from Danny.

Found these extra treasures in the company archives, hope you enjoy them. I'm planning to be in New York next weekend (Sat. 18th), and if you're still interested I'd love to meet you for lunch or a drink or both! XOXO Danny.

They consumed their omelets in leisurely bites between a discussion of the pictures. With Angie seated beside her, Sandy lifted the first. It showed a man, dirt-covered, at the entrance to a mine shaft. The wooden brace above the tunnel read Parker #18. He casually leaned against a gravity railcar and smiled for the camera. Sandy had never seen this photograph; perhaps it had been in safekeeping somewhere. Before even turning it over, she knew what the caption on the back would read. *Daniel Trevor Parker, founder of Parker Mining Company, Plymouth, PA, 1840.*

Apparently the Parker patriarch wasn't afraid to get his hands dirty. The mines had opened in 1807, the coal dug and transported by wagon and later gravity rail to the Susquehanna, where it was loaded onto specially designed boats that carried the heavy weight over the shallow areas of the Susquehanna. By the time this photo was taken, the man in the picture was a millionaire, yet he was still working beside the laborers.

An involuntary gasp escaped her lips as she uncovered the next photo. Her hand reflexively flew to her mouth and her eyes filled with tears as she looked at another man, bearing a strong resemblance to the first, standing beside a woman and a young girl and boy on the grand steps of the house at One Canal Street. "Oh, my God, Angie— this is my house." It took a moment for her to compose herself, to control her emotions. She had forgotten the stress of nearly four days in Pat's company, had forgotten that she'd been shot. She was simply overwhelmed with emotion to once again see the first home she'd ever known. It was the setting of a perfect childhood, of all the memories of her grandfather. Of all the memories of Jeannie.

Angie studied the photo, not concentrating on the people so much as the magnificent structure behind them. "Jesus, Mom, it looks like a museum! These steps, the columns, it's just massive. This was your house?"

Sandy nodded her head. "Yeah, it was! Can you believe I thought this was normal? There were a quite a few coal mansions around the Wyoming Valley, so I really didn't think anything of it. But it was a great house. It was big, with lots of rooms and hidden passageways, and all kinds of cool things like pocket doors and stained glass and a balcony. As a kid I could explore the place all day long and never grow bored." Angie asked her questions and Sandy answered, telling about her house and her life there, her grandparents, and just a little bit about Jeannie. She flipped the picture over and read the caption. "Daniel T. "Bear" Parker III, Madeline Lamoreaux Parker, Daniel T. Parker IV, Eloise Parker at One Canal Street, W. Nanticoke, 1880."

Sandy knew the canal had been built in the 1830s, to help the coal boats through the shallow waters, and from his front porch her great-great-grandfather could monitor the flow of coal down the Susquehanna. The lock operator signaled with a bell that rang in the Parker house, and it was actually Madeline who monitored the boats navigating the canal. Lunches sent to the operator and handsome tips guaranteed Parker boats preferential access to the canals over those of competing coal companies.

She turned the picture over once more and stared at it again. What a treasure this picture was indeed.

The next photo in the stack was yet another she'd never seen, although she recognized all the faces. Her grandfather, his older brothers Dan and Dale, and his father Dan "Cowboy" Parker were positioned side by side, each of them palming the new pocket watches they had been given in celebration of the hundredth anniversary of the Parker Coal Company.

Sandy studied this photo, unsure why, but again with a nagging feeling that she had missed something important the past Thursday when she traveled to West Nanticoke. Was it about that watch Robbie had shown her? The answer she sought eluded her. It would come, though. It just needed a little time.

Sandy was about to flip to the next picture in her pile when her cell phone rang. She glanced at the number and didn't recognize it, but she knew the 570 area code meant the call was originating from a Northeastern Pennsylvania phone. The police? Could they have found the shooter? She hadn't heard a word from them in the forty-eight hours since the shooting happened, and she was planning to call them this morning until she'd run into Angie and gotten caught up in family history.

"I need to take this, I think it's the police," she informed her daughter and headed down the hallway to her bedroom, where she could have privacy.

"Hello," she said in greeting.

"Hi, yes, I'm looking for Sandy Parker, please," a female voice informed her.

"Yes, this is Sandy. How can I help you?"

Sandy nearly dropped the phone when the woman answered. "Hello there, old neighbor. This is Jane Bennett. I understand that you've been trying to get in touch with me." Sandy didn't recognize the voice or the attitude. Jane had never been overly friendly, had in fact been a pain in the ass to her and Jeannie for most of the fourteen years she'd lived in the house next door. But she supposed people changed, didn't they?

She had been expecting a call from Jane's son Bobby—not Jane— and Sandy found herself at a loss for words after the initial greeting and polite inquiries about what they'd both been doing for the last forty years. The conversation she'd had in her head with Bobby began with a basic introduction and history. He would make comments and ask questions that led to the purpose of her call.

Obviously, the discussion with Jane would need a different approach, and Sandy hadn't had the opportunity to rehearse. Certainly she couldn't describe her indignation about the Bennett family's neglect of their younger daughter's grave. Likewise, a confession of her love for Jeannie was out of the question.

She opted for simple facts. "I noticed there's no headstone at Riverview for Jeannie. I'd like to buy her one, if that's okay with you."

"Oh, Sandy, that's so sweet of you! But Jeannie isn't buried at Riverview. That's why there's no marker."

"Well, where is she buried?" Sitting on the bed, furrowing her brow in confusion, Sandy digested Jane's words. Why wouldn't the Bennetts bury Jeannie in their family plot?

"She wasn't. Since she wanted to be a doctor, my mother donated her body for medical students to study." Jane sighed audibly, as if this news troubled her.

Sandy understood Jane's sentiment. She rested her forehead in one hand while holding the phone in the other. This wasn't what she'd expected from this discussion! She'd expected a grateful acceptance of her offer. After all, why would anyone argue this point?

This news, though, was a shock that she didn't know how to handle! Even if she never went back to Riverview in all of these years, Sandy had felt a certain comfort in knowing that she could. She could go and visit her father, or her grandfather, or Jeannie—if she'd had the desire. She could sit in the grass on a sunny afternoon and tell them her troubles, or take a picnic there and enjoy the peace and solitude.

How would she feel if she couldn't go there? If there was no place for her to ever connect with Jeannie again? She didn't realize tears were sliding down her face until Angie wiped them with a tissue. She felt Angie sit beside her and wrap and arm around her and rest her head against her shoulder. It gave her the strength to respond to Jane.

A cough cleared her throat, and she tried hard to feel a truth in the polite words she spoke. "What a wonderful way to honor her, Jane," Sandy said, her voice just a whisper that hid the emotion she felt. After all these years, she would not crumble in front of someone else, most especially the sister who had been a constant thorn in Jeannie's side. When there was no response, and Sandy had once again regained the composure that had made her a bull on Wall Street, facing any crisis with calm, she continued. "Please thank Bobby for me and tell him there's no need to return my call."

"Excuse me?" Jane asked.

Sandy sighed and, using the back of her hand, she wiped away tears as she answered.

"Bobby. He left me a message before leaving for his trip saying he'd call me when he returns. I'm sure he'll have dozens of calls to make, so just let him know we've spoken."

"I will do that. It was nice to talk to you, Sandy. You take care."

When Sandy disconnected the phone without further reply, she slumped onto the bed and continued to cry, feeling sadness and emptiness all over again. Would she never stop crying over Jeannie? No wonder she had kept her feelings buried all those years. Clearly, she couldn't handle them.

She tried not to think, did cleansing yoga breaths, and envisioned the clear-mirrored finish of a lake in the forest, a cloudless blue sky overhead. After a few minutes she felt calmer. Not perfect, but improved. With Angie's arms wrapped around her, she drifted off to a much-needed sleep.

❖

The smell of baking chocolate permeated the deep fog that enshrouded Sandy's brain and slowly brought her back to life. A glance at the clock beside the bed told her she'd slept for more than six hours, and she noticed that she was no longer wearing the clothing she'd had on when she crawled into the bed earlier in the day. Except for a tank and her underwear, she was naked.

Angie's spare bedroom was simply furnished in a modern style, with sleek but deceptively comfortable furniture. The embrace of a pillow-top mattress invited her to pull the blankets up and close her eyes for a few more minutes of rest. She did.

Not thinking of Jeannie was impossible, so she tried to focus on pleasant memories rather than how her life ended and what had become of her remains. Sandy supposed rotting in the earth was no better an end for the human body than dissection in an anatomy lab, but somehow the former, more traditional conclusion was easier for her to accept. She brushed the thought aside and instead remembered snuggling up with Jeannie in a warm bed like the one she was now in, Jeannie's unruly hair falling across her forehead and her eye, Sandy's hand gently pushing it aside. She imagined the feel of Jeannie's hand in hers, could hear her singing. *I wanna hold your ha-ah-ah-ah-and, I wanna hold your hand.*

Just remembering for a few minutes lifted her spirits, and Sandy knew she would be okay with the news she'd received earlier in the day. She'd allowed herself to get excited about doing something for Jeannie, and she supposed she needed to be excited about something. The disappointment was real, but she knew she'd work through it. She took a breath and tucked Jeannie back into that special place in her heart, then pushed back the covers from the bed.

Finding her clothes neatly folded on a chair, she dressed, and with her other senses awakening she saw that Angie had unpacked her bag, and she began to hear the sounds that told her that dinner preparation was under way. After freshening up in the bathroom, she felt ready to face the world again. Or, at least, to face her daughter.

Sandy was torn in her desire to share her feelings about Jeannie with Angie, knowing that she might find comfort in her daughter, yet knowing also that the woman at the heart of her anguish was not Angie's mama. Angie knew that Sandy had loved Diane, and in their twenty years together Sandy had been faithful to her, but it still had to be hard for Angie to discuss her mom and another love. Angie could talk and joke about Pat, and could probably accept Pat's presence in Sandy's life, but Sandy doubted Angie would want *details* about their relationship. Talking about her feelings for Jeannie would involve details that should probably be left buried in the middle of the Susquehanna River.

"It smells wonderful," Sandy said in greeting as she padded barefooted into the kitchen. Angie was sitting at her table, feeding Leo baby mush that seemed to agree with him. He was all smiles, making clumsy attempts to snatch the spoon from Angie's hand so as to get the food more quickly. A pan of brownies was cooling on the counter. Comfort food. She took another deep breath and let the smell soak further into her senses.

"How was your nap?"

"I feel like you put a sleeping pill in my coffee." Sandy kissed her daughter and her grandson on the head before sitting across the table from them.

"Couldn't have been complete physical and emotional exhaustion, could it?"

"Well, if it was, I'm over it now. I feel great." Sandy wasn't lying. She had collapsed onto that bed feeling weary from lack of sleep, from fear and sadness. Things didn't seem so bad now. She had closure. Of course she was still worried that someone was lurking in the shadows with a bullet in a gun with her name on it. How long would she be forced to live with her friends and family? But she felt better than she had over the weekend. The shock of being shot was wearing off, and a restlessness from inactivity was setting in.

She needed to do something. She was an active woman, always had been. She'd played sports and exercised her entire life, and now that she was too old for basketball she still played golf and practiced yoga. She'd always worked, first at Farrell's, then while in college, and for twenty-five years on Wall Street. Even when she sold her firm, she was busy taking care of Diane and doing things with her. This business of sitting around doing nothing—like she had all weekend with Pat— was excruciatingly painful.

"Oh, fuck!" she said as she suddenly remembered she had left

Pat's sister's that morning without letting her know. "Pat's going to be looking for me in Hazlet, New Jersey."

"Relax. She called your phone and I told her you were here. She's happy that you're not alone, and she wants you to call her when you wake up."

"Like I said, Oh, fuck!"

Angie looked at her mom, curious. "I take it your time together didn't go well?"

"I think that's a fair description of the events." For some reason, she didn't feel the same angst in talking about Pat as she did Jeannie.

"What happened?"

"Nothing, really. It's not like we fought or anything. It's just hard to be with someone for days on end with no one else to talk to."

"Mom, if you really like her, give her a break. I think you should just forget the past few days and move forward. This sort of duress can bring out the worst in anyone. And don't forget—she did save your life."

"Yeah, I know. You're right. I guess I'm just stressed. But I think I could use a little break from her. Just some time to think."

"Understandable."

"What's for dinner?" she asked, changing the subject.

Angie raised the cup of baby food toward Sandy. "How's chicken sound?"

"It looks runny."

"Okay, then we can have the lasagna that's in the oven."

With the dinner menu set, Sandy told Angie she wanted to call Danny to thank him for the pictures. Angie's eyes brightened at the mention of her cousin's name, and Sandy knew the few things she had shared about him had left Angie curious and anxious to meet him.

Sandy dialed the number he had written on the note enclosed with the pictures.

Apparently, Danny had her phone number committed to the contacts in his phone, for he answered with an energetic and personal greeting. "Hey, cuz, did you get the pictures?"

Sandy couldn't help laughing at his youthful energy. She instantly felt their connection, even over the phone. It had been there when they met at the lumberyard as well, and in those few moments they spent together that day, Sandy felt sure they had formed a bond that would last the rest of her life.

They bantered for a few minutes, and then an idea came to her.

"Danny, what do you know about the anniversary watches?" Maybe he could help her solve the mystery that was bothering her.

"I know they're very rare and my father would pay a fortune for one if he could find someone willing to sell."

"Really? Why is that?"

"Simple math. There are more Parker heirs than watches. My great-grandfather, Dale—who was your grandfather's brother—actually started buying them years ago. He contacted the men who'd been given watches and even put an ad in the newspaper, but he didn't have much luck. I think he managed to find a handful out of the four dozen that were made. They're not all the same, though—some have more gold, I think. I can't remember off the top of my head."

"Can you find out anything more about them? Like who made them, maybe? Who they were given to?" Sandy wasn't sure why she wanted this information, but her instincts told her to find out as much as she could. She told Danny about the watch that had been given to Robbie Burns's grandfather.

He promised to get back to her. "One more thing—would you like to get together this weekend?" He reminded her of his upcoming plans to travel to New York, and they made a date for dinner on Friday.

"I'll see you in four days," Sandy said.

"Hopefully I'll have some information about those watches to bring with me," he said.

"If you do, I'll buy you dinner," she teased.

"In that case, I'll definitely have something for you."

Laughing, she hung up the phone.

CHAPTER FOURTEEN
A FAMILY SECRET

Danny Parker had always loved history. Perhaps it was the knowledge that the men who bore his name before him had done so much to contribute to it. As a child he listened to stories told by his grandfather, about legendary Parkers who had dined with presidents and died in battle defending the United States. Trains and the history of railroading enthralled him, and he relished the knowledge that coal from the Parker mines had fueled their great engines.

Spending time at the building that served as command central for the Parker Companies would have bored most kids, but not Danny. Reading newspaper articles and company records gave him a great insight into not only his family, but to the world that was spinning around it. Coal had been an asset in war and industry, in commerce and transportation. Danny knew the archives of the Parker Companies as well as anyone who worked there, and he knew just where to look to answer the questions his cousin Sandy had posed about her grandfather's watch.

He had explored the five floors of the office building, climbed the stairs and slid down the railings, hid in the basement and the rafters pretending he was a corporate spy, listening in on important meetings from the floor beneath the boardroom table. In the days before his parents' divorce, he had spent as much time here as he had at home, for his mother's advertising firm provided exclusive services to his father's business. After their separation, Danny still came, but now because he asked to come and not because he was told to.

Arriving at the office building in Plymouth the morning after his conversation with his cousin, he greeted everyone cheerfully. No one questioned his presence or even gave him a second glance when he began pulling file boxes from storage-room shelves. They had seen him do the same thing many times before.

Setting the boxes on the boardroom table, Danny settled into a supple leather chair and leaned back, studying the mural that had been painted on the wall more than a hundred years earlier. Located on the third floor, it had escaped the wrath of Agnes that had done tremendous damage to the wood and marble on the first floor. It was a map of the Wyoming Valley showing the location of all the Parker mines and other business interests. Even though the mines were no longer operating, the map remained as a testament to the greatness of the empire that began right here on the banks of the Susquehanna River.

Turning his gaze, he looked out of the windows that formed a wall of glass on the rear of the building overlooking the river. It was here in Plymouth that the first commercial mining in the United States began. Not far from this office building, the first barges loaded with coal had begun their journey down the Susquehanna to the cities and towns in need of anthracite to heat their homes and fuel their factories.

He couldn't help but feel a sense of awe sitting in this place, so close to where the first Dan Parker had made the bold decisions that would bring him and his family such fortune. It was a wonder to sit in the same chairs that Bear and Cowboy had a century ago when they ran the company. As the son of the man who was currently the head of the Parker Companies, he wondered if he would ever be in charge. As much as he would like to run this little empire, he wasn't sure it would turn out that way.

He'd lived most of the past three years in New York City, where he maintained a blissfully anonymous life. It was hard to be gay in Plymouth, PA, where everyone knew his mother or his father or his uncles or his grandfather. It didn't matter if he was covered in filth after loading wood at the lumberyard, that his hands were callused and his muscles built more by manual labor than gym equipment and kickboxing classes. Even though he'd tried to be a regular teenager, proving his worth and earning his keep, as soon as people heard the name Parker, they treated him differently, scrutinizing his every word and deed. If he worked late, they said he was striving to earn his father's approval. Getting his hands dirty was a sign that he was trying to blend in with the very men and women on whom he was spying.

They were all respectful and polite, and he even felt that he fit in, going out with the guys for a beer after work or hunting with them on the many acres the Parkers still held for just that purpose. He knew, though, that because of who he was, whatever he did was newsworthy. If one of the other guys had three beers and drove home, no one would have said anything. If he did, a dozen people commented on it the next day. If he was seen at a movie, the next day he had to give a review to a dozen coworkers who politely inquired about it. If he told the pro at the club he'd had a birdie on a golf hole, before the sun set that day his father called to congratulate him.

That he didn't date wasn't yet news. He was still blessed with the youth that excused him from the obligatory female companions expected of older men. But he was getting older every day, every minute, in fact. Too soon he'd no longer have the excuse of school as the reason he could refuse the company of the attractive women everyone tried to introduce to him.

When that day came, he was in trouble. He really had no options. If he feigned interest in a woman in order to satisfy his family's expectations, he would be sacrificing his soul. If he satisfied himself, he would be sacrificing his family.

He came from generations of strong men, men who valued family and tradition, conservative Republicans who went to church on Sundays and drove American-made cars and thought that homosexuals should be exiled to a penal colony to spare the innocents of society from the burden of dealing with the homosexual agenda. Even his mother was homophobic, really a female version of his father, so similar to him in values and opinions that Danny still couldn't figure out why they'd divorced.

In New York, everything was so different. People were open-minded and he was anonymous. Just one of thousands of students in the city, he went about his business unnoticed and untethered, researching term papers and carrying a backpack filled with books, reading in Central Park and riding a bike from place to place. No one cared about his name, or what movie he'd watched, or that he'd watched it with a guy with his lip pierced wearing a gay-pride T-shirt.

It was pretty obvious to him that he'd have to leave his home, at least for a while. Perhaps when he'd made his mark and proved himself it wouldn't matter so much who he slept with, but until then, people would have nothing else to talk about.

Sighing, Danny turned his chair and his attention back to the matter at hand and went to work. He had only to look through a few file boxes before he found what he was looking for. The receipt for the Parker Coal Company watches was filed with expenses for 1913, along with a list of the first employees who were awarded them. Cowboy Parker had commissioned the watches from a Swiss jeweler with offices in

New York City in 1913, but because of the turmoil of World War I, the watches weren't delivered until 1919. A total of fifty-two timepieces were ordered, costing the company about two thousand dollars. Most of the watches were identical—stem wound, with the stems on the side, made of gold, the face etched with an image of a Parker colliery. Four of the watches were different, though, costing three times as much as the others. Danny knew these were watches reserved for Cowboy and his three sons. Their gold content was higher and each contained a diamond chip, making them quite a bit fancier than the common variety. The receipt puzzled him, though. It didn't list forty-eight plus four watches, rather forty-eight, plus three, plus one. The individual was priced even more than the other three. He'd have to ask his dad about that. Danny's father had been very close to Dale, his grandfather, the original recipient of one of those special four watches. Plus, his father knew more about the history of his family and the company than any other human being on the planet.

Why was Sandy curious about the watches? Perhaps it was just the reminder of her grandfather. He hoped the information he found helped. He made photocopies of the relevant papers and then returned the boxes to the storage area. While he was there, he began looking through more files, sitting on the floor, not even bothering to take them back to the comfort of the boardroom table.

At first, he concentrated on items that specifically pertained to Sandy's branch of the family, but found few. Her grandfather, Dr. David Parker, had little to do with the family business, so there wasn't much in the archives except pictures of him as a boy and young man before he went off to Philadelphia for his education. The files did contain papers showing the transfer of land parcels made by Cowboy to both of his sons, and Danny copied these as well, figuring Sandy might find them interesting. Sandy's grandfather had inherited the land in Mount Pocono that had been a family retreat, land in Hunlock Creek that housed stables and a hunting lodge, a tract of land in Nanticoke, and the house on Canal Street.

A few hours after beginning his quest, and feeling quite satisfied, Danny put the file boxes back in their places and headed out the door, not thinking much about the papers in his hand. There was little there of interest except to someone like him, a historian. He feared Sandy would be disappointed with his offering. Was he ever wrong.

Since his parents' divorce, Danny and his two sisters had been spending weekends with their father at his home on Harvey's Lake. As they grew to be teenagers and could be trusted for hours by themselves, they had elected to spend summers at the lake as well. There was a boat and a dock, and the siblings had great fun with their neighbors and friends, waterskiing and scuba diving, jet skiing and swimming in the beautiful lake waters.

His sisters, now in high school and college and with cars and lives of their own, were never to be found, it seemed. Danny spent that night at home alone reading while his father golfed and had cocktails at the country club. The next night, after putting in a twelve-hour day at the lumberyard, Danny caught him just as he was about to pour himself a cocktail. He joined his dad on the terrace overlooking the lake. His parents had purchased this house when they married, and unlike most things in his family, it was fairly new. Like most things Parker, though, it was well done, with traditional hardwood floors and cut-glass doors and windows, marble sinks and floors, and antique French doors leading to the terrace. One entire wall, two stories high, was constructed entirely of glass.

The house was set apart from its neighbors, on a rare secluded piece of land right on the water. There were no streetlights on this section of the lake, and at nine thirty in the evening, the only visible light was escaping from the interiors of the homes lined side by side on the water's edge, and from party lights hung on boathouse roofs and railings.

His relationship with his father was an odd one. It hadn't taken Danny long to understand that it wasn't his fault. His father was strange. Of all the people in the world, he thought his father liked him best, but his difficulties in relating to people kept their relationship at a superficial level. Dan wasn't affectionate, and he tended to be harsh and demanding and aloof. His obsessive and compulsive tendencies made him difficult to live with and work for. He was absolutely devoid of humor. He could be compassionate, until someone pissed him off. At that point the killer instinct took over and he became absolutely ruthless. And whether he liked him or not, this man was his father, and he knew for certain that he loved him.

Danny sank into a comfortable patio chair and pulled the sheaf of documents he'd copied from an envelope and handed the top one to his father. "I'm looking into family history and I want to know more about the watches."

"School project?" his father asked, even though it was June and Danny was off for the summer.

"Yes." Danny lied because his father hadn't been happy when he mentioned meeting his cousin Sandy the week before. As much as he loved history, the information surrounding Dr. David Parker's family had always been a mystery. It seemed that David had struck out on his own, and while Dale hadn't officially disowned him, he seemed to have shunned him, for there was a paucity of information about David after he left for school. Without Danny's knowledge of the trust fund and his curiosity about his family, he might not have even known that his great-grandfather had this mysterious brother.

"Was there something special about Cowboy's watch? Is that why one of them cost more money?"

Dan glanced at the paper in his hand and squinted in the near darkness. "Flip the light, will you?" he said. Instantly, a string of party lights provided enough wattage for him to read the document. All he needed was a glance to identify the document and understand its contents. He signaled for Danny to flip the switch again, and instantly the patio was cloaked in darkness. "Oh, no, Danny, that watch wasn't for Cowboy," his father replied, with what sounded like a hint of sarcasm. He took a long sip from his glass and exhaled loudly before continuing. "Like you, David was left-handed. That extra watch was made especially for him, with the winding mechanism on the left side. Cowboy couldn't have his baby boy using his right hand to wind his watch, now could he?"

Danny marveled at his father's knowledge. He could have pored over records and documents for days and not found the information his father had tucked away in his brain. Danny only wished his father made better use of his great mind and didn't poison it with alcohol. He would continue to probe until Dan became argumentative, and then he'd back off before the conversation became too ugly. Like so many men and women Danny knew, his father wasn't a nice man after alcohol began to influence his judgment. And Danny knew before he walked out to the terrace that this wasn't the first bourbon and water his father had poured this evening. Danny nursed his, not really partial to the drink his father preferred, but too polite to ask for something else. Even if he had, he wasn't sure Dan kept anything but bourbon in his den. Dan, on the other hand, was already at the bottom of his glass, causing the ice to tinkle against the sides with every gesture of his animated hand.

Watching him, Danny was overwhelmed by sadness that such an intelligent and capable man had been reduced to this pathetic state.

At times like this he could understand why his mother had divorced this man—he wasn't the same guy who'd stopped by the lumberyard that afternoon, who ran million-dollar companies and golfed with the governor. This man wasn't to be respected and feared; he was to be pitied.

When his dad excused himself to pour another drink, Danny spilled half of his over the terrace wall. "What happened with the land? Why did Cowboy divide it?" Danny asked his father, who was just a dozen feet away, just inside the French doors and close enough that their conversation didn't pause while he poured another drink.

"His sister Eloise had married and moved away, and he knew she wouldn't be interested in having large tracts of land here. Too much of a headache to deal with. So he decided to split things up, giving her the monetary value of the land Bear had left in his control, and then gave the rest to his two surviving sons. Then he set up the trust fund with company stocks and public stocks so everyone would profit equally from the company."

"What happened when your grandfather bought them out of the company?" After Agnes, the first Dale had taken possession of the companies by purchasing the shares held by Nellie and Madeline's descendants. This unilateral control gave him the freedom to make bold moves that resulted in tremendous growth for the companies in the decades after the flood.

Dan laughed. "It was a little sticky. Since the company profits funded the trust fund, some tenets of the trust had to be revised. Everyone who's a descendant of Bear Parker gets an equal share to the trust. It just isn't growing from the profits of the Parker companies anymore."

Danny knew this, his father had complained many times about what had been the folly of his grandfather's decision. What had seemed like a smart move back then had actually crippled the trust fund. It would never grow and never do more than sustain the basic needs to the beneficiaries.

"What about the land, Dad?"

"What about it?"

"What happened to the land Cowboy gave David?"

"Well, Canal Street was washed away by Agnes. David's widow sold the hunting lodge, and his granddaughter still owns the Pocono property."

Danny looked to his father, whose head was thrown back against the lounge chair on which he reposed, as if stargazing on this bright night. His eyes were closed, though. He was just resting.

"What about the land in Nanticoke?"

Suddenly, as if he'd been slapped, his father sat upright and turned toward him, grabbing the papers Danny still held in his hand. "Why don't you major in business? What are you going to do with a history degree, anyway? Sometimes history should be left to rest. Now, no more questions."

With that, Dan rose, and on somewhat unsteady legs, he marched into his study. Danny followed him, unsure what he'd said to piss his father off so unexpectedly. Before he even reached the door to the study, he could hear the sound of the shredding machine chopping up the documents he'd spent yesterday copying.

❖

His typical day at the lumberyard began at five thirty a.m., allowing Danny time to prepare for the six o'clock opening of the doors. To meet those deadlines, he usually set a four thirty alarm, but on this particular day Danny had set his clock for three am. He needed to stop back at the Parker Companies and do some investigating.

He arrived at the offices in Plymouth at three forty-five, entered the security code into the alarm, and then headed back to the boardroom. This time, he didn't need to dig through boxes of papers to find what he was looking for. He simply sat back at the boardroom table and studied the map of the Parker Companies that had been painted over a century before.

His father's sudden change in temperament the evening before had resulted from Danny's questions regarding David's land in Nanticoke. Nanticoke and the surrounding communities—Breslau, Hanover, Alden, Glen Lyon—had been an enormous faction of the Parker's coal interests. These towns were heavily endowed with both coal and access to the Susquehanna for easy transport south. It wasn't easy for Danny to discern from the map which area had been bequeathed to David, and he had to venture to the file room yet again to pull out topographical maps that gave more detail.

His years of studying these documents gave him a familiarity that told him he was on the right track, even though he couldn't find what he was looking for. It was a difficult task to finally discover what exactly

David Parker had inherited all those years before. When he finally figured it out and saw the piece of land on the map, Danny wondered what had rattled his father. The land in question was located to the east of the city and had never been mined. Some notes on the map he used as reference indicated the land was dry, not suitable for farming, and held little prospect for a lucrative coal vein. It seemed like a worthless tract of land, on paper, at least. The question remained, though—what had upset his father so much?

Using a notepad, Danny jotted some details indicated on the map, including the name of the road nearest the land, and looking at his watch, he decided he had just enough time to dash there before he had to get to the lumberyard. Back at his car—he was driving his mother's BMW while she was out of town—he plugged the address into the GPS. Just fifteen minutes later, he pulled the car to the side of the road when the navigation system indicated he'd arrived at his destination.

Because the map at the office was so old, Danny hadn't recognized the location of the land that Cowboy gave his son David. There were no buildings back then, and the current roads hadn't yet been built. Yet Danny had been able to find the place, simply by following the taillights in front of him. Even though it was only five fifteen, there was already a steady flow of traffic on the road, all of it headed to the same destination. Danny pulled his car to the side of the road and watched as truck after truck passed him, their blinkers glowing brightly in the darkness as they turned into the main entrance to the Anthracite Landfill.

Leaning his head against the plush leather headrest, he chewed his cheek, a habit that told those who knew him best that he was troubled. And at this moment, he was deeply troubled. If he hadn't seen his father's reaction the evening before, Danny would have tried to rationalize what he was seeing, would have thought there must be a plausible explanation for what seemed on the surface to be impossible. Yet here he was, at the property owned by his newfound cousin, Sandy, watching as Parker dump trucks and sanitation trucks bearing a multitude of logos hauled their trash to the landfill his grandfather had opened just days after the Agnes flood.

While Danny wasn't privy to the exact details of the company finances, he knew enough to know this was a huge problem. Sandy Parker knew nothing about this place. That could mean only one thing—his family was operating the business on her property without her knowledge or approval.

Revenue derived from the landfill accounted for just over half of his family's annual profits, maybe a bit more. If Sandy sought restitution for the income she'd lost over the years—and Danny's rough calculation put that number at about a hundred million—his family would be bankrupt.

With a heavy heart he pulled the car onto the road and, dodging the line of trucks, made a U-turn and headed toward the lumberyard. He continued to chew his cheek as he realized that his father had been right. He should have left the past alone.

CHAPTER FIFTEEN
HEIRLOOMS

The warm evening was perfect for a walk through the Village, and looking at the traffic on Washington Square, Sandy was happy Danny had chosen a restaurant that was nearby. After she stepped from the landing to the sidewalk, she headed toward Fifth Avenue and Tenth Street to pick up Angie. Tom had graciously offered to entertain Leo for the evening so his mother could meet her cousin.

Sandy had moved back into the comfort of her own apartment after just one evening at Angie's. The security system at her place was designed to protect a Picasso, and while she knew it couldn't thwart a bullet, she felt perfectly safe at home. As suggested by the police, she was paying her environment a bit more attention than she usually did, but she wasn't sure what to actually look for. In the Village, *unusual* was the norm.

Being in her own space was infinitely more comfortable for her than tiptoeing around Angie, and Sandy knew that to stay would be to disrupt Angie's routine with Leo. While her daughter would never complain, Sandy didn't want to put her in a position where she had to. After a very enjoyable dinner of lasagna and a restful sleep in Angie's guest room, she returned to her own home on Tuesday morning. Nothing exciting had happened since. She'd been going to the gym, reading, and had taken in a matinee on Broadway. She cleaned her apartment and laundered her clothes and shopped for groceries. She'd been doing all the things she normally did and was trying hard to convince herself that life was indeed normal.

She'd spoken with Trooper Beers just a few hours earlier, and he hadn't had any news to report. No one had seen anyone suspicious loitering about on the day of the shooting, and no further clues had been discovered in Angie's tree house or in the woods surrounding the property. Every potential heir of the Davises who might benefit from the gas leases was interviewed, and no one confessed to the shooting. The officer had confided that the crime might never be solved unless they uncovered further evidence. Often crimes like this were solved only when a criminal arrested on other charges offered information in exchange for some leniency. But that sort of break was a matter of luck, and totally out of their hands. They had done everything they could, such as investigating the scene and interviewing potential witnesses, with disappointing results. That news had left Sandy rather shaken. Somehow, she'd hoped they'd find the person who'd shot her. Now, the police were telling her the culprit might never be identified. She cringed as she thought of spending the rest of her life on the lookout for a sniper.

Angie was waiting for her on the step, and Leo and Tom were keeping her company. "Hi, everyone." Sandy greeted the trio but looked only briefly at the adults before her eyes settled on her grandson. Leo's big brown eyes sparkled when Sandy reached for him, and the warmth of his smile penetrated directly to her heart. For a moment, she forgot her troubles. Showering him with kisses and squeezing him tight, Sandy had never felt such love. After a few minutes of baby talk and silly faces, she reluctantly handed him back to his father and joined arms with her daughter for the walk to Fonda, a few blocks up on Seventh Avenue.

"How was your yoga?" Angie inquired as they melted into a crowd of pedestrians on Sixth Avenue.

Sandy had always been fit. As a child, she'd taxed her body with outdoor activities, and she still did some outdoor exercise, but these days most of her exercise was in the gym. She did a Pilates class whenever she was in town, worked on the weight machines, and had even participated in Zumba with Angie to help her shed baby fat.

"Good. We had a new instructor today. Lidya sprained something." Sandy didn't mention that the new instructor was a young hottie who'd been flirting with her for the past several months.

"Too bad for her. She'll go insane if she can't work out," Angie commented. Lidya was an ultra-fit guru who spent hours on her daily gym routine. "Any word from the cops?"

"No news. And no news is bad news." Sandy explained what the officer had told her about the cold trail and confessed how troubled she was. "I'd like to go back to the cabin, but it's a little scary right now."

Angie stopped short, turning toward Sandy and grabbing her hand. "Mom, listen to me! You can't go back there!"

"Honey, he could shoot me right here. What's the difference? Since we have no idea who pulled that trigger, I'm in danger everywhere I go."

Angie slowly released her hands. "This is so awful. I can't imagine what you must be feeling."

They were still speaking of the attempt on Sandy's life when they reached the restaurant. At the same moment, a cab pulled up and Danny called to them from the open window. "Do you know where I can get a good margarita in this neighborhood?"

Sandy made the introductions as Danny paid his driver and unloaded his duffel from the car. He easily slung the bag over his shoulder, his long, muscular frame well displayed in a tight-fitting T-shirt and cargo shorts. It was hard not to admire his physique, and Sandy thought instantly of her father, who was just this age when he was killed in a car accident. He, too, had been tall, although leaner than Danny, but just as fair and handsome.

The restaurant was crowded on this Friday night, and as they waited for their drinks Sandy continued her tale about the investigation into the shooting. It was only when Danny's jaw dropped that Sandy realized she hadn't told him what had happened to her so soon after their last meeting.

Drinks were delivered and the waiter was paid, but Danny hardly noticed the handsome young man clearly noticing him. He was focused on Sandy's words, on trying to control the nausea rising in his stomach, on trying to ignore the coincidence that seemed too powerful to dismiss. His cousin seemed genuinely baffled that someone would want to kill her, and likewise, Angie found it unimaginable. Sandy Parker was a very wealthy woman, who knew of no enemies but enjoyed many friends, didn't engage in any dangerous hobbies like drugs, didn't gamble, and could think of no reason anyone would want her dead.

Danny could, though. Just a couple of days earlier he'd uncovered evidence of a fraud so huge it could motivate someone to commit murder. If, in fact, it was fraud. He wasn't sure—it was, after all, entirely possible that Sandy's grandfather had made some sort of agreement with his brother Dale many years ago, allowing him to use his land, and that the Anthracite Landfill was operating legally.

If that was the case, though, why had his dad reacted so strongly at the mention of that land? In doing his due diligence, Danny had researched the deeds at the courthouse and found that the land in use by the Anthracite Landfill was still owned by David Parker. The Parker Coal Company and then the Parker Companies had paid the taxes since the land was acquired in the 1840s. That fact wasn't surprising. The company had paid taxes on most of the private holdings of the family, and since David was in medical school when the land was gifted to him, it made sense that the company continue to take care of the assessments.

Although Danny had originally planned this trip to New York for pleasure, that plan had changed after his discovery. There was no relaxing for him now, not until this was resolved. One of Danny's missions on this trip was to try to determine if his grandfather had made some agreement with his brother, or if his family was operating a business on property they didn't own for some other reason.

Not typically a heavy drinker, Danny ordered a second margarita when the waiter made his rounds. Tonight, he needed it. And unlike many guys who weren't acclimated to the effects of alcohol, Danny knew the drink would calm his frazzled nerves without impairing him in any way.

The opportunity for questions came over dinner, and it flowed so easily with the conversation that it seemed to Danny as if he wasn't making a pointed inquiry at all but merely engaging in conversation about family history. Angie had asked Danny where he grew up, and then he asked the same question of her. When she mentioned spending time in the Poconos, the opening Danny had been waiting for presented itself. "Is that the property your grandfather inherited from Cowboy?"

Sandy told him it was, and relayed the story of how her grandparents had met as children. "Do you still have the hunting lodge?" he asked, knowing it had been sold after David's death. The property in Hunlock Creek had been close enough to the house on Canal Street that Cowboy could escape to the wilderness for a few hours of hunting or riding and return home in time for dinner. The Pocono property had been passed to her grandfather because of its proximity to his in-laws' land. The lodge and the property in Hunlock Creek were given to him because of the love David showed for it over the years. He'd hunted and fished there with Cowboy, then later with his son, and finally with Sandy.

"No, Nellie sold that to Paul Bennett, who was our neighbor and a hunter. Paul loved that land, and she thought he'd put it to good use."

"What about the land in Nanticoke?" He watched her expression closely, anxious for some sign that she was onto the fraud and about to call the FBI. She merely pursed her lips and appeared puzzled, then took a sip of her drink.

Shaking her head she answered his question. "I don't remember any land in Nanticoke. Maybe my grandfather sold it before he died? I know my grandmother didn't sell it, because after he died I helped her with all the business dealings and I would remember that."

So, that settled that, Danny thought. It didn't settle his stomach, though. The Anthracite Landfill, a multimillion-dollar company owned by his family, was operating illegally. An attempt had been made on the life of the woman who could bring this fraud to light. His father knew about the fraud. Was he ruthless enough to kill a woman to cover it up? To kill his own cousin?

His reputation in the business world was that of a ruthless competitor, a man who not only bent the rules for his own gain, but broke them. He bribed politicians and whoever else he needed to in order to make his businesses run to his satisfaction. He was a liar, a thief, and a cheater. Was he also a killer?

Danny wasn't sure. He knew his own heart, and if he were in charge he could never operate in the fashion his father had found to be so lucrative. Danny wanted to study the law, and he wanted to uphold the law. He could imagine a career in politics, fighting for good and truth. Could he take another step forward carrying the burden he now had on his shoulders? He didn't see how he could. He was going to have to find a way to deal with this issue without destroying his family. But how? How, when there had been so much dishonesty? How, when there was so much jealousy and anger? And how, when it might have been his father who shot at his cousin?

After pushing the food around on his plate, taking a few bites without really tasting, and trying to engage his cousins so as to not appear rude, he was relieved when the waiter finally brought their check. As much as he wanted to get away from them both, to have an opportunity to think about what was going on, he accepted Sandy's offer to return to her apartment for a drink. He hoped he could improve his mood by sharing with her the information she'd requested about the anniversary watches.

It was a short walk back to Sandy's, and Angie decided to join them both rather than call it a night.

After opening the door to her apartment and quieting the alarm, Sandy poured drinks while Danny looked around. "Is that a Remington?"

he asked when the statue caught his eye. He walked over to it and ran his fingers along the cold metal, exploring the intricate carving.

"It sure is."

"My dad has one, too. It was Cowboy's at one time."

Sandy looked up from the counter and shook her head. "No, you have the facts wrong, Danny. Cowboy did own a Remington, but it was passed on to my grandfather and was lost during the flood." She sighed. "I picked this one up at auction because it reminded me of the one I grew up with. This is very similar to Cowboy's."

Danny sipped his drink and looked around, thinking…not sure what to think. Since he was a little boy he had been told stories of family history, and he was certain of the facts he'd heard. The statue in his father's den had belonged to Cowboy Parker. Could there be two similar statues? Could his grandfather have lied to him because he was jealous that David had been given the statue instead of him? Would it surprise him if he had? This man had helped perpetrate a multimillion-dollar fraud, one that had been ongoing since before his birth. What did a little lie about a bronze statue matter when compared to that?

He didn't even have to ask for Sandy to elaborate about Cowboy and his Remington; she just continued to talk. "Cowboy was given that moniker because of his fascination with the American West. He loved cowboys and Indians, horses and guns. Throughout his life he collected pieces of American history—Civil War artifacts, guns, anything with a Western theme. One of his prize possessions was from the 1893 World's Fair in Chicago. It was, of course, a huge event. Bear took the family, and while he met with President Cleveland, Cowboy was treated to a private display of marksmanship by none other than Annie Oakley."

At the mention of the fair, Danny's heart nearly stopped, and he looked at the drinks Sandy had poured, anxious for something very strong to calm his nerves. It couldn't be *that*, could it?

Sandy placed their drinks on a tray and carried it into her living room, and Danny tried to appear calm as he took a gulp from the heavy crystal martini glass.

"What did he get at the fair? What was his prize possession?" Danny asked, afraid to know the answer.

"Annie signed a poster for him, one of the promotional fliers. Then she stepped back a hundred paces, and while Buffalo Bill Cody held it by the edge, Annie shot a hole through the poster, right above the 'I' in her name. She essentially dotted the 'I' with a bullet hole." Sandy shook her head and smiled.

"Oh, wow!" Angie exclaimed. "That's incredible. Do you think she did that all the time, or was that something special she did for Cowboy?"

"I'm not sure. I've looked for something like it over the years, at auctions and at exhibits, and I've never seen another. I think it was something special, and Cowboy thought it was something special, because he kept that poster until the day he died. He willed it to my father."

"Where is it now?" Angie asked, and then her hand flew to her mouth and her shoulders sagged in frustration. "No! Don't even tell me, Mom."

Sandy sighed. "Right beside the Remington, at the bottom of the river." Her voice was husky and clearly she fought hard to keep her composure. Even after all the time that passed, her anguish was still there, and very evident to both Angie and Danny.

Danny hadn't said a word, but he'd been listening closely. Sandy was right, Danny realized, but wrong as well. The bullet-riddled poster of the 1893 World's Fair was right beside the Remington bronze of a cowboy on a horse. It wasn't at the bottom of the river, though. It was on the wall of his father's study.

Danny excused himself to use the bathroom. Once inside, he closed the door and leaned against it, and staring up at the ceiling, he let out a long sigh. If he wasn't concerned about his father's involvement in the shooting before, he'd have to be blind to ignore the possibility now. Not only did Dan have Sandy's land, but he had her art as well. The next question was how the hell his grandfather had managed to get his hands on the art?

He needed to get out of this place, so he could think and absorb all of these confusing facts.

A splash of water on his face did wonders to calm him, and he felt a bit more in control of his emotions when he found Sandy and Angie once again in the living room. Before he left, he wanted to give Sandy the information she'd asked him for. He removed the receipt for the watches from his duffel and handed it to her.

"Whatcha got?" Angie asked.

Danny explained to her about the Parker family heirlooms. Sandy and Angie leaned close together to read the simple document, and when they finished both leaned back to sip their drinks. In examining the receipt, both women reached the same conclusion he had—that Cowboy's watch must have been somehow different from the others.

Shaking his head, Danny finally smiled as he explained. "That's what I thought, too. The truth is, Cowboy's watch was identical to the two he had made for Daniel and Dale. It was David's watch that was different."

Cocking her head, Sandy seemed to be thinking as she stared at him for a moment, and he watched as her eyes opened wide. She set her glass down and leaned back, studying him. "How so?"

Danny's smile was genuine as he shared this secret with them. "It was made with the winding stem on the left hand side. David was a lefty!"

"Oh, my God," Sandy said. She brought her hand to her mouth and studied the majestic Remington bronze, remembering quietly for a few moments. Then she turned her attention back to her companions and shared some of her memories with them. "I remember Grandfather holding his rifle, sighting down the long barrel as we shot at targets in the woods near the lodge, how it roared as he pulled the trigger with his left index finger. And the golf clubs he played with. He'd look up to my grandmother after a shot, silently seeking her praise. I can remember the gun and the clubs, which were custom made for him, the lefty. So was the watch. The others were standard side-winding watches, but Grandfather's was different. The stem of his pocket watch was on the left. Just like the one Robbie Burns showed me at Riverview."

She stood and paced in front of him and Angie as she told them about the watch she'd discovered in Robbie's possession.

"So the watch is your grandfather's!" Angie exclaimed.

"Holy shit!" Danny chimed in, reassuring them both that, to his knowledge, David's was the only one made that way. And by studying the receipt, the three of them agreed that had to be the case. The alteration in design had increased the price of David's watch by an additional 20 percent over the cost of the three others. The lot of four dozen cost about half the price of the four made for the Parker family. The receipt seemed to be proof positive that David's was the only left-handed watch made.

"Mom," Angie asked softly, "how could this guy have gotten your grandfather's watch?"

CHAPTER SIXTEEN
THE LAST GOODBYE, JUNE 22, 1972

H ere," Jeannie said as she handed Sandy a piece of paper, sniffling. "This is Aunt Elsie's phone number. Call me as soon as you get to your uncle's."

The worry in Jeannie's eyes brought tears to Sandy's. For a moment she was tempted to go with Jeannie, but she couldn't do that. As tough as Nellie seemed, downstairs at this very moment giving orders to workers and directing the evacuation, her strength wouldn't hold. She hadn't been the same person since her husband's death, and the stress of a flood was enough to put even a well woman over the edge. Sure, Nellie had suffered through floods before, but she'd always had David beside her to carry half the load. Even with Sandy there to help, Nellie still felt responsible for running the show. How long she could keep going was unknown, and Sandy had to be there when her grandmother grew weary.

She'd already invited Jeannie to join them in the Poconos, but Jeannie's parents wanted her close by during the impending crisis. Sandy understood that, but it would still be hard on them to be apart.

Opening her arms wide, she pulled Jeannie close. Her bedroom was dark, illuminated by a single candle on the dresser. The foreman from the power company had been by earlier to shut off their power, so the house didn't have any light. The power that supplied the streetlights was disconnected as well, so only darkness seeped through the windows. With the pounding rain falling, there wasn't a beam of starlight or moonlight to brighten this dreary night.

Furniture from the first floor—a dozen pieces from the dining room, the den, and the living room—had all been moved to the second floor, along with boxes of dishes and crystal from the curio cabinet and lamps and paintings and pictures. Stacked as they were, the combination cast strange shadows in the candlelight.

Sandy kissed Jeannie's hair. Jeannie was tall at five feet eight inches, but Sandy had her by two inches. It was enough to tease Jeannie about, but in truth they were the perfect size for each other. Perfect for hugging, perfect for kissing, perfect for cuddling, perfect for making love. Her lips were just above Jeannie's ear and she whispered into it. "It'll just be a few days."

Jeannie pulled her tighter and whispered back. "Maybe, maybe not. They say this is going to be a bad one, and remember '64? We weren't able to move home for months. I can't go months without sleeping next to you. Shit, I can't go hours without wanting you." A hint of a smile indicated Jeannie was teasing. She might whine, but in the end Jeannie was tough and would do what had to be done.

Sandy laughed at her humor, but in fact, she was just as worried as Jeannie was. The rain had been relentless and the river had risen fast, and she'd heard predictions for a record flood as well. While they would all flee to high ground and survive the river's wrath, their homes would stand and do battle with the Susquehanna. When it was over, the town would look like it'd gone fifteen rounds with the heavyweight champion, and no one would have won the match.

Even though her heart held these fears, Sandy hid them from the woman she loved. What was the sense of causing Jeannie more worry?

They separated as they heard footsteps on the stairs, and Sandy went into the hallway to direct the workers. The Burns brothers, Robbie and his older brother Billy, were struggling under the weight of the large Remington statue of a cowboy on his horse. This piece of art wasn't the most valuable one in the house, but it had been her grandfather's favorite. She directed the two men into her bedroom, and they placed the statue on her dresser, at the back of the room near the door to the balcony. When they'd unburdened themselves, they returned to the first floor for another load.

This had been the scene all day at her home on Canal Street, and indeed in all of the homes in the flood plain of the Wyoming Valley. Hurricane Agnes had settled in the region, rain was falling at record levels, and the river was rising at an equally unprecedented pace. Jeannie had spent her day helping her parents pack boxes. They too had shifted furniture and household goods to the second floor, which was safely out of the river's reach. Floodwaters had never reached the second story of these homes.

"Let's go see what General Parker wants us to do now," Sandy said teasingly, referring to the no-nonsense manner in which her grandmother took charge of the workers.

They entered in the middle of an argument. Nellie's brother Arthur was there to drive them to the Poconos. While Nellie felt comfortable behind the wheel, she didn't drive long distances and certainly not in a hurricane. The siblings were arguing about the Norman Rockwell painting that had stood watch over her dining-room table since the early days of her marriage.

"Why can't I bring it, Arthur? It won't take up much room!"

"It'll get damaged, Nell. Just put it upstairs under a cloth and it'll be safe."

"I'd hate to lose that picture. David bought that for me, you know."

Arthur smiled at Nellie and patted her shoulder. "I know you treasure it. And if I thought for a moment there was any danger, I'd tell you to take it."

Sandy and Jeannie stood near the entrance to the command center in the kitchen, and Nellie called Sandy close. "Get a Buster Brown box for me, and bring my jewelry box. And bring your grandfather's pocket watch as well."

A Buster Brown box was their private code for the cash they kept stored in the attic. Each box held between five and twenty-five thousand dollars, depending on the denomination of the bills. A box would give them plenty of money to hold them over during their exile.

Sandy and Jeannie went back up the stairs, and Sandy went alone into the attic to retrieve the money. She handed the box to Jeannie. Back in her grandparents' bedroom, Sandy picked up the small wooden box that held Nellie's jewels, and then she retrieved her grandfather's watch from the drawer where it had always been stored. She handed the watch to Jeannie, who lifted the shoe-box lid and placed the watch inside for safekeeping. If the stacks of money there surprised her, her face didn't betray her.

Out in the hall as they were about to descend to the first floor, they heard a deafening crash in Sandy's room. She and Jeannie rushed to the doorway and screamed in horror at the bloody mess they found. Robbie Burns was covered in blood, and glass was scattered from the table he'd fallen through after tripping in all the clutter of her room. The sight was all the scarier because of the flickering candle illuminating the room, casting its dark shadows everywhere.

The promising physician Jeannie ran to him, and placing the

Buster Brown box on the dresser, she pulled a few shirts out of Sandy's drawer to use as bandages to help stop his hemorrhage.

"Tell the chief to radio for an ambulance," Jeannie instructed Sandy. The fire chief had been walking into Nellie's kitchen moments before when they'd left on their mission. With the power cut, they didn't have a phone to call for medical assistance, so they hoped the chief was still downstairs.

"I'm okay," Robbie insisted, but he appeared to be a little woozy. A gash on his forehead at the hairline seemed to be the biggest problem, and Jeannie surveyed the rest of him while she held pressure with the shirt.

About to pass out from the sight of blood, Robbie's brother had stepped out of the room, but now he came back to check on the injuries. Robbie's hands were cut from trying to break the fall, but other than the gash on his head, he didn't seem to have suffered from any other injuries. Together, Billy and Jeannie helped Robbie to his feet, then down the hallway and the stairs, where miraculously they met the Tilbury Ambulance crew. They'd been on standby at the entrance to Canal Street.

Candles also illuminated the first floor. At least a dozen reflected in Jeannie's eyes as they met Sandy's.

"Can't you do anything, Doc?" Sandy teased Jeannie after she handed over care to the trained professionals.

"I'm going to do neurosurgery to repair his brain if I can find my needle and thread in this mess," Jeannie responded.

Suddenly Paul Bennett came into the hallway, squeezing around the ambulance crew. "Sweetie, we have to go. Everyone's in the car except you." His voice was kind. He had to know how hard this flood would be on Jeannie.

Sandy's eyes met Jeannie's and she tried to convey all of her love and comfort with a smile. Holding her grandmother's jewelry box with one arm, she hugged Jeannie close with the other. "I love you," she whispered into Jeannie's ear.

"I love you, too."

They pulled apart, except for their eyes, which held until, walking backward, Jeannie stepped out the door and out of Sandy's life forever.

"Sandra." Her grandmother's voice conveyed the stress of the day. "The chief says we have to go, now. The water's reached the road."

Sandy's bag had already been packed and taken to Arthur's car. She followed her grandmother, still carrying the jewelry box, and took her place in the backseat. It wasn't until they were on the road, miles from Canal Street, with no opportunity to turn back, that Sandy realized Jeannie had left the Buster Brown box with the money and her grandfather's watch sitting on the dresser in her room.

CHAPTER SEVENTEEN
SHOWDOWN, JUNE 18, 2011

Washington Square is as quiet a place as can be found in Manhattan. A dozen stories up, Sandy's bedroom, facing the park and the street below, was quiet and peaceful. The double set of blinds on the windows, installed to keep out the afternoon sun when Diane had been sick and sleeping during the day, worked equally well at thwarting the ambient light of the neighborhood. Hers was the penthouse. The neighbor below was a quiet man who never brought his dates home, and so the overall ambience was peaceful.

Still, sleep would not come to Sandy. She lay still in her bed, but her mind was active as she remembered all she could of the man who had somehow come into possession of her grandfather's watch. Robbie Burns had been her classmate since kindergarten, a quiet boy, but always friendly to her. He was never the most popular kid, but everyone liked him. He endured the occasional taunting about his father's job as caretaker at the town's only cemetery, but in a town as small as West Nanticoke, the kids had no real enemies. Everyone looked out for one another. The same boys who teased him as a child were the ones who covered his back when they all transferred to the junior high school in seventh grade and their small class of forty became a class of two hundred.

It was often said that you didn't mess with *anyone* from West Nanticoke, or you'd be messing with *everyone*.

As they grew from children to young adults Robbie became shyer, or at least it seemed that way. Jeannie had suggested on more than one occasion that Robbie had a crush on Sandy, but she thought it was merely that they had a special bond because of their family ties. His father managed the maintenance for all of the Parker rental properties.

Although they had little in common after they outgrew riding bikes and climbing trees, when he worked at her grandparents' house, whether in the garden replacing broken stones, painting, or caring for the lawn, he was always very friendly. He and Sandy often worked side by side for hours, talking Phillies baseball, sometimes listening to games on her transistor radio or singing along to the radio in easy companionship. If she needed someone dependable in that time of her life, she knew she could have asked Robbie for just about anything. The boy she knew would not have stolen anything, especially from her.

Yet someone had robbed the Parker house on the night of the flood; there was no question about that. The watch had been there, in the box of money, on her dresser, when the house was abandoned as they fled the rising river. Jeannie, Billy, and Robbie were the last ones down the staircase that night. Sandy remembered a solitary flashlight as they descended the huge marble stair, the gleam reflecting like a mirror in the darkness behind them. No one was carrying a shoe box. Billy, on Robbie's right, held the light in that hand and supported Robbie with the other. Jeannie held Robbie with her right arm as she held the banister with her left. It was slow progress down all those stairs, with nothing to guide them but the narrow beam of Billy's light and Robbie's weight to throw off their balance.

After finding the chief, who was helping Arthur carry something to his car, Sandy entered from the rear of the house and met the trio on the stairs. She waved her own flashlight on the stairs to guide their way. As they reached the bottom, the ambulance immediately took Robbie, and Mr. Burns and Billy followed. Mr. Bennett came in for Jeannie. Her grandmother came in for her.

Sandy blew out the candles and left through the front door behind the Bennetts. The house was dark and deserted as they left. As they pulled away from the house in the pouring rain, the world was dark save for the headlights of that parade of automobiles, led by the ambulance, with Arthur's car pulling up the rear. As they drove the short distance along Canal Street that night, the car tires were already underwater. It would have been impossible for anyone to go back, unless by boat.

That, she realized, was what had to have happened. After they left, someone who knew about the money must have gone back with a boat to steal it. Her grandfather's watch was just a bonus.

Remembering the night they had fled West Nanticoke, Sandy found it hard to imagine that Robbie could have taken part in a robbery at her grandparents' house later that night. He had suffered deep wounds to both hands, and Sandy figured it would have been at least a week or so before they were working well enough to use them. He might have been able to commit a robbery if the head wound was his only injury, but as Jeannie and Billy had walked with him on the stairs, Robbie had looked shaky. A concussion was likely. She wouldn't be surprised if he had been admitted to the hospital because of his injuries.

It wasn't only the injuries that convinced Sandy of Robbie's innocence, though. She had seen him just the week before, when he had shown her the watch. He had shown no fear, no hesitation to hand over the watch for her inspection. He had been so proud of the watch and what it represented. His grandfather really was a hero, and she had no doubt that Robbie truly believed the watch in his possession belonged to him.

If it wasn't Robbie, then who had robbed the house? It certainly could have been anyone. There was no police presence guarding the house; all someone would have needed was a boat with a powerful motor and enough guts to challenge the current of the rising river.

How had Robbie gotten the watch, then? The answer to that question would answer the first, and it was just the first question she had for him when she met him later that day.

She had another question as well. If someone had risked their life in the swift current of the Susquehanna, would they have settled for a single box of cash? Might they have also stolen the artwork? Between the cash and the art in the house that night, a thief could have walked away with close to a million dollars. And while the cash wasn't traceable, the Rockwell, the Wyeth, and the Remington certainly were. On today's market, the paintings alone were worth four or five million dollars. As her daughter had pointed out the night before, keeping the theft of the Parker art a secret could certainly be a motive for murder.

❖

Less than a mile away on a beat-up couch much too small for him, Danny stared at the ceiling of his friend's apartment. Unlike the luxury apartment that Sandy owned, this place was far from quiet. It wasn't the noise on the streets of Greenwich Village that was keeping him awake, however. The noise in his head was deafening. The things he had learned in the past few days had his head spinning and his heart pounding.

No way could he tell Sandy the location of her stolen art. If things weren't already bad enough, she'd divulged the existence of yet another piece of art that had probably been stolen as well. Of all the pieces in his father's collection, the Rockwell was by far the most valuable. If Danny could twist his thoughts to rationalize Dan stealing the pieces that had been Cowboy's, treasures he perhaps thought were rightfully his, Danny couldn't apply the same thinking to the theft of the Rockwell that hung in his dining room. That piece had never been in the Parker family; it was purchased for Sandy's grandmother to celebrate the birth of her son. Why—except pure greed—would his father want that piece of art?

Danny had no idea what the hell had happened during the flood, and until he did, he planned to keep his mouth shut about what little he did know. He'd already discussed with Sandy a plan to drive to West Nanticoke on Saturday morning, and both of them were so anxious to meet with Robbie Burns that if it weren't for too many margaritas, they'd have left Friday evening.

He was trying to understand what had happened the night of the flood. Had his family orchestrated the robbery, using the rising waters of the Susquehanna as a cover for their crime? It was possible, but it really didn't seem likely. Although it was predicted that Agnes would be a record flood, no one knew the house on Canal Street would be swept away. If not for that fact, the crime would have been detected quickly. Even if the muddy waters of the river had washed away any evidence that would have incriminated those responsible, it would have been a much more dangerous scenario to display the art if it was known to be stolen.

His great-grandfather Dale, or whoever was responsible for the theft, would have recovered the family heirlooms but would have had to sequester them in a closet to prevent their discovery. There would have been no point, and that certainly hadn't been the case. Dale had proudly displayed the pieces as long as Danny could remember, and more recently they had been prominently in view in his father's study. They had to know the pieces were stolen; yet it didn't seem to bother them. The question was why? And was there some connection to the stolen art and the stolen land? Most worrisome of all, as Angie had asked a few hours before—was there some connection between the theft of this art and the bullets fired at Sandy's back?

❖

"Would you like coffee or a doughnut?" Robbie asked them as they seated themselves on the metal folding chairs in front of his desk.

Danny appeared squeamish at the prospect of eating here in this anteroom of the dead, but Sandy had spent her childhood doing just that. "That would be wonderful," she replied, then watched as he prepared the Keurig.

At seven a.m., the earliest hour Sandy felt acceptable to call a near stranger, she'd dialed Robbie's number. Two funerals had consumed his morning, but now at nearly two o'clock he was finally free to talk with them. The cemetery was deserted, visitors and workers long gone, allowing them to speak without interruption.

In spite of his morning duties, Robbie appeared clean and fresh, wearing jeans and a T-shirt rather than coveralls as he had at their last meeting.

Sandy courteously waited for him to complete the task at hand, and when he was seated at his desk she began to talk. Like an actress on the stage, she had rehearsed her dialogue into the wee hours of the morning. Her dress rehearsal had been for Danny's ears only on the ride from New York. Now, seated in front of Robbie, who looked as nervous as she felt, she had a difficult time beginning.

"I came to see you about the watch," she finally explained. Leaning forward in her seat, she rested the coffee on Robbie's desk, suddenly too nauseated to drink. Before she could say anything more, Robbie interrupted her.

"Ms. Parker, I wish you'd just told me that on the phone. I could have saved you a long trip." Robbie's nerves appeared to calm as he spoke, and he looked at home behind the beat-up desk in the old cinderblock structure. Surrounded by the tools of his trade, he was literally in his element, which showed in the confidence that grew as he spoke. "It's true that the Burns family isn't *quite* as well off as the Parkers are, but this watch is our family's greatest treasure. It is not for sale, at any price." He leaned back in his chair when he finished speaking, his body language the exclamation point telling them that he'd made his mind up and his decision was final.

Sandy's script hadn't allowed for Robbie's candid interruption, and she wasn't sure how to proceed as she studied his face. Even more convinced than before that he had nothing to do with the theft, she understood now that this conversation would be more difficult than she'd anticipated.

Saved from a reply by Danny, Sandy watched him hand Robbie a copy of the nearly one-hundred-year-old receipt for the watches. After pausing for a moment to allow Robbie to glance at the paper, Danny began to speak. "We'd like to show you this document, Mr. Burns. This is a copy of the receipt for the purchase of your grandfather's watch, and all the others. No others were ever made except the ones you see documented on this paper." Danny's tone was respectful, and even though he was dressed in another tight-fitting shirt and well-worn shorts, his carriage and demeanor bespoke the lawyer he would one day become. He handed Sandy a copy of the document so she could follow along, and even though she knew the details, knew what the paper said and what it meant, she concentrated on Danny's every word.

"See the top line, here?" Danny pointed to his own receipt so Robbie could follow. "This is the charge for forty-eight watches. They were very nice watches, made of gold, but they had plain stainless-steel faces and no diamonds. They cost the company about forty dollars each, which was expensive in 1918. This type of watch was given to the mine foremen and officers of the company, and to men like your grandfather who were exceptional employees."

Robbie interrupted him, the anger in his voice evident. "My grandfather was a *hero*, Mr. Parker. He saved seven men from drowning. He was more than an *exceptional employee* who did the company's bidding."

Danny nodded in agreement, and Sandy found herself doing the same. She had to suppress a smile when she realized she looked like a bobble-head doll. "You're right, sir. I don't mean to trivialize the heroic act your grandfather performed. I'm merely showing you this paper to explain the differences in the watches the Parker Coal Company gave out in 1918 and the following years."

"My grandfather saved those people in 1920."

"Yes, I know that. My cousin tells me you're quite the historian, Mr. Burns. One day I'd like to take you to the archives at the Parker Company and let you look through the documents we have there. There's quite a bit of information about your grandfather."

Robbie grudgingly agreed. "That'd be nice, but what do you want with my watch?"

Danny pointed back to the paper. "The next three watches were made a little differently. They had gold faces, like yours. They had a diamond chip at the twelve o'clock position. I believe the gold content is also higher. You can see from the receipt that these watches cost a hundred and thirty dollars back then. They were given to Cowboy, Dale, and Daniel Parker V."

Robbie was studying the face of his watch, verifying what Danny had just told him. The face was in fact gold, and the diamond chip was glinting in the sunlight. When he didn't reply, Danny said, "The last watch—the one that cost a hundred and fifty dollars—was similar to the other three, with one huge exception. Just like your watch, the winding stem was set on the left at the nine o'clock position."

"This doesn't prove anything!" Robbie was trembling as he stood. Clearly he understood the point Danny was trying to make.

"Of all those fifty-two watches made, Mr. Burns, there was only one left-handed watch. It was made for David Parker, Sandy's grandfather, and stolen from their home on Canal Street during the Agnes flood."

"Get out! I will not have you accuse me of theft! My grandfather was a hero and this is his watch, not your grandfather's," he said, nodding and pointing at Sandy. Gone was the gentle soul Sandy had once known, replaced by an angry man she didn't recognize and suddenly feared. Perhaps she had been unwise to come here and challenge him in this way. She should have done this with her lawyer.

As they stood to leave, a sound behind them startled them. An ATV bearing a man in full camouflage pulled into the garage and stopped just a few feet from them. A rifle was strapped across his back. When he stood and removed his helmet, both Sandy and Danny took a step back toward the desk.

The man appeared rabid, with wild unkempt hair and a beard that grew down to his chest, a grimace on his face and fire in his eyes.

Sandy and Danny stared at the gravedigger, surveying his camouflage boots and pants and coordinating green long-sleeve T-shirt. Sandy had seen many hunters similarly dressed, so it wasn't his appearance that frightened her. It was the look of evil in his eyes that caused her heart to pound faster.

"Don't you believe a word they told you, Robbie. They're lying." The man spat his tobacco juice onto the floor and it splattered, nearly hitting Sandy's sneaker.

Danny had quickly recovered. "How would you know what we're discussing, Mr...?"

Robbie took the cue from Danny and introduced his older brother, Billy. Sandy wouldn't have recognized him if Robbie hadn't made the introduction. He had been an average-looking young man in his early twenties at the time of the flood, putting him in his early sixties now. He looked much older, with a chilling resemblance to the Unabomber. Seeing him now, she remembered him then. A bit odd. Never very friendly. He hadn't spent much time at the Parkers', but on the night of the flood, when every pair of hands was needed, he'd been there. He was the one who'd stolen the watch!

The gun across his back suddenly made Sandy very nervous. They needed to get out of the deserted cemetery, fast.

"We were just discussing your brother's watch, Mr. Burns." Apparently Danny felt none of the anxiety that was building within Sandy. Like a lawyer on cross-examination, he seemed to be just getting started with his questions.

"Maybe we should go," Sandy suggested, fighting the rising panic surging like bile in her gut.

The quick turn of his head forecast an argument, but he must have recognized the fear in her eyes, because after looking at her for a moment, he nodded. "We'll speak another time, Mr. Parker. Take good care of that watch." As they turned to go, they found themselves staring down the barrel of Billy's rifle. He stood a dozen feet away, his legs spread wide for balance and the gun pointed directly at the two feet of space between them.

"You're not going anywhere! Sit down!" Billy screamed. The gun waved in his dancing arms as he gestured to them, causing Sandy and Danny to jump back into their seats. Sandy didn't dare take her eyes off the gun to look at Danny, but she could suddenly hear his breathing.

Robbie, who was still standing, began to creep out from behind his desk, moving toward his brother. Or perhaps moving out of the line of fire? "Hold on, Billy! This is stupid. You don't want to hurt these people over a watch!"

Billy shook his head. "Stay still, brother. Don't you see? This isn't about that damn watch!"

Sandy had a difficult time pulling her eyes off the gun, so she couldn't see Robbie's expression. Yet she could hear the confusion in his voice. "What's going on, Billy? Why do you want to hurt these people?"

She shifted in her seat, causing Billy to point the gun directly at her chest. "You keep still, Ms. Parker. I might have missed you from two hundred yards, but I won't miss from five feet."

Sandy recoiled at his words. He'd robbed the Parker house on Canal Street and tried to kill her, and now he was going to try again. Suddenly the fears and frustrations of the past two weeks boiled over. "You? You shot me? And you robbed my family? You bastard! What did my family ever do to you? What did *I* ever do to you?" She rose in her seat to confront the gunman.

"You shut up!" Billy screamed, pulling the rifle up to his eye to sight the target at Sandy. "And sit back down!"

As her good sense returned, she sat down, as Robbie began to plead. "Billy!" He tried to calm his brother. "Who cares about the watch? It's no big deal. I'll give it back. It's not worth killing someone for!"

"It's not about the damn watch," Billy repeated, sounding calmer than he had during the entire episode. Shaking his head, he let out a sigh. "Robbie, where do you think Daddy got all that money after the flood? Do you really think he was that great a contractor that we were suddenly rich?"

Robbie shook his head no, denying what his brother was telling him. "No, don't say that! Dad worked hard!"

"Daddy was a drunk! He robbed the Parkers on the night of the flood, and he killed the man who drove the boat to their house. He took their money, their paintings, their statues, their china! He took it all, Robbie! Then he killed the man who wanted to buy the artwork. And I was there! I saw him kill two men so you could have a decent life and a stupid watch. And for all these years I've been sweating it out, hoping no one ever learned the truth, because I was an accessory to those murders. And I do not intend to go to jail. If she hadn't come back here, I wouldn't have to do this. But I don't have a choice, Robbie. It's her or me."

Robbie's jaw dropped. All three of their jaws dropped. They were going to die, ironically, in the cemetery.

Why had Sandy had the idea to come here? Why hadn't she met Robbie at Stookey's or the Wyoming Valley Mall, or someplace crowded with pedestrians where a madman with a rifle wouldn't have followed them?

"This is Pop's watch!" Robbie exclaimed, giving his brother the same argument he'd given just a few minutes earlier to Sandy and Danny.

"Pop was poor, Robbie. That watch cost more than he made in a month. Why the hell didn't the Parkers just give him money for being a hero? He didn't need that stupid watch! He sold it to buy food for his family and to pay the rent. When Dad found Dr. Parker's watch on the night of the flood, he kept it. That was his only souvenir of the robbery. He always thought Pop regretted selling the watch, and he took it for him." Robbie shook his head, laughing. "He thought it was untraceable. He couldn't even get that right, the bastard."

"You can't do this," Sandy interjected, her voice soft, pleading. "No one cares about all that stuff that happened so long ago. But they will care about what happens today. If you kill us, you'll be found. My family knows I'm here." She tipped her head toward Danny. "His family knows he's here. They'll come looking here, and you and your brother will go to jail."

Billy laughed. "I'll take my chances. Now both of you, stand up."

Danny had been silently watching and listening to the events unfold, cursing his vanity. He'd wanted to be the hotshot lawyer and break the case, solve the puzzle about the stolen watch and look like a hero to his father. He'd wanted to prove his father wasn't a murderer. Well, in that, at least, he was successful. If he'd told Sandy what he knew about the stolen art, though, she would have figured out there was more involved in this than the watch. She probably wouldn't have rushed over here like this, and they wouldn't be facing their executioner right now.

Danny didn't want to die. His life was just beginning. He was about to graduate college and was going to law school. He had so much to look forward to.

Assessing the situation, he thought he might be able to take down the gunman. Although Billy was tall, Danny was muscular and younger, and all he needed was a split-second advantage and the element of surprise to subdue the guy. When they were ordered to stand, he'd begun to formulate a plan. He hadn't quite worked out the details when Billy told them to begin walking and he prayed that wouldn't matter.

Sandy was already in front of him, and he fell in behind her as Billy pointed the way out the open garage door and toward the woods behind the cemetery. They began their death march with the brothers behind them, arguing. Robbie's frantic pleas to his brother might be all the distraction Danny needed.

He slowed his stride a bit as the hill behind the garage steepened, narrowing the gap between him and his would-be assassin. Sensing Billy was close enough to him, Danny suddenly stopped, leaned forward, then sent a ferocious back kick into the man's abdomen. He spun and, as Billy faltered, Danny blasted him with another kick and a sequence of punches to the gut and then finally a knee to the face that knocked him to his knees. Danny kicked the rifle away and Sandy, alerted by their scuffle, grabbed it, pointing it at the man who lay moaning on the ground. His nose was broken, blood poured from both nostrils, and his ragged breathing indicated a few ribs were probably injured as well.

Robbie stood helplessly, staring first at his brother on the ground and then at Sandy holding a powerful gun in her hands. Not sure she could trust Robbie, Sandy ordered him down beside his brother.

She glanced at Danny, who was catching his breath after the sequence of kicks and punches he'd thrown. He caught her eye and she nodded her approval. "Nice work," she commented. "And I thought kickboxing was just for exercise."

Danny rubbed the knuckles on his right hand. "So did I."

When the police arrived ten minutes later, the Burns brothers were still sitting there, side by side on the hill behind the cemetery. What had started at Riverview with Nellie's funeral just three weeks earlier was finished there as well.

Sandy thought she might just give it another forty years before she came back again.

CHAPTER EIGHTEEN
A SMOOTH-TALKING LAWYER

S andy sipped her coffee as she read the complimentary copy of *USA Today* offered at the East Mountain Inn. Located at the foothills of Bear Creek Mountain, this hotel was in an area that had been entirely wooded when she lived here as a young girl, an area like nearby Mountaintop that had exploded with development in the wake of Agnes. The flood that reached this area would have to cover 95 percent of the planet with water.

She had arrived early for this meeting—she always felt it gave her the upper hand—and was killing time as she waited for the two other members of the Parker family to arrive with their attorney. This morning she was conferencing with Danny and his father, the cousin she hadn't liked as a child and who she now knew was a thief. It was likely not him but rather his grandfather, Danny's great-grandfather, who purchased her family's art from Bill Burns, but she was certain her cousin knew where it had come from. The pieces were too unique, and famous within their family, to put their ownership in doubt. Likewise, he might not have orchestrated the opening of the Anthracite Landfill on her land, but for the last three decades he'd been running it, and to keep his fraud from discovery he'd been paying the tax bill sent to her dead grandfather. He'd been reaping the profits as well.

For a reason probably known only to them, her grandfather and his brother had never been close. Their children weren't either. Their parents hadn't encouraged the cousins to form a bond, and without that push, they just didn't have enough in common to develop a lasting relationship. That was one reason Nellie and Sandy had been able to walk away after Agnes. With David dead, and then Jeannie, neither of them had a tie to the Wyoming Valley to keep them there. Nellie's relationship with her own family was by far the better one, making the move to Mount Pocono the right choice for her.

Sandy often thought the gods must move the chess pieces on the board of life. Losing her home in Agnes had been the worst thing that ever happened to her—other than the death of the women she loved, of course—but it had shaped her life in a wonderful way. With Nellie in Mount Pocono it had been so much easier for Sandy to leave for New York. Just an hour away by bus, she was comfortable knowing she could easily return if her grandmother needed her. And she knew Nellie wasn't alone, for her siblings and their families always welcomed her grandmother as their own.

As she sipped her coffee, Sandy hoped this meeting would go better than the last meeting with their branch of the family tree. That was the day that Dale, Danny's great-grandfather, had been sent packing when he tried to convince Nellie to sell him her shares of the company and her real-estate interests. Dale must have developed an ulcer when Nellie refused to sell him the land he'd already used to open his landfill.

After the events at the cemetery a week earlier, she and Danny had both been quite shaken. When they had finished their statements to the police and were excused, Danny had silently climbed into Sandy's car for the ride to Wilkes-Barre, where he'd left his own vehicle the day before when he'd boarded the bus for New York. Once at the bus terminal, instead of climbing out of her car, Danny unbuckled his seat belt and turned toward her. He then began a confession that sent Sandy's head spinning yet once again.

When he finished telling her his story—about all the pieces of stolen art he knew were at his father's house, about his reasons for not telling her earlier, and about his speculations about how it must have come into his great-grandfather's possession—Danny apologized profusely for not informing her earlier. He blamed himself that they were nearly killed.

Sandy didn't necessarily agree with him. She already knew that someone had robbed her house on Canal Street and suspected they had taken much more than the watch, whose discovery had seemingly set the wheels of this drama in motion. Having known that her great-uncle's family possessed the art probably wouldn't have altered her decision to meet Robbie at the cemetery that day. She couldn't have anticipated the actions of a madman, which Billy Burns seemed to be.

Over the course of the week since his arrest, information had poured forth from many sources, describing the strange behavior and volatile personality of the man who'd attempted to murder her. The police told her he'd been in and out of trouble his entire adult life, not for serious crimes, but for the types that would indicate an underlying mental illness that periodically flared up, causing dramatic behaviors that drew the attention of the law. He opened packages of food in the grocery store, sitting in the middle of the aisle and eating as other shoppers navigated around him. When he finished his meal he'd leave, not bothering to clean up his mess or pay for what he'd eaten. He shoplifted. He displayed road rage. He caused fights at sporting events.

When his misdeeds happened close to home, usually someone around who knew him steered him back on track and on his way home. If he ventured too far away, though, he usually found himself in police custody until his brother Robbie could bail him out.

The police had found four Buster Brown shoe boxes in his house, fitting the description of the boxes of cash stashed in the attic of the house at One Canal Street. The boxes contained more than a hundred thousand dollars, mostly in bills dated from the 1950s. They described the house as meticulously clean and equipped with high-tech computer equipment and the most modern television on the market. On the bookshelves they found volumes of classic literature ranging from Shakespeare to Mark Twain, all of the books stolen from local libraries. They also discovered all manner of mechanical devices, including engines and generators, fans, and radios, all built from parts of other machines that this rather remarkable man had disassembled and reconfigured.

Obstinate in the first days of his incarceration, Billy had finally decided to cooperate with the police when they offered him the simple exchange of a book of Robert Frost's poetry. He confessed to aiding his father on the night of the Agnes flood when the elder Bill Burns hired an acquaintance with a motorboat to drive them to the Parker house. He described the difficulty of keeping the boat stabilized in the swift current of the river, of the boat's owner threatening to abandon Billy and his father as they entered the house one last time for the Remington statue. They had gone in through the rear, climbing up onto Sandy's balcony to gain entry, and had made a dozen trips in and out of the house, hauling out boxes of money and other valuables. The boat had been tied to a rail, but the current was knocking it against the balcony, and the owner became anxious. He decided they had collected enough and commanded Billy and his father to return to the boat. Billy's father had almost killed him then, but knew he needed him to navigate the boat in the rapidly rising Susquehanna. Later, after the boat was emptied of its treasures, his father had drowned the man.

Billy didn't know the man's name or the name of the man in the Cadillac who was contacted to sell the Parkers' art collection. He did know exactly where his body was, though—buried atop Nancy Stewart, who had died in July of 1972. Using missing-persons' reports from that era, the police were easily able to identify the two men and exhumed the body of the second from the double grave.

His father had never told him who eventually took the pieces of art off his hands; he only knew the elder Bill Burns was very disappointed with the hundred thousand dollars he received in trade. They had pulled over a million dollars in cash out of the house, with little difficulty. They had nearly drowned hauling out that damn statue, and in the end they profited very little from it.

Finding the watch in the box of money atop Sandy's dresser had been an omen, according to Billy. That watch, the symbol of his grandfather's heroism, was a sign that the Burns family was meant to have all the Parker money.

Although Danny couldn't have known it at the time, Billy Burns would never have been able to identify his father as the buyer of the stolen art. Danny's confession to Sandy had implicated him, though. Danny had formed his own conclusions and followed his conscience, and for that Sandy was grateful. Knowing that Agnes didn't destroy the treasures of her family meant more to Sandy than she ever could have guessed. The thought of recovering her grandmother's Norman Rockwell, of hanging the painting in her own dining room, filled her with a tremendous peace.

The other pieces of artwork weren't really that important to her. They were more historically significant than of personal interest. It was the Rockwell that she missed. So when Danny surprised her still further by telling her of a plan he'd devised, Sandy listened closely, pleased at what she heard.

As a history major, Danny had a great appreciation for his family's contribution to the growth of the region and the country. The company archives held thousands of documents relating not just to the history of the Parker Coal Company, but to the history of the region and the country. Deeds and contracts and maps documented the Wyoming Valley's growth over a two-hundred-year period. The company had artifacts as well. Shelf upon shelf held the tools of the old miners—helmets and lanterns, picks and shovels, lunch pails and blasting caps. Samples of coal of different grades were kept, from peat and bituminous to anthracite and graphite. Telegrams from governors, senators, and presidents to the heads of the company hung on walls in handsome antique frames. Photographs of the common people who lived here, as well as the politicians and business moguls who led them, were filed in boxes at the Parker Companies' headquarters.

The archives held a treasure, hidden away in the building in Plymouth where no one would ever get to appreciate it. Danny wanted to change that. If Sandy would agree, items from the archives and any pieces of the stolen art she chose to donate would be used to create an exhibit at King's College to celebrate the rich history of the region and of the Parker family. The college was founded to educate the children of coal miners. The altar in the school chapel was crafted from a two-ton piece of coal. And while coal miners no longer toiled in the Wyoming Valley, King's continued to provide an outstanding education to the descendants of the men who'd worked and died in the mines generations ago. The school was the perfect place to display such a collection.

As she sat next to him that day, Sandy knew she loved Danny's idea. Yet she was still reeling over the events of the days and weeks before. She told him she needed some time to think about his proposal, and he agreed that her request was understandable.

Already in shock, Sandy was in no way prepared for the next segment of her conversation with Danny.

"I need to ask you something, and I'm pretty sure I know the answer, but I can't find enough information to prove my suspicions." Sandy watched him closely. He'd seemed nervous before telling her about the art. Now that emotion seemed to be replaced by another—sadness, perhaps? Frustration? Letting go of a tremendous breath, Danny asked her a question. "Did you, or perhaps your grandparents, ever lease any land to my grandfather for the Anthracite Landfill?"

A bell rang in Sandy's brain and she was suddenly more alert. A landfill! When she'd met Danny for the first time, he'd informed her that the landfill was going strong. The news didn't register at the time, but in the back of her mind she'd asked—what landfill? The Parkers owned coal mines and businesses related to destruction and construction, and a landfill seemed like a logical business to complement those others, but no landfill had been in operation when she lived on Canal Street.

"No," she answered simply, but she watched him, eager to hear what he would say next.

Danny nodded. "And to your knowledge, your grandfather never sold any land to his brother?"

Sandy still searched his face, and all she saw was the sadness in his eyes. "He never mentioned any land to me, so it's possible. Maybe it was sold before I was born, or when I was very young? And now I have a question for you. After what we've been through, I'm almost afraid to ask, but why do you want to know?"

Danny reached into his duffel bag, retrieved the paper he'd copied at the office, and handed it to her. It documented the transfer of land from Cowboy to his son David. "First, let me say I've been trying to verify this, but I'm not a hundred percent certain what's going on. There may be some paperwork somewhere that explains all of this, and I honestly hope there is."

As Sandy looked at the paper he'd given her, he spoke again. "This land is still registered to your grandfather, and the Parker Companies have been paying the taxes on it since the 1920s." Danny sighed again. "It seems we've been using your land, Sandy, without your knowledge or approval. In the days after Agnes, my great-grandfather opened a landfill on this piece of land. Over the years that place has brought in more than a hundred million dollars in revenue to the family, and we don't even own the land. You own it. You've never been paid a cent."

Sandy thought back to the meeting Dale had with her grandmother after Agnes, wanting to buy her shares of company stock and all her land. He was trying to cover his tracks then, only Nellie wouldn't cooperate.

After confirming this swindle with Sandy, Danny proposed he broker a deal between her and his family that would compensate her for her losses while allowing the company to maintain solvency. He informed her in plain terms that any litigation she engaged in would break the family business. There were simply too many shareholders and not enough income to go around. They were by no means poor, but the money made in the days of coal mining was no more. The only Parker with enough assets to survive a lawsuit was Sandy.

After speaking with his father, who developed chest pains and subsequently underwent a stress test after learning what Sandy knew, they were meeting today to finalize the agreement she and Danny had forged over their smart phones.

She was cordial to the man who'd kept her family heirloom from her, controlling her anger because she knew she wouldn't accomplish anything by arguing with him. Men like Dan, who thought they could break all the rules and never get caught, were all the same. Just like with the crooks she'd dealt with on Wall Street, Sandy didn't bother trying to convince him of his crimes. It wasn't up to her.

She had wanted to be civil for Danny's benefit as well. She adored this young man, and the deeds of his father shouldn't have come back to haunt him. Yet he'd nearly been shot and gone through tremendous personal turmoil to make his confession to Sandy, and she appreciated his effort. She wouldn't embarrass herself or stress him further by arguing with his father.

She'd agreed to donate most of Cowboy's art to King's, with the exception of the Annie Oakley print, which she kept for herself. Playing with Cowboy's guns in her grandfather's study, she'd pretended to be the great gunslinger, and the print brought back fond memories. A few paintings would be sold to generate cash to maintain the museum. As for the Rockwell—it brought Sandy to tears, and she was overjoyed to see it again. She would keep that piece as well, and it would always hang over her dining-room table, as it had at Nellie's on Canal Street.

A million dollars annually in leasing fees would allow the Parkers to continue to operate the landfill and still compensate Sandy for what she'd lost in earnings. It was only a fraction of what she was owed, but to take any more would have put the company in financial jeopardy, and no good would come of that. Thanks to her grandfather's financial investments, and her own hard work and financial planning, she was a wealthy woman. She had no interest in taking over the Parker Companies. The million dollars was a nice bonus for her, though, and when Danny offered it as a part of her "settlement" with the family, she'd agreed.

Sandy had made only one other request, and a few minutes into the meeting, the elder Dan in the room handed it to her. It was a right-hand, stem-wound Parker Coal Company watch, with a stainless-steel face. Forty-eight of them had been given out to employees such as Bill Burns, heroes who had made the company great.

This watch was a true sacrifice for Dan, and Sandy understood that. Split between all the shareholders, the lease fee paid to her wouldn't cost him very much. Cowboy's art had never been his to begin with. The watch, though, was priceless. But as much as she despised her cousin, Sandy didn't ask for it to punish him. She just thought someone else would appreciate it far more than anyone in the family ever could.

After signing where indicated, Sandy hugged Danny. His negotiating skills had brought them here, had brought closure to her family, and had brought back her grandmother's painting. Since he was going back to New York for his final year at NYU, she knew as they hugged that she'd be seeing him again soon.

Their meeting was over in twenty minutes. There was no small talk, just business, and since she and Danny had ironed out the details beforehand, the meeting was actually a formality. Still, it felt great to conclude it.

A half hour later, Sandy was back in West Nanticoke. Robbie Burns appeared nervous when he arrived at Stookey's for his meeting with her. Considering what had happened the last time they were together, she couldn't blame him. She understood the police had held him overnight before deciding he was harmless, but they'd ransacked his home and questioned his friends. His brother was in jail. It had been a tough week for Robbie, and Sandy was sorry for her part in his anguish.

As she watched him, it occurred to her that life had not been fair to Robbie Burns but that he had still turned out to be a good man in spite of life's best efforts. He broke into tears when she gave him the watch. "It's not the same," she said apologetically, her own eyes brimming with tears, "but who knows? It may actually be the one your grandfather owned."

He'd surrendered his treasured watch to the state police, and they'd mailed it to Sandy. It was in her safe at home at the moment, out of harm's way. "There's something I have to tell you," Robbie confessed when he regained his composure.

"Do I want to know?" She was teasing him and laughed.

"I think you do. Sandy," he paused, staring at her, "Jeannie Bennett isn't buried at Riverview."

Jeannie was still a hard subject for her, and the sudden change in topic threw her. Swallowing tears that threatened to erupt, Sandy nodded. "I know," she said simply, staring into the water she was swirling in its plastic glass.

"You do?"

"Jane Bennett told me."

"She did?"

Noting the total surprise in his voice, Sandy watched him closely. "Yes, she did. Why do you ask?"

"If she planned on telling you herself, then why on earth did she pay me five thousand dollars *not* to tell you?"

Sandy's jaw dropped. "You've got to be kidding me! She paid you five grand? Why?"

Robbie told Sandy about the weekly payments, and she simply shook her head. It was almost too bizarre to believe. But if Robbie had come clean on everything else, why would he lie about this? And what the hell was up with Jane Bennett? Sandy thought about it for a moment, then dismissed the thought. A few weeks earlier, she might have pressed the matter further. But after all she'd been through since first coming home, she was too tired to care. Whatever Jane was hiding was none of her concern.

CHAPTER NINETEEN
YOU CAN PICK YOUR FRIENDS

An ice-cream cone seemed to be just the comfort food Sandy needed
to soothe her after the morning of emotional meetings. She'd come
out of her efforts richer by one poster, one painting, and one million a
year for life, but she didn't feel she'd won anything. It saddened her to
know that her grandfather's family had been so devious, and righting
the wrongs hadn't lessened that burden. She hoped Robbie would be
okay. He was an innocent victim, too.

Sitting at the picnic table at Maureen's, the local ice-cream stand,
she looked around at the homes nearby. She couldn't help but feel
sad as she wondered what had become of all the people who'd lived
in them. They had been her friends and neighbors, and she had left
them at their darkest hour, running off to hide from her sorrows. A
good friend, and a good neighbor, would have come back. Sandy was
young and strong in 1972, and there was much she could have done
to help these people in their recovery. Suddenly ashamed of the way
she'd behaved, she glanced up at the mountain in front of her, the one
she'd climbed with Jeannie and her friend Linda Grabowski, who'd
gotten married just before Agnes. Linda was planning to move up to
the Heights after her wedding. Was she still living there? Was she even
still alive?

Finishing her cone, Sandy decided to find out.

She'd never driven to the Heights, and she wasn't sure how to get
where she was going. Paths and stairs of stone set into the mountain had
once led to Jimmy Anderson's land at the top, and Sandy had to find the
dilapidated stairs to get her bearings. She drove slowly, watching for
familiar landmarks, and turned and turned yet again until she came upon
a one-lane road that seemed to be in the general direction she'd hoped
to go. There was no street sign, and a bank of mailboxes had house

▪ 178 ▪ JAIME MADDOX

numbers but no names. She didn't know if she was in the right place, and even when she came upon a cluster of homes, she wasn't sure. If this was Jimmy's house, it had certainly changed over the years.

In a terrace dug into the mountainside, a dozen cars were parked side by side. Below the road, four houses, cottages really, were arranged in a semicircle. At the rear of the house closest to her, a party seemed to be in full swing. Children were swimming in a beautifully landscaped pool, while the adults sat beneath the shade of huge umbrellas, watching them. A man and a woman were cooking at a grill, and off in the distance a group was gathered at a horseshoe pit.

This quiet corner of the universe was too remote for anyone to discover by accident, and no doubt every car driving on their road was quickly noticed. Indeed, just about everyone turned to assess the stranger who'd disturbed their idyllic afternoon. She seriously considered just turning around and driving back home, but before she'd made up her mind to stay or go, one of the women had thrown on a cover-up and was walking in her direction.

She parked the car in the first available space and hopped out. As she walked she marveled at the landscaping that had made this mountainside so beautiful. Retaining walls scattered on the hillside created flattened areas where the horseshoes were tossed or a basketball could be dribbled, and the pool was set in the bottom terrace to the rear of the very last house. Plants covered every inch of space on the hillside. Towering pines bordered all edges of the property, insulating it from the world.

Descending a staircase of stone set into the hillside, Sandy was able to more closely survey the woman approaching her. Forty years and ten pounds hadn't changed Linda's face a bit, and even though huge Jackie Onassis sunglasses concealing the woman's big green eyes, Sandy knew it was her old friend. They met at a landing halfway down, Linda offering a cautious smile to this presumed stranger. Not wanting to raise Linda's concerns, Sandy introduced herself immediately.

A hand flew to Linda's mouth as she recognized her. A smile quickly replaced the shocked expression, and then Linda opened her arms in a welcoming embrace. They hugged for a long moment, exchanging pleasantries, until Linda pulled back. "I read about your grandmother in the paper. I couldn't find an address to send a card. I'm sorry. She was a great woman."

"We should all be so lucky as Nellie," Sandy said in acceptance of Linda's condolence.

Nodding, Linda took Sandy's hand and pulled her toward the pool. "What can I get you? I don't drink Genny anymore, but we have plenty of other beer."

Sandy laughed as she remembered the Genesee Beer most of her friends had preferred back then, mostly due to its affordability. "Anything cold will do. It's getting to be a scorcher. And it's legal now!"

Linda laughed. "Well, come with me and join us. We're having a pool party. You remember my kid sister, Lisa, don't you? It's her birthday, so the whole family's over for a cookout."

Sandy stopped, uncertain. She didn't want to intrude and told Linda so.

"Don't be silly. The more the merrier. Besides, everyone will be glad to see you after all these years."

They'd reached the first umbrella where five women sat and reclined on patio furniture, all of them talking and laughing and seeming to be having a good time. A young boy was reclining in a chair reading a book. In the pool at least a dozen children of various ages were splashing and having an even better time. A few yards away, near the rear of the house, a brick fire pit was burning, and Sandy could smell burgers cooking. The man and the woman tending the grill glanced over and waved at Sandy before turning back to their work.

"Annette, do you remember Sandy Parker from Canal Street?"

Annette Rosen's jaw dropped and she stood to offer Sandy a hug. Sandy marveled that Annette hadn't changed much either over the years. Half Italian, she'd inherited her classic beauty from her mother and was still striking. "Oh, my God, of course I do. Sandy introduced me to Chaz."

Suddenly Sandy's brain made the connection. Chaz and Linda were brother and sister. Annette was at Linda's pool party. "You married Chaz?" Sandy asked.

Annette smiled. "We're married thirty-five years." She nodded at a beautiful young lady seated beside her. The woman was no doubt Annette's daughter, with the same facial structure and dark eyes, but with Chaz's brown hair. "This is our daughter, Tara."

Sandy shook the woman's hand. "It's nice to meet you."

Linda continued to introduce Sandy. "My sister Lisa and her partner Susan, and their son Jamison." Sandy shook hands with Susan and Jamison, then hugged Lisa, who'd stood to greet her. "Wow, what a birthday surprise. My sister never ceases to amaze me!"

Sandy would never have recognized this woman, who was just a little girl at the time of Agnes. She was amazed that Lisa remembered her, and told her so.

Lisa laughed. "How could I forget you? I poached cookies from your house, stole your bike, and chiseled free cones from you at Farrell's. And you taught me to dribble a basketball!"

Sandy laughed as she remembered all those details and a few others, which, to Lisa's dismay, she shared. "You were a quite an energetic little girl," Sandy summarized her recollections, drawing the laughter of everyone in the group. Lisa had been the most precocious four-year-old in the world, smart as could be and with a sense of curiosity that bordered on dangerous. Her fascination with the river often took her to Sandy's block, where Nellie fed her cookies and Sandy shot hoops and rode bikes with her until one of her older siblings came to escort her safely home.

"Why didn't anyone tell me these things about her before I agreed to have children?" Susan asked of the crowd.

"Mama," Jamison exclaimed, to everyone's delight, "are you suggesting that I've inherited Mommy's bad qualities?"

All the adults laughed again, but Sandy could see more than a physical resemblance between the little boy and his mother. He was a smart one, and if he was anything like Lisa, they certainly had their hands full.

"Not you, your brother," Susan answered.

"How many children do you have?" Sandy asked, when the laughter died down.

"Just two. Twin boys." Lisa pointed at another boy in the pool. "That's our son, Max."

Sandy smiled as she looked toward the other boy splashing around with his cousins. In a few years, Leo would be doing the same thing. "That's wonderful," she replied after a moment, then turned her attention to her other old friend. "How about you, Annette?"

"Tara has two brothers, and all together I have six grandchildren. They're all in the pool."

Linda contributed without being surveyed. "I have two boys and five grandchildren." She handed Sandy the promised beer and asked, "How about you?"

Looking at all of them, she smiled. "My partner and I adopted a little girl who's now all grown up. She just gave me a grandson." Sandy noted a smile of recognition on Lisa's face when she mentioned her partner. None of the other women seemed to notice the comment, or perhaps they just didn't care. They were obviously very accepting of Lisa and Susan, so she supposed news of another same-sex couple wouldn't bother them.

"That's exciting. When was he born? Just recently?" Lisa asked.

"November. He's starting to get interesting."

"Crawling yet?" Lisa asked.

"Yeah." Sandy laughed, nodding.

"Let the games begin!"

"What's his name?" Jamison asked.

"Leo."

"Cool, like from Little Einstein's."

Sandy already knew about the Baby Einstein series and had met the Little Einsteins as well. "Do you like that show?" she asked him.

"When I was four I watched that, but now I'm eight."

"What do you watch now?"

"Game shows. I want to be a game-show host when I grow up."

Sandy nodded and told him that sounded like a great job.

"Where's your partner?" Lisa asked.

Sandy had answered this question a thousand times, and she was happy to say it had become easier. Still not easy, though.

"She died a few years ago. Breast cancer," she answered, knowing that would be the follow-up question.

"I'm sorry. Cancer sucks." Lisa offered a smile and a supportive hand on Sandy's knee.

"Yep."

"I'm a breast-cancer survivor," Linda said. "Five years in February."

"Keep up the fight." Sandy offered her beer in a toast, and all of the women raised their bottles and glasses.

"To boobs," Lisa added, and her sister frowned at her, but then they all laughed.

Their pleasant exchange was interrupted by a booming male voice. "Who the hell is this?" someone demanded. Turning, Sandy saw a much balder and heavier Chaz smiling at her. She stood and hugged her old friend. "Where the hell have you been?" he asked. "We all thought you'd died!"

"Really?"

"Hell, yeah! No one ever saw you again after the flood, so I figured the rumor must've been true."

Sandy shook her head in disbelief, then searched the face of her old friend. "Linda?" Sandy asked. Linda didn't seem to think she was dead when she'd greeted her on the hillside.

Linda nodded sadly. "It's true. I don't know where or how it started, but that's what we all heard."

"How did I die?" Sandy asked.

The siblings looked at each other and shook their heads. It was Linda who answered. "There was such chaos after the flood, half the town was displaced. I don't know what happened to half the people who lived here before Agnes. They were just gone. So when I heard you were dead, I just accepted it, no questions asked."

Although her pain was great and she hadn't wanted to return to her hometown after Agnes, Sandy occasionally wondered what had become of all of her friends, and why they never tried to track her down. Now, she knew.

"Where did you go?" Annette asked.

It seemed to Sandy that everyone wanted to hear the answer, so she sat back down and told them about moving to Mount Pocono and then to New York City.

"Do you live by the Plaza?" Jamison asked.

"Not really. It's about fifty blocks from my house."

"I want to go to the Plaza and order room service, like Kevin did on *Home Alone*. My two moms are going to take me there for my birthday. And I have to bring my brother Max, because we're twins and it's his birthday too."

Sandy couldn't help but laugh. "Well, maybe you can come visit me when you're in New York."

"Okay, I'd like to meet Leo. We'll go to the top of the Empire State Building and ride around on a bus that doesn't have a roof and we'll see all the tall buildings."

"That sounds like fun."

The woman who had been grilling delivered a tray loaded with burgers and hot dogs and placed it on a table already laden with cold salads, chips, pickles, and condiments. When she put the food down, she came to Sandy and offered her a hug.

"Babe," Sandy said when she recognized yet another sister. Carol was the leader, Linda the fun sister, and Babe the bookworm. She'd worked with Annette and Sandy in FBLA, and although she was a year younger than the others, Babe was by far the smartest in the group. She was sweet and funny and brilliant, but so shy she wouldn't speak to anyone she didn't know.

Babe sat beside Sandy and Lisa as they ate their burgers, and they caught up. She and her husband ran several successful businesses in town, which didn't surprise Sandy. She traveled to New York often to shop and take her children and grandchildren to the theater. She was still a Phillies fan.

"You haven't become a Yankees fan since moving to New York, have you?" Babe asked to tease her.

Babe and her brother Lute had been the Parkers' guest at Phillies games every year, but it was Babe who talked for hours with Sandy's grandfather about their favorite team.

"Mets, actually," Sandy admitted. "But not when they play the Phils. How about you? Do you still go to the games?"

"Lisa and I have season tickets, so we go a few times a year. In fact, talk about a small world—our tickets are in the row behind Jeannie Bennett's."

The look on Sandy's face must have showed confusion, for when Lisa spoke she looked directly at her.

"You remember Jeannie, of course. Of course you do, you were neighbors," Lisa said, letting out a little nervous laugh.

Sandy faced her, trying to remember to breathe. "You're friends with Jeannie Bennett?" The sun suddenly seemed a million times brighter, and the features of Lisa's face were fading in contrast to the light surrounding her. Her words echoed and caused an unpleasant pressure deep in Sandy's ears. The pulse in her throat was choking her, seemingly preventing air from reaching her lungs.

"She was one of my instructors in medical school. Our moms remained friends over the years, and when I was thinking of medical school, Jeannie really helped me out. We're friends to this day. We stay with her when we go to Philly."

It took a moment before Sandy could speak. She needed to clarify Lisa's words, Babe's words, because what they said just didn't make sense. Jeannie Bennett was dead, so how could she be a physician? How could she own Phillies tickets? How could she be friends with Lisa? Sandy didn't want to overreact and appear insane, but one of them was, because Jeannie couldn't be dead *and* living in Philadelphia.

"Are you okay?" Lisa asked, leaning toward Sandy, the physician in her taking over.

She wasn't okay, but how could she explain that to all of these people? She looked from Lisa to Babe, waiting for one of them to laugh at their cruel joke. Jeannie was dead, and it was wrong for them to say the things they did.

"Let's get you in the house, out of this heat."

Lisa and Babe walked Sandy inside and she tried to focus on making her feet move. "Just the heat, I think," Lisa said to everyone as she asked Sandy a series of questions about medication and her health status.

Inside, a cold cloth on her forehead and the cool air helped to revive Sandy a bit. Babe, always a bit squeamish, took advantage of her sister's medical skills and excused herself. "She'll fix you up in no time," she said as she closed the sliding-glass door behind her.

It took a few minutes for Sandy to regain her composure. When she was sure she could speak, she looked directly at Lisa, who sat beside her. "So, you're friends with Jeannie Bennett."

"Yeah." Lisa smiled. "She's been a very positive force in my life."

Sandy leaned back into the cool embrace of the leather couch. "I haven't seen Jeannie since the flood." She sipped the water Lisa had proffered and remembered that afternoon at Hazleton General Hospital forty years earlier when she'd been looking for Jeannie and instead met Helen Bennett in the lobby. *"She died an hour ago."* Jane's words from just a couple of weeks back rang in her ears. *"Jeannie isn't buried at Riverview...my mother donated her body."* Robbie's voice from an hour ago. *"She paid me five thousand dollars NOT to tell you."*

It was so obvious now, looking back with the gift of 20/20 hindsight. Somehow, Helen had discovered their affair and told the mother of all lies, told Sandy the only possible story that would have kept her from Jeannie. And Jane was in on the charade as well. Forty years later, Jane was still lying to her.

Knowing that Lisa—who had a partner of her own—might understand this, she decided to share her story. After shaking her head in disbelief, Sandy sipped the water. "I think I need a stronger drink," she said as she leaned back into the couch and turned to face her. The concern was evident in Lisa's eyes, and Sandy was comforted by the hand that gently rubbed her shoulder. "I thought she was dead."

"What?"

"We were lovers," she began after a few moments, but tears quickly choked off her voice and she simply sobbed. Once again, Sandy found herself crying for Jeannie, not because she was dead, but because she was alive and because of hatred and prejudice she'd been taken from Sandy just the same. "Her mother must have found out...about us..." Sandy tried again, but she couldn't finish. She closed her eyes and leaned into Lisa, whose arms pulled her tightly against her.

Lisa gently stroked Sandy's hair, as tears fell from her own eyes. She told Sandy that her confession didn't surprise her, and she shared her own story with Sandy.

Lisa said that although she was just turning five when Agnes struck, she already had an understanding that she liked girls much better than boys. Boys were great for building rafts and climbing trees, but when it came time to lie down and rest inside one of their cool forts beside the Susquehanna, Lisa always wanted her friend Cindy beside her. Even at that young age, Lisa had felt a special connection to both Sandy and Jeannie, and although she didn't understand it at the time, when she was old enough to grasp the concept of sexuality, she often wondered about the girls from Canal Street. As a medical student, when she reconnected with Jeannie, she discovered the topic of Sandy Parker made Jeannie very sad. After that one time, neither Lisa nor Jeannie ever mentioned Sandy's name again. Lisa drew her conclusions, and Sandy just confirmed them.

After many, many minutes, Sandy pulled back and looked at Lisa. "Can you tell me about her?"

Lisa laughed. "What would you like to know?"

Brushing away her tears, she smiled. "Everything."

Lisa laughed. "What she was in 1972 she is now. Beautiful. Vibrant. In charge. Smart as hell. She is an incredible physician. She owns a clinic in North Philly, and everyone who knows her loves her."

Sandy reflected for a moment. None of this surprised her. Jeannie had been an amazing girl and was destined to be an amazing woman. "Is she...with someone?" Sandy asked tentatively. Instead of an answer, Lisa just shrugged.

"What does that mean?"

"She's married. To a man."

CHAPTER TWENTY
YOU CAN'T PICK YOUR RELATIVES

Having the Parker name had given Sandy many privileges during her lifetime, but she'd never really taken advantage of her name and the power of her family. Until this day.

She parked her car on North Franklin Street, in the heart of the King's College campus, and wandered into the first building she found.

"I'm Sandy Parker," she told the security guard. "My family is making a donation to the college, and I was hoping to look around and see what you do here."

The man smiled and offered his hand in greeting. "It's a pleasure to meet you, Ms. Parker. Your family has done a lot of good things for this region, and I'm happy to hear you're going to be helpin' out the college."

After showing her identification, she received a visitor's pass and a campus map and was directed toward the library. She'd used her smart phone to try to find information about Jeannie, but she'd struck out. Lisa had offered to contact Jeannie and pass along Sandy's number, but Sandy wasn't sure she wanted to do that just yet. If ever. Although Lisa didn't go into detail, it seemed that Jeannie had a good life in Philadelphia that included a husband and children, and the last thing Sandy wanted was to upset the order in her universe by calling and opening up old wounds.

After the initial shock faded and Sandy began to think about it, she was absolutely mystified to learn that Jeannie was in a relationship with a man. Jeannie was by far the more liberal of the two of them and was ready to come out when they were still on Canal Street. There was no doubt in her mind that Jeannie was a lesbian. How the hell had she ended up married to a man? She might never know the whole story of

Jeannie's life after 1972, but Sandy was determined to find out what she could. King's College was the first stop.

She might be on a wild goose chase, but it occurred to her that the Bobby she'd contacted might in fact be Jeannie's son, not Jane's. She had assumed he was Jane's child based on her understanding that Jeannie was dead and therefore couldn't have a son. Since she was alive, perhaps the grandson who'd taken care of Helen Bennett's funeral was Jeannie's boy. She wanted to find out. When she left Linda's house, she dialed the number she had for Bobby and left him another message. All she'd be wasting was time, but she had plenty of that. She decided to head to King's College and investigate a bit.

In the library, Sandy began with the yearbooks from 2010. The current year wasn't yet available. Bobby could have been anywhere from a freshman to a graduate student when his grandmother died, so Sandy decided to look through them all until she found a name that sounded similar to his. She only hoped he'd stuck it out and graduated and that Bobby wasn't a moniker for a dissimilar name like Theodore.

As she flipped through the pages, she marveled at the number of female graduates. When she'd lived here, King's had just started accepting women, and now half the student body was female. It was good to see it.

There were no candidates named Robert in 2011. Ditto for 2010, 2009, and 2008. But there in 2004, just after the Ms, Ns, and Os was a handsome young man named Robert T. Percavage, Jr. He hailed from Philadelphia and had Jeannie's hair color, her eyes, and her smile.

This boy from Philadelphia, who looked so much like the woman Sandy had loved, had to be Jeannie's son.

She stared for a long time, breathing, calming herself, thinking that this boy wouldn't be alive today if her own life had turned out as she'd planned. Jeannie had gone to medical school, married, and had a son. According to J.R., the monument salesman, Bobby was an exceptional young man. It didn't surprise Sandy at all, knowing his mother. How wonderful for Jeannie.

Sandy knew she had no business feeling sad about this turn of events, either. Her life was blessed. She'd traveled and explored and enjoyed life with Diane beside her; she'd loved her daughter and now her grandson. If she'd been with Jeannie, none of those people would have been part of her life.

It was so simple, wasn't it? Then why did she feel such sorrow?

As she carried the yearbooks back to their place, ignoring the sign that instructed her not to return them to their shelves, she looked at the other books and wondered. Could Jeannie have come to college here? Kings was educating young women back then. She grabbed the 1977 volume. They were the same age, and that was the year she'd graduated from Queens College, so it was a logical place to start.

Only a few names began with the letter *A*, and she was still skimming them when she saw the face of her memories and dreams. Jeanne Marie Bennett.

Her hair was still long, but her eyes didn't twinkle, and her smile seemed forced. She had a haunted look about her that no makeup or camera lens could hide. In a picture that should have been proclaiming joy and triumph, Jeannie looked sad. Yet she was even more beautiful in 1977 than she'd been when Sandy had last seen her five years before.

And she was alive! Lisa and Babe had seen her and talked to her. She went to Phillies games, and practiced medicine, and had children. Sandy had no reason to question them. Why would they lie? Helen Bennett had a motive to lie, and Sandy knew she had done just that.

It was so senseless! She shook her head, cursing her anguish all those years ago and the chances she'd blown to learn this secret. If she'd just asked to see Jeannie's body, she'd have figured out the truth—but that would have been too much to bear. If she'd gone to the funeral, like any best friend would have, she'd have known. If she'd just once taken a flower to Jeannie's grave, it would have been evident. If she'd come home to West Nanticoke and talked to any one of their friends, she would have uncovered this awful lie.

And everything would be different now. Not better, and very arguably worse. But the course of her life should have been in her hands. Hers and Jeannie's. For better or worse, they would have followed the course they themselves dictated. They should have had the right to decide their own fates, no matter what the outcome.

With a last look into Jeannie's sad eyes, Sandy closed the yearbook. She found her car and climbed in, opened the windows to vent the sweltering heat, and leaned back as hot air blew into her face. When it turned cool, she closed the windows and dialed another number from her phone's memory.

"It's Sandy Parker," she said when Jane answered.

Sandy wasn't sure this call would do her any good, but she needed to make it anyway. "Yes?" Jane asked.

"Why?" she asked simply.

Apparently Jane understood the meaning of Sandy's cryptic comment, because she didn't hesitate to begin her tirade. "Leave my sister alone, Sandy," Jane hissed into the phone. "She's not like you. She's normal. She has a wonderful husband and two beautiful children, and she's happy in her life. The last thing she needs is for you to barge in, unearthing her dirty secrets! If she wanted to see you, don't you think she would have done so by now?"

"She thinks I'm dead, Jane."

"No," Jane said with a confidence Sandy couldn't question. "She knows the truth, and she doesn't want to see you. Leave her alone."

Sandy sighed in defeat. She wasn't sure what she hoped to accomplish from this call. She'd thought of screaming at Jane, hurling profanities, asking why?—but she figured she knew why. She supposed she hoped Jane would apologize after all these years and tell her Jeannie was gay and single and would love to see her. Or even just affirm that Jeannie would appreciate a call from her old friend. Of course, the conversation didn't go that way at all. It simply confirmed what Sandy had feared. Jeannie, the love of her life, was a straight girl who'd had a lesbian fling that she wanted to forget. She'd moved on. She didn't want to hear from Sandy. "I don't want to hurt her," Sandy whispered at last.

The venom in Jane's voice stung. "If you care about her—if you ever cared about her—you'll just leave her alone. Jeannie's happy! She and Bob were meant to be together."

Chapter Twenty-one
Namesake

"Your father and I were never happy. We were never meant to be together." Jeannie Bennett Percavage admitted this to her daughter, Sandy, not for the first time, but she hoped for the last. The remains of her marriage had been autopsied before, but unfortunately never buried. She was willing, had always been willing, to walk away and divorce, but she and Bob could never agree on the terms.

Unfortunately, her husband had found a new love, and now he wanted to pronounce dead the patient who had been comatose for ten years. The discussion of division of assets brought back painful memories and feelings she had successfully buried for so long. Now her children were trying to coerce from her an empathy toward their father that she just didn't feel.

Sinking back into the soft, plush couch, in the living room of her home in the northwest corner of Philadelphia, Jeannie curled her legs beneath her as she watched her daughter pace the room. This was her favorite room in a house boasting a dozen of them, a warm and cheerful room with its lemony painted walls and large stone fireplace. The wooden floor shone beneath scattered rugs, and French doors opened onto a terrace garden. Pictures of her children adorned the walls and mantel, and potted plants added color and vitality to the room. Jeannie had restored the house with care to preserve its historical integrity but sacrificed tradition for comfort by adding central air. On this hot day, it was keeping her comfortably cool.

She sipped iced water from a tall glass, appreciating the woman Sandy had become—graceful, poised, confident. While Sandy was a carbon copy of Jeannie on the outside, their mannerisms and personalities were totally opposite. Usually calm, Sandy now reminded Jeannie of herself, with her restless energy driving her to wear a hole in the carpet.

Jeannie was truly sorry that her husband was putting their children between them, and she was tempted to give in to his demands to spare them further anguish. She loved Bobby and Sandy and wanted more than anything to protect them, but at the same time she wanted them to learn from their parents' mistakes. The picture of Bob's financials was worth a thousand lectures from her about investing and saving and responsibility. She was as tired of the ordeal as the kids were, but she knew she was doing the right thing.

Sandy's cell phone rang and she looked at the caller ID. "It's Bobby."

"You should probably answer it, then." Jeannie's children were close, and after growing up beside Jane, Jeannie was grateful that they shared the warmth and love they did.

She watched as Sandy ran a hand through her long hair, a habit that told her Sandy was frustrated. Jeannie softened a bit. She'd never intended to hurt her children by taking a strong stance with her husband. In fact, after watching them suffer through the pain of their father's betrayal, Jeannie would have done just about anything they asked to lighten their burden. And she did. What they asked had seemed such an easy compromise at the time, yet had become the albatross around her weary neck.

A decade earlier, after she had discovered her husband's infidelity, Jeannie had simply asked him to leave. Her marriage had never been a good one, but it had always been good enough for her. Bob had been her medical-school classmate, a colleague and a friend when they began dating, and though she later discovered they had virtually no common interests, they did share two that were so vital they could bear the load of their flawed relationship: both practiced their professions with passion, and they loved their children above all else.

Medicine was an exciting topic of books and television shows and equally good conversation for two people so inclined as Jeannie and Bob. They could fashion an entire discussion lasting the duration of the journey from the city to the mountains from the opening statement, "I saw an interesting case today."

These two factors were enough to keep them together for nearly twenty years, even with no other common threads to bind them. Sports and homework and traveling with their kids kept them busy and provided ever-changing topics of conversation. And with an orthopedic trauma surgeon and family doctor inhabiting the same house, there was always medical dialogue. But while they loved and respected one another, after a while the friendship dissolved. They never really had any passion.

Jeannie wasn't surprised when a receipt for jewelry confirmed her suspicions that Bob was screwing around. She suspected he had planted the receipt because the alternative—that he was actually that stupid—didn't seem possible. He was happy to leave, too, when she confronted him. He took the essentials to get by and set up an apartment where he could play with his paramour. She was the sales rep for the artificial hips and knees he often used to piece bones back together. They carried on for about a month, when reality poured rain on their party. After the younger woman discovered that the successful orthopedic surgeon, who had been spoiling her with lavish gifts, was actually near bankruptcy, her affections for Bob quickly faded.

Crawling back on his knees and begging Jeannie's forgiveness got him nowhere, so Bob used the empathy of his children to get what he wanted. They begged their mother's compassion, and not wanting to hurt them any further, she agreed and allowed her husband to move into the carriage house at the back of their property. They had remodeled it as a guesthouse, with a kitchenette, full bath, living room, and bedroom. Apparently, the tiny space was all he needed, because ten years later, even though they barely acknowledged each other, he was still living there. She had grown tired of running into him in their shared driveway but didn't have the energy to throw him out.

A divorce a decade earlier would have been a much more compassionate way for them to end their marriage, but Bob had reached the sad conclusion that he really couldn't afford a divorce. After hiring an accountant to make sense of his finances, he learned that he spent just as much money as he made, had saved too little, and didn't have the necessary credit scores to get a loan for a car or a house or even a new credit card without Jeannie backing him. Realizing how expensive a divorce would be, Bob had put the idea on hold and was content to live in the carriage house, where he could see his children and control his expenses.

The piece of paper that would officially end her marriage wasn't important to Jeannie, and she'd never pressed the issue. In her mind, the marriage had ended with his infidelity. She didn't even consult a lawyer.

Upon his rather anticlimactic exit from her life, Jeannie was once again so very grateful to her mother, who had always given her such good financial advice, for while Bob's accounts were in disarray, hers were in perfect order. She didn't need him or his money because she had taken care of her own over the years. And while she would have found it a financial hardship to buy him out of the house, she celebrated the fact that she would never have to. The house was hers.

Upon meeting her future son-in-law for the first time all those years ago, Helen Bennett had been unimpressed with him and concerned about his future. That had inspired her to put her assets into a trust fund that would protect them from financial indiscretion. Soon afterward, she made a rare appearance in Philadelphia, under the guise of shopping, but really to sit and talk with Jeannie. It was a conversation she would never forget. Their afternoon together was one of the most intimate times she had ever shared with her mother, with whom she seldom saw eye to eye and often argued. That day changed their relationship forever, brought them closer and opened a door through which both of them could freely travel to reach the other.

"You know, Jeanne Marie"—her mother always called her by her given name—"having a baby is no reason to get married these days," she'd said.

Jeannie's jaw nearly dropped and she stammered in response. She hadn't really felt nervous confessing to her mother that she'd become pregnant and was planning to elope, thereby shattering her mother's illusions that she was a virgin and her vision of another country-club wedding. She wasn't worried that her mother would cause a scene because at that stage of her life, Jeannie didn't care.

She wasn't surprised that Helen hadn't responded angrily. Helen had changed in the years since the flood, becoming kinder and more understanding. Jeannie's loss had just the opposite effect on her—she no longer felt emotion. She had changed after Sandy's death, had lost the ability to truly feel anything, and she knew that keeping what few feelings she experienced in a tight orbit prevented her from experiencing any more of the pain that had nearly crushed her. As it was, she didn't have much happiness in her life, but she was protected from sadness.

When Jeannie couldn't articulate an intelligent response, her mother continued. "We aren't poor, Jeanne Marie. I can help take care of you and the baby. There's no need to marry someone you don't love. You should wait until you find the right man."

Jeannie sighed, and in that moment she looked into her mother's eyes and saw a love she hadn't often seen, or at least had been too young or brash to recognize. That love pierced her armor, and before she could think, she spoke. "I was in love once, Mom. Madly, perfectly in love. And it didn't work out so well. I don't think I can ever give my heart to someone like that again."

She saw in her mother's eyes the questions—who, what, when? For a moment she thought her mother would ask, and for a moment Jeannie thought she would tell her what she'd never told another soul, about her love affair with Sandy Parker. But then something shifted in Helen's eyes and the moment passed, and she brought the conversation back to the matter at hand.

"Don't marry him, Jeannie. Don't sentence yourself to a loveless marriage. You deserve more, someone like your father. Just wait— you'll find him."

Sitting there and watching her mother's face as she mentioned her late husband, Jeannie gained an understanding for the first time that, once upon a time, her mother had been more than a mother and grandmother. She had been a wife and a lover. Simultaneously a million thoughts poured into her brain, of her parents humming to the radio in the kitchen as they cooked side by side, of them rocking in the swing on their front porch on Canal Street, of them dancing together at a wedding.

For the first time she thought of not what she had lost in the flood, but what her mother had lost. Her friend, partner, breadwinner, co-parent. Through all of what must have been very difficult months after her father's death, her mother had been a rock, concentrating on helping Jeannie recover from surgery and helping her get her life back in order. All the while, behind the scenes, she had been dealing with flood issues and setting up a new home, as well as handling financial concerns that had been the sole responsibility of her father, and she'd accomplished this without so much as a hint that she was aching for the man she'd loved. Helen had been only forty-five years old in 1972, still a young woman, really, but she never even looked at another man until she died three decades later.

Fighting tears, Jeannie had reached across the table to hold her mother's hand. "Thank you, Mom, for your concern. But I'll never have what you and Daddy had." Her mom swallowed, acknowledging that loss as Jeannie continued. "I think this is the right thing to do."

It wasn't long after the wedding that Jeannie discovered the severity of her husband's financial crisis. While Jeannie's parents were fairly well off, Bob was the middle child of seven, born to a family of limited means. Throughout her four years of medical school, Jeannie had never seen a bill for her tuition. Her mother simply paid it. Every month a check would arrive, with an ample sum to cover Jeannie's rent and utilities, as well as supply her with food and all the necessities of a medical student. Bob, on the other hand, had relied on credit cards to cover what his student loans didn't. He'd purchased everything from his rent to his razor blades with someone else's money. Just as he married Jeannie, all those creditors began demanding payment on their loans.

Jeannie tried to help him to straighten out his finances. She had worked with her dad over summers and during tax seasons, as had her mom, and money issues were a topic of conversation at the Bennett table for breakfast, lunch, and dinner. The problem, Jeannie began to realize, was not so much Bob's poor start in life, which left him climbing out of a hole that she had been blessed to avoid. That hole wasn't so deep that he couldn't make it out, especially on the salary of an orthopedic surgeon. The problem was far more complicated and difficult to remediate.

During his formative years, Bob had done without. He hadn't worn the best clothing or gone swimming at the country club. Dining out was an extravagance his family simply couldn't afford. His only childhood vacation was a trip to Atlantic City with neighbors who needed a playmate to occupy their little boy's time during their week at the beach.

These circumstances had created a very needy man who wanted it all, and wanted it now. He worked hard, Jeannie couldn't deny him that—but he played hard as well. He made money, and he spent it. Unfortunately he spent money he hadn't yet made, using credit cards to sustain him during school and residency, with the idea that he'd have the money to pay them later.

Understanding the inherent danger in this practice, Jeannie decided it would be best to keep their finances separate, and Bob didn't care. Money was simply not a concern to him. As long as he had the plastic in his wallet, he didn't bother with the details.

While Bob was working endless hours, Jeannie worked half days so she could spend time with Bobby. She had always loved the outdoors, and even when she could afford more, her tastes remained simple. She walked with Bobby, as much as her leg allowed. It had never been right after the accident, and she would always limp, but it didn't stop her from doing anything she wanted. She took him to the park and pushed him on the swings, took him swimming at the apartment complex's pool.

His birth wasn't an instant cure for her broken heart, but over the days and nights of caring for her squirming, scrawny, helpless baby boy, Jeannie's heart opened once again. She loved this child more than life, and giving birth to him saved her. She had been dead, walking around in a fog, powered by a broken heart, and Bobby's birth was the medicine she needed to restore her. She was never the same—she would always miss Sandy—but life was still precious and, thanks to her son, wonderful.

As Bobby grew and began to explore his world, their small and affordable apartment became crowded. Jeannie began house hunting, and the gods were on her side. She found an old home in Mount Airy, not far from Temple University Hospital, where she and Bob taught and practiced. The place was in simply deplorable condition, but it had land and character, two essential qualities. The rest could be remedied.

With Bob's debt and credit rating, they couldn't get a mortgage. It was difficult to ask her mother to help, but when desperation set in, she overcame her hesitancy. She loved, loved, loved this house. It reminded her of their house on Canal Street. It was a huge old Victorian with original molding and pocket doors, stained glass, hardwood throughout. She needed to put down roots, felt as if she had been drifting since the flood. Her mom, of course, had bought a new home, but Jeannie started college soon after the flood and lived on campus. The house in Mountaintop never felt like home to her. A series of apartments in Philadelphia provided shelter from the cold, but she'd moved so many times during school and residency that she couldn't even remember all the addresses. This house, though, would finally bring her home.

She decided to ask her mother to co-sign the loan that would give her the house of her dreams. Not willing to risk a rejection over the phone, and wanting her mother to know how important this was for her, Jeannie drove to the mountains.

This wasn't the first time she'd taken Bobby "home" by herself. Since that day at the restaurant, she and her mother had become closer than ever. After Bobby's birth, her mother made frequent trips to Philly—unprecedented in the nearly seven years Jeannie had been there before that. Helen helped design the nursery, and she paid for everything her new grandchild could ever desire, from a crib to clothing to a giant stuffed giraffe. Giraffes had been a favorite of Jeannie's when she was a child. It wasn't surprising, then, when Jeannie phoned to tell her mother she would be paying a visit.

Never one to waste time, Jeannie sat down with her mother and asked her to co-sign her mortgage. While bouncing a giggling Bobby on her knee, Helen looked across her living room and stared her in the eye.

"Under no circumstances will I ever enter into a financial agreement with that man," she informed her.

Before Jeannie's shoulders had a chance to sag, however, her mother said, "However, I think a home is a good investment, and I'll be happy to help *you* in any way I can. I'll give you the money for the down payment and help you with the loan and any repairs to the house, whatever you need, Jeannie. But you must promise me to never put his name on the deed. It'll be your security some day, and I don't want his financial misdeeds to come back to haunt you."

So Jeannie entered the realm of homeownership, not with her husband, but with her mother. Bob had no objections to the arrangement; in fact, he was thrilled that his mother-in-law was making the down payment on a house he would get to enjoy. He couldn't count on his own parents for anything, and there was no other way for them to obtain a mortgage.

Helen didn't stop with the loan, however. Her years at her husband's side hadn't been wasted, and in fact, she'd been completing tax returns and helping people with investments since Paul's death. She was explicit in her instructions to Jeannie, and Jeannie in turn followed them to the letter. She set up three checking accounts—one for Bob, one for herself, and a joint account. Out of his account, Bob issued a monthly check to his wife to cover the costs of the house. Jeannie deposited this "rent" into her own account, which she used to pay the mortgage and all expenses related to the house—landscaping, appliances, roof repairs, everything a house needed. From their joint account came the money for the utilities and other common expenses.

The young Jeannie had been a social creature, but after Sandy's death, she became more of an introvert. She could bury her pain in work and study, but found that socializing and relaxing was difficult. Filling her hours with caring for her son was not only easy, but it was also fulfilling. Her life was simple, a clean division between work and motherhood, and with the birth of her daughter Sandy three years after Bobby, it was even more so. She worked twenty hours weekly curing disease and spent the rest of her time raising her children. They spent much of their time at parks and playing in their yard, and when Sandy turned one, Helen decided the trip to Philly was getting to be too much for her and she bought Jeannie a house in the mountains, where she could spend all the time she wanted to out of doors.

While Jeannie took such pleasure in the simple things that had always made her happy, Bob hadn't changed either. The Porsche he drove had to be the most current model. The lake house her mother had bought them wasn't satisfactory without a speedboat at the dock. His season tickets to every Philly sports team kept him away from home, but when he was there he listened to the finest stereo equipment and watched the biggest television on the market.

Jeannie saved, Bob spent. Then one day, when he left her for a woman half his age, he expected Jeannie to give him her house so he would have some financial security. That didn't sit well with her. Not because of the affair. Not because of his reckless approach to finances. It was her house, something she loved, and she had promised her mother she would protect it from this man. She had made a wise investment in the house, and it would have come back to haunt her if not for her mother, because the property value had increased so exponentially in the nearly thirty years they were married, she could not have easily afforded to buy him out. To give him half of the value of the house in cash, she would have to sell it to someone else and would be set adrift once again. She would have lost her husband, broken up her family, and lost her home in yet another catastrophic event. Divorce.

So Jeannie had done nothing to push the divorce. Bob hadn't either, until now, when he apparently needed the money for a home to share with his new bride. Jeannie guessed the carriage house wouldn't be a suitable abode for the wife of a prestigious orthopedic surgeon.

Jeannie watched her daughter pacing as she talked to her son and worried that what was best for her would be so hard on her kids. "Is everything okay?" she asked when Sandy hung up the phone.

"I have no idea! He needs to talk to me, and I didn't want to get into it until I finish talking to you. I can only handle one crisis at a time." Shaking her head, she plopped down on the other end of the sofa and put her feet in Jeannie's lap. Without being asked, Jeannie placed her water glass on the table and began to rub Sandy's feet.

"You're the counselor in this family, my darling. That must grow tiring." Sandy had been born a peacemaker, with negotiating skills she began to reveal as soon as she could formulate words. Jeannie often thought her marriage would have collapsed years before it actually did if Sandy hadn't been between them, coaxing her and Bob into a compromise they both found palatable. From choosing color swatches to paint the family room to choosing food for dinner or family vacation destinations, when a disagreement erupted, Sandy negotiated until someone gave in or gave up.

No one had ever asked this of her; it was simply a role she was born to. And Jeannie knew she loved it, was thrilled to be in the middle, solving other people's problems. Law had been a natural choice for her, and she had just finished law school at Penn. Jeannie thought her daughter would make the perfect judge one day. She was fair and impartial and pursued justice with a passion. Sometimes, though, she needed a break, even from a job she loved so much. And this particular job—as mediator of her parents' separation—had been ongoing for a decade.

Sighing in acknowledgment, Sandy appeared defeated as she drew a shading hand over her eyes. "I just want everyone to be happy."

"Honey, no matter how much you love someone, you can't make them happy. You aren't responsible for your dad, or for me, or your brother, either. We all have to take responsibility for ourselves."

"But you won't listen to Dad."

"Why is that your problem?"

"Because he's my father and I care about what happens to him."

"I'm your mother. Don't you care about what happens to me?"

"Of course I do! But you're just so much more…capable than he is. And you have more money than he does."

"Says who?"

"Says Dad."

Jeannie had never discussed any of their troubles with the kids, and it frosted her to think that Bob did. They didn't know of his liaisons, not from Jeannie, anyway. They didn't know about gambling debts or credit-card bills. They only knew that the guy who had tucked them in at night was asking them for something that seemed reasonable, and they expected a fair and reasonable response from their mother. Sandy and Bobby had no idea how Bob had screwed things up for himself, and Jeannie loved them too much to expose his flaws for them to see.

Sipping her water, Jeannie leaned back and looked at her daughter's troubled face. She debated telling Sandy everything, but only for a second. She'd had this discussion with herself before, and she knew it was wrong to rat him out to their kids. She'd try a different strategy instead.

"You realize, don't you, that to give him half of this house means

I'd have to sell it. I don't have that kind of money to just hand it to him. And if I sell the house and give him half the money, I won't have it to give to you one day. If he takes it and blows it on—" Jeannie had to choose her words carefully. What was the word she needed? *Whore? Bimbo?* She decided to drop that train of thought. She cleared her throat and paused, then changed the subject.

"As things stand, you and Bobby are my heirs. If I give twenty dollars to the Girl Scouts for cookies, that's ten bucks less for you and ten bucks less for Bobby."

Sandy sat up and looked pleadingly at her. "Dad needs the money, Mom. All of his money is tied up, and he always thought he had the house to fall back on."

This was a lie, told by a desperate man to an impressionable child, and Jeannie had to fight hard to control her anger. Bob knew the terms of her mother's loan and had wholeheartedly agreed to it. Why couldn't he just be decent enough to walk away without dragging this on and dragging their children down?

"You can afford it, Mom. What's the big deal?"

Apparently, Sandy hadn't heard a word she'd said. The big deal was an agreement with her mother. The big deal was adultery and recklessness. The big deal was her children's future. The big deal was her house, the safe haven that had sheltered her for nearly three decades. It was on these floors that her children learned to crawl and walk. She'd listened to them practicing the piano from the kitchen while she'd cooked her family dinner. She'd taught them to throw balls in the yard and ride bikes in the driveway. So many memories were made under this roof, that she couldn't bear the thought of losing it. She'd lost her house on Canal Street and she didn't want to lose this one, too.

But Jeannie was tired of arguing. If this was what her children wanted, and if this made peace for them, Jeannie would do it. She would sell her house. She would move downtown, close to the theaters, and take the subway to the office for rounds. She could do it…but she didn't want to!

Jeannie sighed. She never regretted marrying Bob, because their union had resulted in her children. She tried to not dwell on the past, on the *what ifs* and *what could've beens*. Yet, sometimes, she couldn't help herself.

Why hadn't she just insisted on the divorce years before? It would have been all over now, and she'd be sitting in her living room having a much more pleasant discussion with her daughter. Dragging it out hadn't made it any easier. Yet she knew it wouldn't have been easier then, either. In truth, it had been a pretty bad time in her life.

She hated to admit it, but Bob's infidelity stung. She had cared for him, and about him, and his betrayal was a blow to her spirit. Her mother had been ailing at the time, battling advanced colon cancer, with surgery and chemotherapy and a multitude of issues that pulled Jeannie to the mountains for days at a time. Her son was threatened with expulsion from college after hosting a party where no one in attendance, including him, was old enough to drink alcohol. And just before her discovery of her husband's infidelity and his subsequent move out of their home, their daughter confessed that she was a lesbian. It was a difficult argument to convince Sandy that her father didn't leave because of her sexuality, and it had taken months for her to settle down after coming out.

Although that was a difficult time, it passed. Since then, she'd had plenty of time and opportunity to finalize this divorce, and she sat there now wishing she'd just gotten it over with.

Now, Bob had the children convinced that she, Jeannie, was the bad guy. They had no idea about their parents' finances; they only knew what he told them. Jeannie wished she could show them, in black and white, without having to go into the details of Bob's transgressions. But how? Then an idea occurred to her.

"I just have one thing to show you, Sandy. Wait here."

Jeannie was back in a moment with a large white envelope. She opened it and pulled her tax return from it. She found the item she was looking for and showed it to Sandy and asked her to read it.

It was Jeannie's income from wages for the prior year. The sum was a little over a hundred thousand dollars.

"Is that all you make? You save people's lives! This is an atrocity!" Sandy's sense of fairness always prevailed. It was why she waged this misguided fight for her father.

Rubbing Sandy's shoulder, she laughed. "Somehow, I manage."

Sandy laughed softly, apparently getting the joke, and when their eyes met, Jeannie could see the tension had left her eyes. Jeannie took her hand and squeezed.

She had completed her husband's taxes for years, and she was intimately familiar with the disparity in their incomes. If she looked hard enough, she might even be able to produce a copy of one of Bob's old tax returns for Sandy to view. That wouldn't be right, though. It was Bob's business, and she had no right to share that information without his consent. There was another way, though. "I want you to ask your father for a look at his tax return. After seeing it on paper like this, if you're still convinced I should give him half of this house, I will."

CHAPTER TWENTY-TWO
OUT OF THE MOUTHS OF BABES

Hey, little sister." Bobby greeted Sandy with a kiss on the cheek. "I hope I'm not keeping you from that hot babe of yours." He noticed she'd been texting as he approached the bar, and he knew he was probably interfering with her Saturday afternoon plans. Unlike him, she was a social creature, always on the move, always doing something.

"As a matter of fact, you are." She sipped her margarita and smiled tellingly. "Jennifer is sitting on the beach in Rehoboth, and as soon as I finish this drink I plan to head south to join her."

"Why are you drinking if you have to drive?"

"Tough day," she said simply.

"I'm sorry for holding you up, but I really need to run something by you."

"What's up?"

"I'm not sure, but knowing Jane—it's trouble."

Sandy sighed. "Why? What did Jane do now?"

Bobby shook his hair out of his eyes and looked at her. The scowl on her face told him she understood his concerns. They'd spent a good part of their childhood in the mountains, and that time inevitably involved some encounter with Jane and her family. Their summer home on Lake Nuangola wasn't far from their grandmother's and Jane's houses, and while they'd loved seeing Helen, Jane was always a pain in the ass. Even as children they could sense the resentment Jane felt for their mother, the hostility she often displayed toward her. Jeannie was able to somehow ignore her sister, and in fact he knew Jeannie loved Jane, but neither Bobby nor Sandy was fond of their aunt. Bobby had been named executor of Helen's estate, and he would never forget the trouble Jane had caused after her mother's death. It infuriated her that Helen had chosen Bobby over Jane's son Steven and over Jane herself. The arguments over trivialities like canned goods left in Helen's cupboard were simply ridiculous, and finally the Percavages as a group just picked out a few personal items from Helen's house and told Jane everything else was hers. She of course then complained that they'd left her to dispose of all the garbage. There was just no winning with her.

Bobby turned toward Sandy. "About two weeks ago, just as I was boarding my flight for Paris, I received a call from a woman named Sandy Parker. She told me she was an old friend of my aunt's. I called her, but I missed her and told her I'd call her when I got back." Bobby sighed and sipped his water. "So, I walk through the gate at the airport when I get back, and there's Aunt Jane waiting for me in a golf cart, escorted by security guards."

Seeing the look of surprise on Sandy's face, Bobby nodded in agreement. "Bizarre, right? I immediately panic, figuring you or Mom or Dad or all three of you are dead. I go running over to her and ask her what's wrong. She tells me there's an emergency, but she won't say what." Bobby sighed again. "So we retrieve my luggage, and when I can't stand the torture any longer, she sits me down on a bench by the luggage carousel and tells me a crazy woman's going to be contacting me and I should ignore her."

"She was talking about Sandy Parker?" Sandy asked.

"Yeah. She told me that Sandy had done something awful to Mom when they were kids, and now she wanted to make up with Mom, but I shouldn't help her. Jane said that it would only upset her. I was so relieved that you guys were okay I just agreed. It was no big deal. But today, Sandy called me again." Bobby pulled out his smart phone and manipulated the screen with his thumbs. "Listen to this."

"Hi, Bobby, this is Sandy Parker calling again. Bobby, I was your mother—Jeannie Bennett's—best friend when we were kids. I've spent the last forty years thinking your mother was dead, killed in an accident on the night of the flood. I just found out that isn't the case. I really don't want to upset her by contacting her directly, but I hope you can call me and advise me about this—about whether your mother would like to hear from me after all these years. Please call me, either way. Thank you."

They looked at each other. Sandy Parker's voice was so emotional as she spoke, it sounded like she was fighting tears. Although the story was unbelivable, the woman telling it didn't sound crazy, as Jane had suggested. She sounded like she cared a lot for their mother.

"What do you think? Should we tell Mom? What if this woman

really is crazy? She must have done something awful for Mom to write her off like that and let her think she was dead."

"How do you know Mom was involved? Maybe Jane just wanted Sandy to think Mom was dead."

Shaking his head, Bobby shrugged. "That doesn't make any sense. Why would Jane do that?"

Sandy shrugged as well. "Who knows? But something tells me Mom wasn't mad at Sandy Parker."

"Why's that?"

"I would imagine she's the old friend I'm named after."

❖

Jeannie carefully unrolled the garden hose from the large bracket that held it neatly in place beside her shed, pulling carefully to avoid the vines and ground cover surrounding the building. When she'd freed enough of the hose, she began spraying a mist over the beds that took up most of the area behind her house. She would have preferred to water her flowers later in the evening, but a social obligation would have her out until well past the suitable time for wandering about in the garden.

Her longtime nurse manager, Ellen Foster, had invited her to her husband Emmett's retirement party, and it was one of those events she couldn't politely refuse. She'd known the Fosters for over thirty years and was fond of them both. First as a staff physician and later as the owner of the clinic, Jeannie had worked closely with Ellen, and they'd become friends both in and out of the office. Most of her staff would be there as well.

Jeannie breathed in the scent of the butterfly garden, awash with color as all the flowers bloomed. The blue and purple asters and the yellow and white hollyhocks brightened their corner of the yard, next to the patio where Jeannie enjoyed the morning sun before office hours.

Since her children were technically grown and no longer needed her—a point she often debated with them—Jeannie kept a busier work schedule than ever. She loved her job. Owning the clinic required a combination of skills that challenged her every day. Of course, she had to be on top of all the latest developments in the medical field, and since she was a family practicioner, that included all the specialties. She had to play politician with the medical school because of the residents and students that trained at her clinic. On any given day, a half dozen of them were learning their craft under the watchful eye of Jeannie and her associates. She had to play referee to all of the staff who bickered and squabbled over nonsense. And she had to run the business aspect of the practice, which entailed everything from arguing with insurance companies over how much they reimbursed for pregnancy tests to negotiating better rates on malpractice insurance to paying the electric bill. It was a ton of work, but it was rewarding and she loved it.

If she were a different kind of person, she could have made her fortune in medicine. Instead, she gave much of what the clinic brought in to the uninsured and underinsured, and to her own staff, who enjoyed excellent salaries and benefit packages. Jeannie had everything that she needed, and what she gave always made her much happier than what she took for herself.

Satisfied that her flowers wouldn't shrivel from thirst, she turned off the water and began to wind her hose. The sound of a car on the narrow drive beside the house interrupted her. The property was set back from the street and bordered on three sides by hedges that stretched a dozen feet high, insulating the yard from noise. It was easy to hear the approaching car, and Jeannie was at first happy to see Bobby's car, then concerned when Sandy's pulled in right behind him.

She knew Sandy was anxious to get to Rehoboth Beach to spend the remains of the weekend with her lover, and she was quite surprised that her son wasn't in the mountains. They were up to something, and she figured she was about to find out just what it was.

"What's up?" she asked as Bobby stepped from his car.

"Hi, Mom." He kissed her softly and then began helping her with the hose. His sister took a moment to exit her car; Jeannie could see her lips moving and assumed she was talking on the phone.

"Are you going to tell me what's going on, or will I need to whip you with this hose?"

"I'm going to let Sandy tell you," he said.

"Well, then, get her out of the car. I have to shower and get to Bucks County, and the clock is ticking."

As if she heard them, Sandy opened the door to her car and stepped out into the heat. It was no cooler in the late afternoon than it had been earlier in the day.

"Okay, spill," Jeannie commanded her.

"Let's go inside. I'd prefer you to be sitting, in case you pass out or something."

Chapter Twenty-three
Face-off

Steaming. Jeannie was steaming. She actually felt heat venting through the ears that felt as if they were on fire. Looking up at the ceiling in Jane's townhouse, she wished her sister had a yard with some privacy so she could go out on the deck and scream. But she didn't. Jeannie paced instead, taking deep breaths in a futile attempt to calm her frazzled nerves.

The morning certainly hadn't gone as she'd imagined it would. She hadn't left her Philadelphia home with murderous intentions, but somehow her sister always managed to bring out the very worst in her, and at this moment Jeannie felt homicide would have been justifiable. It had been that way since they were little girls, with the two of them barely able to agree that the sky was blue. Jeannie always hoped their differences would change as they grew older, but somehow, they never did. Not after Jane married the doctor she'd always coveted, not after bearing a delightful son, not after buying the mansion and joining the country club. It seemed Jane never outgrew her need to outdo her sister, and the years only brought more trouble to them as Jeannie lived what seemed to Jane to be the great life.

Still, Jeannie didn't really harbor ill feelings for her sister. In fact, she loved her, and she often pitied Jane and her insecurities and jealousy and need for superficial pleasures. In spite of all she'd lost, Jeannie had managed to find some happiness in her life. And in spite of all she had, Jane was still miserable.

After her children broke the news about Sandy the evening before, Jeannie had been in such a state of mental disarray that she felt absolutely nothing. Not anger, not joy. Not even curiosity. Just shock. She had the wherewithal to pry what little information her children possessed from them before issuing a dismissal, but unfortunately, their knowledge was limited to the few words left on Bobby's voice mail.

To the dismay of her professional colleagues, she called and issued her regrets to the Fosters just as soon as her children were out the door. She was in no state of mind to travel, and socializing was out of the question. She didn't think she could string three words together to form an intelligible sentence if her life depended on it.

So she sought the peace of her garden, where a bench swing had offered her solace on many troubling occasions over the years. She brought with her a book, which sat unopened beside her. Adjusting the cushions, she reclined on her swing and looked over her flowers and shrubs, across the expanse of lawn to the same blue sky she'd gazed at with Sandy from the mountaintops of her childhood home. As the evening light faded and the stars appeared, they found her in the same position, staring at the sky.

A casual observer would have assumed her to be deep in thought, but for most of that time, her mind was truly blank. Ironically, upon learning that Sandy was alive, Jeannie felt much the same as she did all those years before when she heard the false tale of Sandy's death. Numb. As the sky turned a deep navy and the moon shone down, Jeannie finally felt the fog lifting from her brain, pushed out by the sunshine of memories of Sandy.

She had so many happy memories, but during all of the years since Agnes, Jeannie hadn't allowed herself the joy they now brought her. With Sandy's return to life, the memories came back in full force. Sandy's blue eyes twinkling as she pondered something mischievous. Their intensity as she focused on the basket, flying through the air with a basketball in her hands. Smoky with passion as they made love. Jeannie could picture Sandy's long blond hair flying behind her as she rode her bike, and she still could see it splayed out on the pillow beside her. She could feel the softness of Sandy's skin next to hers and the strength of her arms around her.

All of these memories filled Jeannie with a happiness that left no room for sadness or anger, but as the night grew older and the world around her grew still, her mind came back to life, bursting with questions. What the hell happened?

What happened to them—that was an easy one. Jeannie knew her mother must have discovered their affair. Somehow, she'd realized what was going on between her and the girl next door, and when the opportunity presented itself to end their relationship, she grabbed it. As Jeannie dredged up the horror of her time in the hospital, of her mother telling her the sad news that Sandy had died, she wondered at the cruelty of someone who was otherwise a kind and charitable human being. But how had she figured it out? The only plausible explanation was that Sandy must have told them. Jeannie could picture Sandy arriving at the hospital and demanding to see her, and Helen attempting to send her away because she wasn't a relative. And under that awful stress, Sandy might have told all. It would have been out of character for her, but under the circumstances, it could have happened.

But then what? Why had Sandy walked away, given up on her and their dreams of a life together? Why didn't she contact Jeannie later, after she left the hospital? Or at some time in the forty years since? That question brought tears to her eyes. When she calmed herself, controlling the bitter disappointment that Sandy had abandoned her when she needed her most, another almost morbid curiosity settled in. How had Sandy lived her life? Had she gone to New York as they'd planned or stayed in West Nanticoke? Had she played basketball and traveled, exploring exotic corners of the planet? Did she still hike and bike, or had she found new hobbies? Did she have a husband, or perhaps a lover?

Was Sandy open to the idea of reconnecting with her, or had she moved on? Would that husband or lover feel comfortable with their relationship or feel threatened by it and discourage her from reviving their friendship? Did Jeannie even want a reconciliation, considering that Sandy had allowed her to suffer for nearly four decades?

This curiosity tickled her brain through the night, forming question upon question, forcing her from her bed in the early hours of the morning so she might learn more about the woman she had once loved so long ago. And who better to answer her questions than the one who'd no doubt been at the heart of this great deception. Her sister.

After that fitful sleep, Jeannie had done something unprecedented: she canceled her office hours. Not just for the following day, Monday, but for the entire week. That would give her time off through the Fourth of July holiday, nine whole days to get her thoughts in order before she had to focus again. Given her current state of mind, she couldn't do her job. People's lives depended on her being able to give them 100 percent concentration, and her attention to detail and keen observations were what made her a good physician. She needed to stay out of the office, or she was likely to hurt someone.

After canceling her patients' appointments, Jeannie packed for the week and climbed into her Jeep. Jane lived in Mountaintop, just a short ride from Jeannie's lake home, and a getaway to the country was just what the doctor needed.

Still filled with curiosity, and a tiny bit of hope that she might see Sandy again, if only to give her a piece of her mind, Jeannie had knocked on Jane's door. An honest and heartfelt confession was what Jeannie needed from her sister before she could make her inquiries about Sandy. But a confession was not to be had. It was, still, all about Jane.

Jeannie was blown away by her sister's reaction. Although she had no doubt their mother was the mastermind of this plot, Jeannie knew that Jane was in on it, too. Pulling off this scam had been an amazing feat, and her mother couldn't have done it alone. If there was any doubt, it was erased by Jane's recent conversations with Bobby.

Yet, when she arrived at her door, Jane had feigned surprise, at first standing by her story that Sandy was dead, then later admitting that she'd recently heard rumors that Sandy was alive. What an actress she was! Bobby had described Jane's pleas for silence, about her appearance at the airport, about her wish to protect Jeannie from a crazed former friend.

Did Jane really think Bobby would keep this from her? Was she that delusional? Or had she spent the past few days plotting, worrying, awaiting this confrontation with Jeannie? If that was the case, Jeannie was happy to put her out of her misery.

The happiness that Jeannie felt in learning Sandy was alive had held in check an underlying anger at her mother and her sister. The dam quickly broke in the face of Jane's continued deception, unleashing all Jeannie's fury. She screamed, almost incoherently at times, pacing the room, wishing for some sort of reaction from Jane. Tears, or perhaps a hug. Something, anything to show that a heart beat in her chest. But Jane simply sat still, staring into the distance in a punishing silence.

Suddenly Jeannie stopped her tirade and studied the walls, trying to distract herself. Jane's diplomas from Misericordia and the University of Scranton were handsomely framed and hung above a table in her living room. Unlike Jeannie, who put her degrees to good use, Jane just used hers for wall décor. She had only gone to college at her parents' insistence, and had only chosen nursing so she could meet a doctor to marry. On that count Jane had been successful and had lived the dream for twenty-five years. Funny how dreams came to an end, though.

Jeannie had once fantasized of a life with Sandy, and Jane had helped to end that fantasy. She could remember Jane so well, sitting at her hospital bedside with Helen, comforting her as she cried after they told her Sandy was dead. Thoughts of Sandy were the first thing on her mind coming out of surgery, and for an entire foggy week her mother and her sister had been there with her, shushing her and telling her to rest. Finally, when she was clear enough to notice her father was missing and tried to climb out of bed—body cast and all—her mother had broken down. Sobbing, Helen told Jeannie that Paul had been killed in the accident that had nearly claimed her life. And in a bizarre, tragic twist, Sandy Parker had drowned after she and her grandmother went back to their house to try to save some artwork.

Jeannie nearly died, not from her injured body but from her broken spirit. She'd spent her senior year of high school at home, working with a physical therapist to walk again, learning twelfth-grade schoolwork from a private tutor hired by her mother. She never had an aide to help her deal with losing her father and her lover, though, and she buried that grief, unearthing it only in small pieces over time as she grew stronger and could manage it.

She had managed. She'd moved on, gone to school, married, raised two amazing children, and lived an enviable life. But her heart had never healed, and for forty years it had bled for Sandy Parker. The scars over her spleen and hip had faded, but not the ones on her heart.

Jeannie forced herself to face her sister, whose denial was infuriating her. "Bobby told me about your calls, Jane. You didn't want him to, but he did. Now you tell me, what the hell happened?"

Jane sat and, lighting a cigarette, stared at her, seeming to contemplate her options. After a few moments, she leaned back in her chair and looked at Jeannie. "Okay, I admit it. I knew about the whole thing. Are you happy now?"

"But why?"

"Mom threatened to disown me if I told you. What was I to do? I was twenty, penniless, and my father was dead." Here Jane paused to wipe tears that seemed to appear on demand. "I needed Mom. I'm sorry for looking out for myself, but I didn't have any choice, Jeannie."

"Okay, maybe that was true, then. But why would you continue this charade for so long? After you were married to the surgeon and didn't need her money anymore, couldn't you have said something? Or how about when Mom died? Did it slip your mind, Jane?" Jeannie was pacing, which was never good for her left leg. Sitting and elevating it would help, but she wasn't about to show Jane any sign of her weakness.

And she was weak—totally exhausted, mentally and physically. Lack of sleep was catching up to her. Thoughts whirled through her mind as if driven by a tornado, here and then gone. She had no focus. She thought of Sandy, whom she'd loved so desperately, and the pain she'd felt for years after her death. Years. She'd cried for Sandy Parker until she just couldn't cry anymore. If she hadn't made a decision to live—a conscious decision—to put Sandy to rest and move on with her life, she was sure she would still be crying. Her heart had been shattered, though, and nothing—not the man she'd married or the children she'd carried—had mended it.

Jeannie was growing more frustrated as she paced, wanting and needing answers to her questions. How had this happened? Why? What would happen next? How long had Sandy known Jeannie was alive? Why had she never contacted her? Why contact her now?

In spite of her agitated state, Jeannie had to laugh when she thought about it. In reality, unless Sandy had changed dramatically, the fact that she'd called now was amazing. Jeannie must have thrown a million hints to Sandy in their early days, but she was certain that if she hadn't made the first move and kissed Sandy, it never would have happened. Even then, after their kisses led to a frenzied excitement that neither knew how to assuage, it had been Jeannie who undressed Sandy and took her to bed. Not that Sandy hadn't been a willing and eager partner. She was. She just lacked the courage to put her heart on the line and take that chance.

At least she did back then. Perhaps Sandy had changed.

Why wouldn't she have changed? It had been so many years. They'd grown up, and when Jeannie looked at her wrinkles and the traces of gray in her hair, she had to admit they'd grown old.

"Tell me what happened!" Jeannie demanded again.

Jane stood, marched to her kitchen, and returned with an ashtray. She offered a cigarette to Jeannie, who declined, before sitting again, this time on the edge of the chair. She flipped her auburn hair and for a moment, Jeannie admired her sister's beauty. She knew Jane had had work done, but it was hard to tell, and she looked great. It amazed her that they could look so much alike on the outside, but have such different minds and hearts.

"Mom found your diary," Jane confessed at last. She sighed in defeat and leaned back into the chair. Looking directly at Jeannie, she raised her eyebrows, as if trying to tell Jeannie she knew the sordid contents without having to say it. Then she turned on what seemed to be feigned nonchalance. Jane almost pulled it off. Almost. She was so fucking phony Jeannie wanted to throw up, but she remained silent and still and controlled her nausea so she wouldn't interrupt Jane's confession.

Staring at her, allowing no break from the inquisition, Jeannie forced her to continue. "And?"

Jane waved her hand dismissively, as if these trivial details were unimportant. Nothing could have been further from the truth. The details were so very important to Jeannie. "It was in a bag of our belongings the police recovered from Dad's car. He was in the morgue, you were in the hospital, and the police showed up at Aunt Elsie's with four Pomeroy's shopping bags filled with our stuff. Remember, we didn't have a thing with us when Elsie picked us up at the hospital. We rooted through those bags like they held Blackbeard's treasure. Of course Mom recognized your diary immediately. You were always writing in that book! Why she never read it before I can't imagine. Anyway, a few hours later she came out of her room and looked like she'd seen a ghost. I didn't know it then, but later at the hospital I figured out that she read it. Jesus, I figured out about you and Sandy without reading the goddamn diary. Who ruptures their spleen and shatters their leg and comes out of the surgery asking for their best friend? It wasn't normal, but Mom didn't know, not until she saw it in your own words. So she told you Sandy was dead. Mom blamed your…transgressions on Sandy and figured with her out of the picture you'd find a nice man and be normal. And you did! So why are you so pissed at me?"

Jeannie walked to the end of the room and turned again, a look of complete shock on her tired face. "Why? Because this is my life, Jane, not yours! You had no right! Do you know how I…" Jeannie looked at her sister and saw nothing but defiance on her face. She was not sorry. There was no concern or compassion on her face. She didn't care what she'd done to Jeannie, how much Jeannie had suffered because of the lie she'd told.

Finally, Jeannie gave in to her fatigue and sat down. She didn't think her legs could hold her anymore. "You broke my heart, Jane."

"Please!" She said it in three syllables, and with much sarcasm.

Jeannie was quiet for a minute. She sat staring at the wall, focusing on her breathing. After a moment she spoke again. "What about Sandy? What did you tell her?"

Jane actually looked remorseful now. "Sandy already knew about the accident. She knew that Dad was dead and she came to the hospital looking for you. Mom intercepted her. She told Sandy you died. There was no reason for her to question Mom. Mom was prepared to make up some story about a closed casket and all that baloney, but it never came to that. Apparently, Sandy preferred the memories she had of you alive and never asked to see your body. She just walked out of the hospital and disappeared. Mom worried for years, but after that day, we never heard from her again. Mom even paid Mr. Burns, the manager of the cemetery, to keep an eye open for Sandy in case she came looking for your grave. And she wanted to know if Nellie died so she could keep you away from the funeral. But nothing ever happened. She never showed up. Until now."

The pain of Sandy's death came back in a wave that toppled her over on the couch, and she couldn't control the cry that escaped her lips as she clenched a pillow to her chest. She knew the anguish Sandy had to bear in learning she was dead. She knew it, because she'd had to bear it herself. The tears fell and just wouldn't stop. And her pathetic, evil, homophobic sister simply sat in her chair and did nothing to offer comfort.

After many minutes, Jeannie escaped to the powder room. Splashing cold water on her face finally helped to calm her. Her makeup was a disaster anyway; what did it matter? She patted her face and noted how weary she looked, how old. Did Sandy look the same? Would Jeannie even recognize her if they met on the street? She wondered if she'd ever have the chance to answer that question.

Returning to face Jane, she was unsure what to say. Unlike Jeannie, who literally looked like shit, Jane was impeccably dressed and coifed and looked relieved to have shed this secret. Jeannie just stared at her, silent, lost in her own thoughts of the young girl who'd stolen her heart at the age of three and still had it.

"Are we done?" Jane asked, sighing dramatically.

Jeannie thought she was numb, but still her sister's choice of words stung. The way Jane handled the aftermath of this disaster would determine if they could heal this wound. If Jane was truly remorseful, if she cared for Jeannie at all, she'd help right this wrong and help Jeannie understand and forgive. So far it wasn't going well.

"Excuse me?" Jeannie asked.

"Are you done with this inquisition? Because I really need to talk to you about the gas lease."

Jeannie stared in disbelief. She knew a gas company had been pursuing Jane, hoping to sign a lease that would give them the rights to drill on the Bennetts' land in Hunlock Creek. They had done all the work, verifying land ownership and such, and her signature this day would mean a check for a hundred thousand dollars for both of them by the end of the week. It would mean similar checks quarterly once the drilling process began. It would mean the end of Jane's worries.

Jeannie suspected her sister's finances were worrisome, because for six months Jane had been encouraging Jeannie to sign the lease, but lately the requests and pressure had become more frequent and firmer. Jeannie had agreed to meet with representatives from the gas company, but even after they answered all of her questions, Jeannie was still hesitant.

Although she hated her mother at the moment, Jeannie had to admit that Helen had been a smart lady when it came to finances. She'd made sure Jeannie was safe from Bob. And she made sure Jane was protected from herself. Helen had put all of her assets into trusts so none of the heirs could squander the estate. She'd helped Jeannie set up a similar trust for her own children. Helen's heirs jointly owned thousands of acres of land in northeastern Pennsylvania, land that sat above valuable beds of natural gas, and without the other's approval, neither sister could do anything to harvest it. Any decision involving something as radical as gas drilling involved mutual consent.

Jeannie had been stalling. She was concerned about the environmental risks of hydraulic fracturing, and the health risks hadn't been studied. She hoped the state would step in and impose some limits, or that the gas companies would lose interest in the Bennetts' land so she wouldn't have to make a decision on the matter that might anger Jane. She hadn't been so lucky.

Yet, suddenly it didn't matter anymore. She was no longer concerned about Jane's feelings; she could follow her own heart and her own instincts. She didn't need the money, and she wasn't going to do something she didn't believe in just to make a quick buck. "I'm not signing, Jane. As a physician I have grave concerns about the purity of our drinking water and these chemicals seeping into the ground and causing God only knows what kind of cancers. So I've decided I'm not going to let them drill on our land."

Jeannie stood. The conversation, and their relationship, was over. It was time for her to leave.

"You're just being spiteful!" Jane said. "If I hadn't done what I did, you wouldn't have married your husband. You wouldn't have Bobby and Sandy. How can you be mad at me?"

"If you have to ask that question, Jane, you wouldn't understand the answer."

With the weight of sadness crushing her drooping shoulders, Jeannie turned her back to her only sibling and went to the door. She opened it and walked through before turning and looking Jane in the eye.

"Good-bye, Jane."

❖

It took Jeannie five minutes to calm down enough to dial the phone, but as soon as she was able, she did. She needed to hear a friendly voice. Her son answered on the first ring.

"Hi, Mom. How's your day going?"

Her smile was reflexive, and instantaneously her mood lifted. Of course she'd known that would happen. That's why she'd called Bobby.

"It's been pretty shitty so far. How about yours?"

"Oh, no. Did one of your patients die?"

She hadn't told either of her children about her plan to drive to the mountains, and she really hadn't decided to make the trip until the middle of her sleepless night. Bobby's concern was so genuine Jeannie had to laugh. "No, darling, nothing so devastating as that. I just had it out with Aunt Jane, and I'm never going to speak to her again."

"Wow. I wish I could have been there to hear that." Bobby was naturally polite and generally got along with everyone, but Jeannie knew he wasn't a fan of Jane.

"I thought she was going to faint, mostly because I told her I wouldn't sign the gas lease. I think she's broke. She was as pale as a ghost when I left."

She heard Bobby's breath. "Wait. Are you here? At the lake?"

"I will be in a few minutes. You?"

His laugh was deep and mirthful. "Mom, if you wanted to have dinner with me we could have done it at home. You didn't need to make a two-hour drive."

In truth, Jeannie probably could have had it out with Jane on the phone. But Jeannie had wanted to come to the mountains. This was where she felt most relaxed. This was where she'd loved Sandy. This was where she should deal with what she'd buried for so long.

Bobby was waiting on the deck of the Swiss-style chalet when she arrived a few minutes later. He helped her with her bag and pulled the cooler she'd packed to stock the fridge. These days, her children spent more time at the lake house than she did, and while they usually did a good job of keeping the kitchen stocked, she was never sure what she'd find. The basics like creamer and milk and cereal would get her through at least the first few hours in the wilderness, so she always brought them with her.

"So what did she say?" he asked when they were both resting comfortably in lounge chairs on the deck that overlooked Lake Nuangola. Jeannie already felt better, just getting her feet up and looking out at the water, allowing the warmth of the sun's rays to chase the chill she'd felt since the evening before. Bobby had made them iced coffee, which they sipped as they caught up.

"Basically she admitted that she and my mom lied to me about my best friend's death. That my mom forced her to do it. And at no time in the past forty years was there ever an opportunity to set the record straight."

Bobby's puzzlement showed. "It's just so bizarre, Mom. It doesn't make any sense. Why would they do that?"

Jeannie looked at him and sighed. Never, never had she told a soul. After Sandy's death, when she was grieving so badly, no one was around except her family and a therapist and a tutor. They'd moved to the mountain, far away from all of her friends, and Jeannie was alone. There was no one she could have told, even if she'd wanted to. And after a while she had no reason to tell the story. She dealt with her grief and went on with her life.

Now, she had a reason.

She'd loved her children unconditionally, had been there for them through every dirty diaper and illness, for help with every sheet of homework and science project, to talk to and to laugh with. She hoped with all her heart that the feeling was mutual, their love unconditional, and that what she needed to say wouldn't in any way change the way Bobby felt about her.

She took a deep breath and looked right at him. She had no other way but right at it. "Bobby, Sandy was my lover. She was my best friend and my lover. My mother found out about our relationship and thought that if she got rid of Sandy she could cure me of my homosexuality. So she lied to me and let me think the girl I loved was dead."

Bobby's jaw dropped and he leaned toward her. For a moment he simply stared at her, speechless. Jeannie met his gaze, so relieved he wasn't turning away she almost cried. "Mom, does this mean you're a lesbian? Is this why you left Dad?"

Jeannie shook her head in frustration. "No, no, no. You know the reason I left him, right?" She looked for Bobby's response and he shook his head. Neither of them wanted to speak of it if they didn't have to. "Yet I have to say, Bobby, that I loved her so much that your dad really never stood a chance. No one did."

Bobby sat and turned to face her, his arms resting on this knees, a sweet smile on his handsome face. "Well, Mom, I don't want to talk about your sex life with Dad, okay, but the rest of it—that wasn't your fault. You were a good wife and a good mom. You made our house a home, made our life exciting and fun. You didn't make him gamble or blow his money on young nurses and sports cars. That's no one's fault but Dad's."

For a moment, Jeannie was speechless. She'd tried to keep these things from her children, to protect them, but apparently it hadn't worked. They knew about their father, anyway. "No secrets from you, huh?" She teased him in acknowledgment of his kind words without opening up any more discussion of Bob.

"Well, apparently there's quite a big one. This Sandy Parker. What's up with her? Are you a lesbian?" His inflection went from teasing to tender in a heartbeat. Whatever the answer, she knew he would accept it, and her.

If someone had asked her this in her time with Sandy, her answer would have been a confident and cocky "yes." But she hadn't been with any other women after Sandy, and only one man. Over the years she'd asked herself the question a few times, at first when she contemplated marriage and again when that marriage ended. When her daughter came out, she couldn't help wondering if there was some predisposition in her genes. She reflected on her own sexuality when she met women like Lisa and Susan, happily raising a family together and living a wonderful life, just the sort of life she'd planned to live with Sandy. More and more frequently she met colleagues and other professionals who were openly gay. These encounters caused her to think of Sandy, but never of the hope for that kind of love with another woman. She knew that wasn't possible. And she honestly never felt an attraction to anyone.

So, she figured she wasn't gay. She'd simply once loved a truly remarkable girl.

"No," she responded truthfully.

"So you aren't going to call her?"

The question shocked Jeannie and the look on her face reflected it. "Of course I'm going to call her!"

Bobby shook his head and frowned. "I will never understand women. But if you're going to call her, you should do it now. Afterward we can go out for a nice lunch. If you wait you'll be too nervous to eat."

Jeannie shook her head. "I'm not ready to call her. I can't. What do I say? 'Hi, this is Jeannie and I'm not dead, but I'm kind of hungry. Would you like to have lunch?'"

Bobby roared. "Maybe you should!"

CHAPTER TWENTY-FOUR
THE REUNION

Jeannie soon realized the impossibility of concentrating on her conversation with Bobby. Her mind continually wandered back to Sandy, and she realized how desperately she wanted to see her again. Decades-old feelings were awakening within her that she found difficult to control. Even if just for a moment, she wanted to look into those blue eyes and see the brilliant smile that had never failed to melt her heart. And if miracles did happen, and old dreams did come true, she would have more than one such moment of happiness. Finally accepting what Bobby had jokingly predicted earlier—that she wouldn't relax until she had spoken to Sandy—Jeannie excused herself and headed for the solitude of her bedroom. Whether Sandy wanted to meet with her or not remained to be seen, but Jeannie knew for certain that she'd never know until she made that phone call.

In the end she didn't need a script. Bobby gave her the number, and before she reached the privacy of her bedroom she found herself hitting the send button on her phone. And before the door was even closed behind her, she heard her call answered on the other end.

"Hello?"

"Is this Sandy Parker?" Jeannie asked as she walked across the room, but she already knew the answer. She'd heard that voice in her dreams since she was a child. With a few steps Jeannie covered the distance to the sliding-glass doors that granted access to the balcony overlooking the lake. Fumbling with the lock, she finally managed to open the door and stepped out into the morning. It was a cool day, just as it had been on that last day in West Nanticoke, and not a soul was on the water. Unlike that day, though, when she'd last heard Sandy's voice, this one was bright and clear, with no rain in the forecast. Jeannie hoped this day would end better than that one had.

Sandy's breath escaping was her first reply, and then Jeannie listened as she cleared her throat. "Yes," she finally answered, and Jeannie suddenly felt weak. She walked back into her bedroom and sat down on the bed before her legs had the chance to give out. Running her fingers along the smooth cool fabric of the bedding, she tried to focus her eyes as her head began to spin. Using the back of her hand, she wiped away tears and cleared her own throat. Then she stood again, too nervous to sit. How could this be so hard, when everything with Sandy had always been so easy? *Well, except that first kiss*, she thought, and the memory made her smile and gave her the courage to go on.

"Who makes a better banana split? Farrell's or the Treat?" Jeannie demanded as she paced her bedroom floor. The Treat was Mr. Farrell's main competition.

Sandy was out on her deck, reading a novel, trying to occupy and calm her mind and recover from the emotional storm of the day before. She looked up into the clear blue sky and smiled at the question.

"Farrell's, definitely. But don't get it upside down, 'cuz you get cheated on the portion of ice cream." Sandy chuckled as she remembered her first job, at Farrell's. She didn't tell Jeannie that both places were now gone.

"What's the best pizza in Nanticoke?"

"Stuccio's." Mr. Stuccio had made great pizza, and they spent many Friday nights in his shop with their friends, eating pizza and drinking Cokes and listening to music on the jukebox.

"Which is—without question—the best Beatles song ever?" They'd listened to every Beatles song ever recorded, but there was one that had been their song.

Sandy didn't simply answer the question. She sang it. "'I wanna hold your hand.'"

After another pause in the conversation Jeannie finally answered. "So, it is you," she whispered at last.

"It's me, all right." Sandy's voice was just as soft as Jeannie's when she replied.

Jeannie didn't say anything immediately, but Sandy heard her clearing her throat. She cleared her own, then wiped her tear-streaked face.

"Please excuse me," Jeannie asked. "I'm just in a little bit of shock here. I thought you were dead."

"What a coincidence." Although sarcasm might have been warranted, there was none in Sandy's voice. She didn't want to be angry or bitter about what had happened so long ago. She just wanted today. And perhaps tomorrow.

"So what do we do now?" Jeannie asked.

Sandy laughed. "You still get right to the point, huh?"

"Always. And besides, don't you think we've wasted enough time?"

Sandy laughed softly, running a hand through her short hair. "You're right. How about breakfast tomorrow?"

Jeannie sighed. "Sandy, honestly, I don't think I can wait that long to see you."

Sandy laughed. She'd just glanced at her watch, wondering how she'd be able to pass twenty more hours before she could see Jeannie again. "I have some cold beer in the fridge. I could make you lunch."

"Right now?" Jeannie asked, sounding panicky. As anxious as she was to see Sandy, the thought was simultaneously terrifying.

"No hurry, Jeannie. Whenever you're ready, I'll be here."

"I'm ready, I'm ready! I'm coming right now. Hold on." She ran from her bedroom to the kitchen and picked up her purse, then onto the deck where she rushed right by her son without issuing an explation for her sudden departure.

"Do you want to call me back?" Sandy asked.

"No, no, no!" Jeannie exclaimed. "Give me your address. I'll put it into my GPS."

Sandy heard a car engine start and she relayed the information. "Okay, I found it. The computer says you're thirty-five miles and fifty-three minutes away. Oh, hold on…"

Sandy could hear Jeannie speaking to someone else. "I'm meeting Sandy. Parker. I don't know when I'll be back. I'll call you, Bobby. Love you.

"That was my son," Jeannie explained, then she laughed. "I got so excited I forgot to tell him I was leaving!"

"Is that Bobby?" Sandy asked.

"Yes, that was Bobby. And I have a daughter, too. Sandy. I named her after you."

Sandy couldn't believe what was happening at this moment. That she was talking on the phone with Jeannie. That Jeannie was coming to meet her. That Jeannie was alive. That she'd named her daughter after her. She stopped pacing her deck and sat on the stairs.

"Wow, that's quite an honor. I hope she hasn't turned out too badly?" Sandy had always loved to tease her.

Jeannie laughed. "She's wonderful, but I'm sort of prejudiced."

Sandy asked questions and they spent the next few minutes talking about Jeannie's children. After listening to Jeannie's descriptions, Sandy had to agree that they sounded like great kids. It wasn't her two offspring that piqued Sandy's curiosity, though. It was their father. From the moment she had left that second message for Bobby, Sandy had been holding her breath, waiting and hoping for some news from Jeannie. She could tell herself that all she wanted was to see her again, to be friends again, but the truth was that she still loved Jeannie and would always want more than friendship. And while she was a fierce competitor on the playing field and in the boardroom, Sandy was much more demure in matters of the heart. That phone call had taken every ounce of her courage, and she hoped the risk she took would be rewarded. She needed to know if Jeannie was free.

"What about their father?" Sandy asked, tentatively.

"Urgh!" Jeannie groaned. "His name is Bob. He's an orthopedic surgeon. What else can I tell you about him? He's a jerk. I left him ten years ago."

Sandy laughed at Jeannie's declaration. "I guess I don't know what to say, except are you happy? Is life good?"

Jeannie grew quiet for a moment before answering. "For almost thirty years I've filled my life with my children, and they've brought me tremendous joy. Now they're all grown up, though, and I'm not sure if they need me anymore. It's awful."

Sandy could relate. She shared her recent concerns about crowding Angie and Tom as they welcomed their son into the world.

"So you have a daughter, too? That's wonderful."

"It is. She is. But back to you…do I have to call you 'Doctor'?"

Jeannie roared. "Yes, you do. Just once. I'd like to hear you say it one time."

"Okay, Doc, you got it. So what's that like? What kind of medicine do you practice?"

Jeannie talked a little about her job at the clinic, and Sandy asked thoughtful questions. It was a far different world from the one where her grandfather practiced medicine out of two rooms on the side of their house. Finally exhausting that topic, Jeannie changed the subject. "Enough about me! What about you? Is there a Mr. Parker?"

Sandy gasped, then chuckled. "Oh, my God, no. There used to be a Mrs. Parker, but she died a few years ago. Breast cancer."

"Oh, Sandy, I'm so sorry." Sandy could hear the compassion in

Jeannie's voice and she thought of how lucky her patients were. Jeannie always had a big heart, and Sandy could tell from their conversation that she still did.

"Well, thank you. The wounds are healing. I've started dating again."

"Anyone special?"

"I'm having lunch with the most beautiful woman I've ever known."

Jeannie cleared her throat before she spoke again. "Sandy Parker, you flirt."

"Should I take that back?"

"Absolutely not! Do you drive a black Mercedes SUV?"

"Huh? Yes. How'd you know that?"

"I'm here."

It was hard to imagine that thirty-five miles and fifty-three minutes had passed so quickly, but as long as they'd been friends they'd managed to pass the time without ever growing bored. Sandy was happy to know that hadn't changed.

Sandy stood, wishing for a moment she'd changed her clothes and brushed her hair, but it hadn't occurred to her. She'd been totally preoccupied with Jeannie. Just like always. She surveyed the stone-washed blue T-shirt and white golf shorts she wore and hoped she looked presentable. The shirt suited her eyes, and the shorts fit nicely, although they were a bit wrinkled after the hour she'd spent in the hammock. It was as good as it was going to get, she supposed, so she summoned her courage again and took the first step toward Jeannie. Sandy rounded the deck at the back of her cabin just as Jeannie was stepping from her Jeep, and she stopped dead. The hand holding her phone dropped to her side and she thought her legs would collapse next. They didn't, though. They moved again, bringing her closer to her Jeannie.

Their eyes met from fifty feet away, and Sandy's heart pounded as they silently approached each other. They'd talked nonstop for almost an hour, and now they were both speechless. Sandy could see the young girl Jeannie had been in the face of the woman she had become. Her hair was the same dark color, now streaked with red highlights and cut shoulder-length. As she moved toward her, Sandy noticed a slight limp, but it didn't seem to slow her down. When they were close enough to touch, finally, tentative smiles formed at the corners of both of their mouths. They stopped, each staring at the other.

Then wordlessly, Sandy opened her arms, and Jeannie's smile

widened as she stepped into her embrace. Hearts pounding, they both shed silent tears as they held each other. Then Sandy pulled her head back to look at Jeannie and gently wiped a tear away with her thumb. She looked into the speckled green eyes she'd always loved, at the woman she still loved, and then kissed her gently, chastely. When she pulled back to look at Jeannie, there was a twinkle in her blue eyes. "Now, where were we?"

About the Author

Jaime Maddox grew up on the banks of the Susquehanna River and still makes her home in Northeastern Pennsylvania, where she shares space with a beautiful woman, two little boys, and a furry white dog. *Agnes* is her first novel, but certainly not her last.

Books Available From Bold Strokes Books

The Quickening: A Sisterhood of Spirits novel by Yvonne Heidt. Ghosts, visions, and demons are all in a day's work for Tiffany. But when Kat asks for help on a serial killer case, life takes on another dimension altogether. (978-1-60282-975-6)

Windigo Thrall by Cate Culpepper. Six women trapped in a mountain cabin by a blizzard, stalked by an ancient cannibal demon bent on stealing their sanity—and their lives. (978-1-60282-950-3)

Smoke and Fire by Julie Cannon. Oil and water, passion and desire, a combustible combination. Can two women fight the fire that draws them together and threatens to keep them apart? (978-1-60282-977-0)

Love and Devotion by Jove Belle. KC Hall trips her way through life, stumbling into an affair with a married bombshell twice her age. Thankfully, her best friend, Emma Reynolds, is there to show her the true meaning of Love and Devotion. (978-1-60282-965-7)

The Shoal of Time by J.M. Redmann. It sounded too easy. Micky Knight is reluctant to take the case because the easy ones often turn into the hard ones, and the hard ones turn into the dangerous ones. In this one, easy turns hard without warning. (978-1-60282-967-1)

In Between by Jane Hoppen. At the age of fourteen, Sophie Schmidt discovers that she was born an intersexual baby and sets off on a journey to find her place in a world that denies her true existence. (978-1-60282-968-8)

Under Her Spell by Maggie Morton. The magic of love brought Terra and Athene together, but now a magical quest stands between them—a quest for Athene's hand in marriage. Will their passion keep them together, or will stronger magic tear them apart? (978-1-60282-973-2)

Scars by Amy Dunne. While fleeing from her abuser, Nicola Jackson bumps into Jenny O'Connor, and their unlikely friendship quickly develops into a blossoming romance—but when it comes down to a matter of life or death, are they both willing to face their fears? (978-1-60282-970-1)

Rush by Carsen Taite. Murder, secrets, and romance combine to create the ultimate rush. (978-1-60282-966-4)

Homestead by Radclyffe. R. Clayton Sutter figures getting NorthAm Fuel's newest refinery operational on a rolling tract of land in upstate New York should take a month or two, but then, she hadn't counted on local resistance in the form of vandalism, petitions, and one furious farmer named Tess Rogers. (978-1-60282-956-5)

Battle of Forces: Sera Toujours by Ali Vali. Kendal and Piper return to New Orleans to start the rest of eternity together, but the return of an old enemy makes their peaceful reunion short-lived, especially when they join forces with the new queen of the vampires. (978-1-60282-957-2)

How Sweet It Is by Melissa Brayden. Some things are better than chocolate. Molly O'Brien enjoys her quiet life running the bakeshop in a small town. When the beautiful Jordan Tuscana returns home, Molly can't deny the attraction—or the stirrings of something more. (978-1-60282-958-9)

The Missing Juliet: A Fisher Key Adventure by Sam Cameron. A teenage detective and her friends search for a kidnapped Hollywood star in the Florida Keys. (978-1-60282-959-6)

Amor and More: Love Everafter, edited by Radclyffe and Stacia Seaman. Rediscover favorite couples as Bold Strokes Books authors reveal glimpses of life and love beyond the honeymoon in short stories featuring main characters from favorite BSB novels. (978-1-60282-963-3)

First Love by CJ Harte. Finding true love is hard enough, but for Jordan Thompson, daughter of a conservative president, it's challenging, especially when that love is a female rodeo cowgirl. (978-1-60282-949-7)

Pale Wings Protecting by Lesley Davis. Posing as a couple to investigate the abduction of infants, Special Agent Blythe Kent and Detective Daryl Chandler find themselves drawn into a battle over the innocents, with demons on one side and the unlikeliest of protectors on the other. (978-1-60282-964-0)